In the Black Veins of the Earth

A John Black Novel

Keith Soares

Bufflegoat Books

© Copyright 2018 Keith Soares. All rights reserved.
First paperback edition August 9, 2018
ISBN 978-0-9977707-6-6
Original publication date August 9, 2018

Edited by Christopher Durso

Dedicated to my own superhuman family, Layla, Yasmin, and Simone.

Also from Keith Soares

∞

The Oasis of Filth

The Fingers of the Colossus *(Ten Short Stories)*

<u>John Black</u>

For I Could Lift My Finger and Black Out the Sun

If Only Every Moment Was Black and White

And It Arose From the Deepest Black

The Night Is Black, Without a Moon

On a Black Wind Blows Doom

The Black Eye of the Beholder

In the Black Veins of the Earth

Cloak of Black, Mantle of Sorrow (forthcoming)

I

KEITH SOARES

1

When the bastards came for us, it was quick.

We were at home, sleeping. Time had passed — you know, just enough time to lull someone like me into thinking I had it all figured out, that I knew what was going on. So on the night they came, all three of us went to bed without any sense that things were about to get nuts.

The world knew I had power, and knew my sister, Holly, did, too. But Mom was a different story. After my thorn-filled blood brought her back from the brink of death, up on Sol's rooftop in the city, she rounded out our little family of superhumans quite nicely. But other than a scant few, no one knew my mother had the same abilities.

Or, at least, she sort of did.

Because there were two problems. First, she was new to it all, and it takes time to figure our special powers out, even with me and Holly around as would-be tour guides. Second, Mom simply *didn't like* messing around with her abilities. She said she'd lived her whole life not having power and it was just too strange to suddenly be different. Still, thorns are gonna do what thorns wanna do, so if she had an accident, like the time she almost chopped off a finger while making dinner, well, wham bam, no thank you ma'am. Her finger just sluiced out of the way. Mom shuddered. "I will *never* get used to that."

I remember that I was dreaming when they broke down the door. Weird that I would remember a dream in such an extreme situation, but it's probably more accurate to call it a nightmare. I was with Sol, and we were somewhere in the dark, about to face off. I couldn't see him so much as *sense* him. We circled each other, both eager, both cautious. Then a light appeared, first just enough for me to make out Sol's gleaming teeth. Then it grew, until it was as bright as day, then as bright as the sun, then brighter than a thousand suns. As Sol and I turned toward the source of the light, I realized something. We were *both* afraid.

There was a thump, a loud crack, and then a crash as our door was pounded out of its frame, startling me awake. Men rushed in, maybe as many as two dozen. I'm estimating because the whole night got chaotic quickly.

Hearing the commotion, I got out of bed and stretched, confident that, whoever they were, some fools had broken into the wrong damn house. Was this a reformed band of the Way of the Sun, thinking of revenge?

The door to my bedroom flew open and men with body armor and guns piled in. White letters on their black vests read TFSA.

Son of a bitch, it's the government, I thought. *Task Force on Superhuman Affairs. Barry Wilk's bunch.*

I raised one hand, and they wisely stopped dead in their tracks. Only, something wasn't right. *I* hadn't stopped them. They stopped on their own. Probably out of fear for what I might do.

Which is when I realized that I felt funny. Something was wrong, and I couldn't do a thing. My powers were completely gone. "What the —"

"John!" Mom called from her room. "Holly!"

The men rushed toward me and with practiced skill turned me around, pushed me up against a wall, and cuffed me. In minutes, I was being led outside. So, there it was. The easiest take-down of a superhuman in history. Pride was not something I was feeling at that moment.

Blazing lights rendered the people on my driveway as dark silhouettes, and I was amazed at just how many of them there were. Not only the TFSA agents, organized and directed in their movement, but also reporters and camera operators, the ones who had been stationed outside our house since we got back from Sol's city. They formed a ring around the government's secured perimeter, flashes popping like fireworks on the Fourth of July. Also, thanks for the heads-up, reporters. *Pssst, someone's about to bust down your front door!* We weren't really pals before, but this instance sort of sealed that deal forever. Jerks.

The air was acrid with the scent of whatever they used to blow off the front door. As my eyes adjusted, I realized my mom stood cuffed just like me, and held firmly by some nondescript agent. To one side, Holly sat in her wheelchair. The jerks even handcuffed my sister to her chair. How low can you go? Sure, with her powers, she could destroy every one of them in a heartbeat, but really? It just seemed uncool.

Still, that wasn't the worst of it. You won't be the least bit surprised to learn that Barry Wilk, the agent I had bumped into when I first went to confront Sol in the city, stepped forward. Unlike the others, Wilk wore a normal brown suit with an even darker brown tie. His clothes were pressed and neat, and what remained of his hair was well-trimmed and combed, but no one would ever mistake Barry Wilk for a fashion model. Efficiency seemed to be more important to him than style. A career government guy. "I'm sorry about this, John," he said.

I was dragged to stand next to my mother. "Yeah, I bet you're really broken up about it."

Wilk stepped in front of me and looked into my eyes with an air of seriousness. "I mean it. My job is to protect the citizens of this country, and I'm going to do that job to the best of my ability. People like you — well, you might be good, you might be bad, but one thing's for sure: You're a risk. I wouldn't be doing my job, or being true to the oath I took, if I didn't try to mitigate that risk."

"So, what then? Take away our powers and kill us? Eliminate the threat?"

Barry Wilk grimaced and scratched at the top of his head, the place where his hair was nothing more than a nest of thin wisps. "John, I'm a government agent, not a barbarian. I don't want to kill you. In fact, I kinda like you. You're nothing like that scumbag Sol. Or at least, I hope you aren't."

"Either way, if Sol was here, would you treat him any differently?"

"Yes, John, I would. I've seen what Sol can do, and the way that he enjoys doing it. If you were Sol, we wouldn't be having this little conversation. Sol would already be packed away, and heck, maybe because he's so good at avoiding injury, my boys might have to take a few potshots at him. You know, just to make sure his powers really got turned off. But you aren't Sol, and so, despite the rudeness of the late hour and the fact that we have you in handcuffs, I'm trying to treat you with some respect." Wilk gave me a long look, then turned toward the agent on his left. "All right, enough chitchat. Load 'em up." He left the agents to the task, heading toward a black SUV parked at the curb.

Mom and I were prodded toward the open back doors of a larger vehicle, some kind of prisoner transport van, the only vehicle of its kind around that I could see. I assumed it was enough to hold the three of us easily. They lifted Holly and her chair toward the doors, agents guiding her in, then helped my mother inside. Next, an agent poked at me to follow.

As soon as I stepped up, I froze. "You!"

Sitting toward the front of the van, in an area separated from us by iron bars, was a dark-haired woman with olive skin. Dr. Naima Ramadi. Strangely, she wore the same dark-blue outfit as the other agents, a badge pinned on her chest, with her last name written in clear block capitals just above. You know, just in case I could forget the name of the one person on the planet who could take away my powers just by being near me.

She didn't speak.

"You're with *them*?" Mom asked.

Naima only nodded, a slow and shallow movement. It seemed like she barely wanted to look at us.

I couldn't believe it. This was the woman whose son Bobby Graden had died trying to save. And now she was helping the government capture us? I was confused. I was livid. If I had been able to use my powers at that moment, I can't say what I might have done to her. "What the hell is going on?"

Head slightly down, Naima spoke. "I — I'm sorry, but this is what has to happen."

"My *best friend* saved your kid's life, and this is how you repay us? We're the good guys, remember?" I seethed, hoping though doubting that Naima would suddenly see the light, run off, and let us use our powers again.

She turned at last to face us, to face me. "Yes, John Black, I remember. I remember how, before all these powers, I had a normal life. My son had a normal life. But now that's not possible. Did you think I could just go back to my career after what happened? Do you care that I would have to live in hiding for the rest of my life? I had to think about what that would do to me, and to Sharif. He doesn't deserve to live like a fugitive."

"So that's it?" I said. "The government shows up with the offer of a steady job, and *boom*! You're sold?"

Her eyes tightened, almost like she was studying me. Well, she had been a psychiatrist, so maybe she actually *was* studying me. "It wasn't so simple as that, John, but yes, stability is important to me. Stability in my life. The stability of my family. Even stability in my *mind*." Her eyes felt like probes, digging into my head the way I had so often done to other people using my powers. "But you, John Black. What about you? Are you stable? I saw what you did on that rooftop. I saw the rage you have inside, the way you exploded at Sol's men and killed them. Compared to you, they were no more powerful than ants, yet you killed them. So how can *you* be trusted? You even killed Sol once, at least according to him, which tells me a lot about how much power you have. So much power, and so little control, either because you *can't* control it or you don't *want* to."

I tried to speak, to object. It was her eyes that stopped me.

Naima continued, her voice perfectly even, her rationale perfectly sound. "Given all that, how can we — how can *I*, knowing that I can do something about it — simply sit back and hope that John Black won't be the next evil in the world, the next one to take Sol's place?"

2

What if the defining moments of your life already happened? Could you still change who you are?

I mean, why me? Who chose me to have superpowers? Why was I special?

Was there some rationale, some benchmark? Was I picked because I had the moral fiber to be the good guy? For that matter, was Sol picked because he had the immoral fiber needed to be the bad guy? Is that even a thing, immoral fiber? Sounds like a bad commercial for bran flakes — *Now with more immoral fiber!*

Hell, is any label correct? Depends on your perspective, right? Maybe Sol was the good guy and I was bad.

Nah, that's impossible.

But these things can mess with you, screw up your head. The so-called experts on TV liked to say we all have the potential to be a superhuman. If so, we must all have the potential to be a supervillain, too.

There was a lull after we returned home. And yeah, we went to our own home, not back to Marcos's house. Well, crap. He did, we didn't. Marcos went to his house and we went to ours. And Pip went to her apartment in the city. Gah. So specific. Everyone went to their own homes, okay? That took way too long to clarify.

Yes, the news crews and paparazzi hounded us. I envied Pip, living in her high-rise. It gave her a buffer. For us, the cameras were just outside our front door.

Pip went back to fighting crime or putting out fires in the city, whatever came up, but with Bobby gone, she worked solo.

Sol hadn't been heard from since he was sucked into the swirling vortex of doom my sister created.

And Holly, Mom, and I just went home.

You know the phrase *You can't go home again*? Well, it's true and it isn't. Sure, we physically could go home again — no one stopped us from walking in the front door. But *nothing* was the same any more.

We were older, wiser, wearier, and — all three of us — more powerful.

To save my mother's life, I had to give her the same powers that I had, the same powers Holly had. Now all three of us were superhumans, and you know what? That's a weird freaking household to live in. Dinners were quiet. Just a lot of utensils clanging and mouths chewing. Not a lot of talking. Everyone was living in their own head.

Here's one thing about living in a superhuman household. You don't need bandages. That's just *not* a thing you need anymore. So the ones you have sit there in the bathroom cabinet mocking you any time you open the door. Like they wish you'd give them away to a needier home before they just desiccate into nothingness.

Here's another thing, and one you might not expect. You *do* need hot pads. You know, when you plop some soup in the microwave for a quick snack and reach in to snatch it out when the timer beeps, but the bowl is lightning hot? Guess what our powers do. Sluice our hands right out of the way! Yes! Except then nothing is holding up the bowl and it smashes on the floor, throwing lukewarm soup everywhere. You need to use a hot pad to avoid that. Speaking from experience here, folks.

In a way, I welcomed the change when it came, when the TFSA broke down the door. Home life had become too bizarre, and frankly, more than a little boring. I don't remember a single conversation of more than 10 words between us back then.

So maybe the government showing up at our house with a brigade of black-ops ninjas wasn't such a bad thing after all.

Nah, it was crappy.

3

I reached out with my mind, in the direction of the large mirror that covered most of one wall. Sitting alone in the sort of holding cell/efficiency apartment the agents had tossed me into, I assumed there was someone behind that wall, that it was really a two-way mirror. So I reached out...

Nothing.

Because of course I had no power.

I didn't know what Naima's radius of influence was exactly, but I assumed it had kept growing since the last time I saw her on Sol's rooftop. Maybe it was upwards of 50 or 60 feet now. Which meant she had to be nearby, and considering there was only one of her, that meant Mom and Holly were nearby, too. Adjacent rooms? Probably. Or maybe that simply indicated two-dimensional thinking. They could be above me, or below. One thing was for sure: The government had worked out some arrangement of rooms to ensure we were never too far away from each other. And yes, that even included the bathroom. Mine was in a corner of the cell, with only a wash basin and toilet, shielded from the ever-watchful eyes of the two-way mirror by nothing more than a basic half-wall.

Sure, they kept a relatively clean shop — some sort of antiseptic was the primary smell most times — but nothing masks the odor of a nearby toilet forever. Despite the fact that it was *my* toilet, if you get my meaning.

My mind churned through every prison escape movie I'd ever seen, trying to find some useful nugget. And, like reaching out with my mental powers, the end result was the same.

Nothing.

I didn't have a spoon to slowly dig a hole under my bed. I wasn't in a chain gang out working the fields with an opportunity to cut and run. And nope, I didn't have a convenient motorcycle available to jump the German fortifications.

So I was stuck, with no way out and no power.

In the beginning, the government was surprisingly hands-off. Maybe they hadn't thought it would work, capturing us all. So maybe they were trying to figure out what to do next.

I remember having one recurring thought. *You better hope Pip doesn't find out about this, you jerks. Then you'll see a real jail break.*

We had driven for hours to get wherever we were, through the entire first night, all during the next day, and into the evening. Driving in a straight line, we could have been halfway across the country. Or maybe they'd gone in circles while we dozed, simply to throw us off, so we would never have a good sense of where this particular bat cave was located.

A buzzer sounded, followed by a click. I'd heard it before. It meant one of my captors was paying me a visit. Sure enough, the door opened seconds later, and Barry Wilk stepped inside. "Morning, John," he said.

"Oh, is it morning? I must have forgotten to set my alarm. And darned if there isn't a window to be found in this place. Well, thanks for the wake-up call. I guess I'll be going now." My tone was hardly pleasant as I stood up from the bed and took a step toward the door.

Wilk held up one hand, palm outward. "Take a seat, John." No *please*, no *thank you*.

But what was I going to do? Fight him? With no power, and without the agent training that I assumed even an old fart like Barry Wilk had, I would just find myself back in handcuffs. I sat down roughly on the bed.

"Thanks for not making this any more uncomfortable than it already is," Wilk said. "I know we've got you in an awkward spot. Your sister and your mother are here, just like you, against their will. And you don't have your special powers. I'm sure you're unhappy with us all."

"*Unhappy*," I echoed. "Yeah, that's certainly one word to use."

"Like I told you —"

"You're just doing your job, I know. Get on with it."

Wilk shot me a look — annoyance or admiration? Then he nodded. "I need to ask you a few questions, and of course, I'd appreciate it if you answer as honestly as you can."

Well, *there's* a loaded phrase. *As honestly as you can.* What if I couldn't be honest? Then, even lying would be acceptable. So of course, I agreed.

He began with some softballs. "How long have you known you had special abilities?"

"I don't know, half my life or so." Not lying so far.

Wilk didn't bother writing anything down. He didn't even have a pen or notepad, which wasn't really surprising. I was sure he didn't need any of that. No doubt the team of agents watching us through the two-way were videoing the entire conversation.

"So, you're telling me you weren't born this way, is that right?"

"Right."

"What happened to change you?"

Here we go, I thought. "I don't know for sure." Also not a lie. Not the complete truth, but not an actual lie. I was being *as honest as I could be*.

"When did you first realize you had powers?"

I smiled. "I got hit by a car as a kid, and I didn't die. In fact, I healed in an oddly sudden fashion, after just a little while." Still truthing up the joint.

"Tell me more about that," Wilk said, seeming truly curious. So I told him the whole story, about Bobby being a bully, chasing me in the snow, and the car crash. Then I told him how my knee was sort of like a bag of broken glass, and that somehow it reconstructed itself one day.

"And you had no idea at the time how or why this was happening?"

"Nope, none whatsoever."

"Were you exposed to any chemicals, or radiation, or anything else unusual that you can recall, at or around that time?"

Now this one was tricky. No, I hadn't been exposed to chemicals or radiation, but I had been exposed to snow. And of course, I believe that the thorns in my cells — the source of my power — came from that snow, and that the snow came from a passing comet. But I didn't really want to tell Barry Wilk and the entire government all that. First, it sounded nutty, and second, it seemed like giving them too much to work with. So I thought about his wording. *Anything else unusual.*

It was winter when Bobby and I were hit by the car, and it was snowing. Snow in the winter is far from unusual, right? That was my out. "Nope, nothing unusual," I said.

Barry Wilk's face twisted, considering my words. "So you have no idea how this happened? How you came to have what they call *superpowers?*"

All right. It was time for me to stretch the boundaries of what it meant to be as honest as I could be. Which, in this case, meant to lie. "Nope." I mean, sure my theory about the thorns was just a theory, but it was backed up by my little experiments. Since I had no desire for the government to start their own little experiments on me, I figured it was in my best interest — and the best interest of my family — to lie.

"All right, then, John. That's all the questions I have for you now. It's time we move on to the next phase."

Wilk stood up and turned to go, but I stopped him with a question. "*Next phase?* What's the next phase?"

Facing the door, Wilk paused. He knew I wasn't going to like whatever he had to say next, so he answered with only two words. I guess we were both being *as honest as we could be*. "Physical examination."

I blinked. "You mean *experiments*. On me. And, presumably, my family, too." Crap. My coy answers didn't exactly get me out of trouble, did they?

There was a buzz and a click, and Wilk opened the door. Standing on the threshold, he tilted his head back to me, just for a moment. "Yeah, something like that."

4

"We're going to start with the basics," a woman in a light-blue lab coat said as she guided a cart full of medical gear to the side of my bed. She smelled vaguely of soap, but there wasn't a whiff of perfume about her. She wore a badge featuring an overexposed head shot in front of a red background that made her skin look pasty and strange, in contrast to its slightly over-tanned natural color. Below the photo was her name: Jennifer Brooks, RN.

I sat on the edge of the bed, feet on the floor, scanning the things she had splayed out on the top shelf of her cart. Syringes in sterile packaging, swabs, test tubes with rubber stoppers. But no large carving knives, no jars of formaldehyde to hold my dissected body parts. At least there was that.

"Will it hurt?" I said, half joking. I had been the government's captive for days. The first days without superhuman power in such a long time. I began to wonder what Naima's presence was doing to me. Would my powers ever come back?

Nurse Brooks paused, head down, opening a container of swabs, then shifted her humorless eyes up to me. "It won't hurt today. At least not much."

Gee, that's reassuring, I thought. *"Today?" How many days of this did they have in mind?*

Still, it wasn't pain I was worried about. It was revelations.

It wouldn't take much digging for a scientist to see there was something different in my cells — the thorns. And I knew all too well that the thorns would do almost anything to survive. So if I let this person — this government researcher — take samples, those samples would contain thorns, and those thorns would want to find a new host, or risk death.

Did I want to think of a world where Barry Wilk or some other government agent suddenly became superhuman? Worse, did I want to live in a world where the government had the means to create as many superhumans as they wished? Even with the best of intentions, what would that mean? A superpowered army most likely, able to defeat any enemy the world could throw at it. And I'd already seen plenty of evidence of the many ways that people dealt with superpowers. Sure, Bobby, Pip, and I tried to do the right thing, be the good guys. Holly and my mother were fairly neutral, in my mind. But Sol, Walter Ivory, Margrethe, Petrus… they weren't nice people. Looking at that ratio, about half of us with power were bad. If the government had a way to give other people my abilities, I had to assume that about half of them would go bad, too.

I simply didn't have the energy to fight a thousand Sols.

And wasn't that what Sol wanted anyway? To make more of himself? Did it matter that the source of power would be me and not him, if the people to receive it decided to abuse it?

Nurse Brooks snapped on a pair of plastic gloves, then pulled out a long cotton swab. "Open wide and say *ah*, please."

Saliva first, huh? I had tried that. Not a lot of thorns to find in spit. I opened my mouth and she swirled the swab near the back of my tongue until I gagged. She didn't apologize. The swab then went into a protective sheath and she set it down on the far side of the cart. She repeated the process three more times, gagging me each time.

"Pull up your left sleeve, please." I did, and she examined my arm, twisting it slightly as she looked for a good vein. Once she was satisfied, she wrapped a rubber tourniquet around my upper arm.

"Make a fist." She unwrapped a cotton-tipped stick coated in a brown liquid, then began to swirl it around on the inside of my elbow to disinfect the site, releasing a sharp, metallic smell. Next came the syringe. She opened the package and inspected the needle.

In moments, the government would have my blood, along with the ability to give power to anyone they wanted. I had to do something.

I admit, what happened next was far from subtle.

I slapped the syringe out of her hand and it went clattering to the floor, sliding toward a corner.

Nurse Brooks looked at me with what could only be called mild annoyance. "Mr. Black, why did you do that?"

"I'm… afraid of needles." I added a nervous laugh and a shrug.

She wasn't amused. "John Black, the superhuman who has faced untold danger, is afraid of needles?" I nodded. "The same John Black whom I watched fight 200-foot-tall monsters? Who supposedly killed Sol? Who can dodge bullets? *That* John Black is afraid of needles?"

"I can't exactly do any of that stuff at the moment, now, can I?"

She smirked. Not a friendly smirk. Her eyes stayed flat and emotionless. "I haven't threatened to have you restrained so far, because there seemed to be no need. However, I can change my mind." She reached for a second syringe without another word, then repeated the same routine.

When she made her move to insert the needle into my flesh, again I jerked away and swatted at it. This time she held on, but the force pushed her hand into the cart, snapping the syringe in the middle.

Nurse Brooks didn't bother to ask for a second explanation. She stood, pulled the cart back from the bed several feet, and turned toward the mirrored wall. "Deputy Director Wilk, if you want this done, I'll need a moment of assistance." Oh, so Barry Wilk was a *Deputy Director*, eh? Well, la-ti-dah.

In seconds, there was another buzz and click. Two burly agents entered, each with close-cropped hair and muscles that looked like they might burst through their well-pressed dark-blue suits.

I did try to resist. Honest.

But in what seemed like milliseconds, I was strapped down. Prior to that moment, I didn't even realize there were restraints hidden in the bed structure, but wouldn't you know it? There were. Soon enough, I was on my back, strapped down, and immobile.

Nurse Brooks stood over me, a third syringe prepped and ready. "This didn't need to be so difficult," she said. It didn't sound much like an apology to me.

With an almost gleeful amount of force, she plunged the needle into my flesh. Immediately, viscous crimson fluid flowed into the reservoir. Over the next several minutes, Nurse Brooks collected untold vials of my blood, each one teeming with superpowered thorns.

When she was finally done, she removed the needle, briefly applied pressure with a small gauze pad, then affixed that to my arm. Silently, she turned and rolled her cart toward the door, where it once again buzzed and clicked. She left, not even bothering to say thank you. Once she was gone, the goons undid my restraints before they too left without a word.

Sitting on my bed, looking at my arm, I thought it was a pretty unfair trade. I got a single crappy bandage. The government got the ability to make superhumans forever.

But here's the funny thing. At the moment that Nurse Brooks rolled her cart away, nobody knew my power was in my blood, let alone that it could be transferred by blood. Not yet. Nobody knew that.

Not even Naima.

5

It's funny how helpless I started to feel after that, with no power of my own, and fearful that a newly created army of government superhumans suddenly would break down the door.

But first things first.

The next day, Nurse Brooks reappeared, this time with Agent Wilk — sorry, *Deputy Director* Wilk — standing over her left shoulder as she set about her work. Oh, and the goon squad was back, both of them. Apparently they weren't going to mess around anymore. A fourth person, holding a camera, rounded out my group of visitors for the day.

"Mr. Black, today we will need to restrain you from the start," Nurse Brooks said unsympathetically. As she stared at me with her dead, fish-like eyes, I noticed the objects on her cart. Not exactly the bone saws and organ-donor ice packs I feared, but awfully damn close. "Particularly after yesterday's... *shenanigans*." She said the word like it tasted bad in her mouth.

Once again, I was deposited in the bed and the restraints were applied. Lying there, pretty ticked off, I took out some of my frustration on the man in the back of the room. "So, *Deputy Director* Wilk, you like to watch the gruesome stuff, huh? Sicko." Wilk didn't reply.

Nurse Brooks snapped on a pair of gloves, then unwrapped a long, gleaming scalpel. "I will explain to you what I'm going to do so that you can approach this process sensibly. It will hurt, but it won't kill you. I will be as surgically precise as I can, and none of this will even take long unless you are excessively problematic." She was going to cut me up with a scalpel, and *I* was the one who might be problematic? Sure. "Normally, I would apply a numbing agent before these next procedures, but I'm afraid in your special case, I can't. *Fear of contamination of the samples.* That's the official reason. So we have to do it the old-fashioned way." She held up a strip of new leather. "I can give you this to bite down on, if you like. Personally, I think you'll want it."

I was floored. "What kind of masochists are you people?" I writhed on the bed but could hardly move from the restraints. "Wilk? What the hell is this? You know, I'm still a *citizen*! I still have *rights*, don't I?"

Barry Wilk remained quiet. I guess he had the right to remain silent. Yeah, I know, not funny. I was just making bad jokes to try to distract myself from impending dismemberment.

Standing over me, Nurse Brooks shook the leather strip. "Do you want it or not?"

I didn't answer. Well, not with words. I pulled at the restraints, trying to get away, shouting from the strain and frustration. Nurse Brooks must have taken some part of that for a yes, so she jammed the leather into my mouth. Suddenly, I felt like a roast pig primed for dinner, complete with a ruby-red apple stuck between my teeth. Except that my apple tasted like dirt and smelled like an old cow.

I spit it out.

Nurse Brooks barely raised an eyebrow. "Well, Mr. Black, that's your choice. But I think you're going to regret that decision." She raised the scalpel.

I continued to writhe, best I could, as she examined the bare skin of my inner forearm, around the same area where she had previously drawn blood. At least that procedure had been generally painless and mess-free. Not this one.

The man with the camera came forward and began to snap photos. I only remember the insanity of feeling like a movie star on the red carpet even as a psycho was about to cut me to pieces.

Bringing the point of the scalpel to bear on my skin, Nurse Brooks made a long, slow, careful incision, downward from about the inside of my elbow, approximately four inches long. From there, she turned the blade 90 degrees, made another cut of about an inch, then continued back up and over until she had carved a perfect rectangle on my inner arm.

I screamed. The camera flashes continued.

For a moment, she paused. "Apologies, I did say I was going to explain what I was doing. In my line of work, that's not very commonplace."

Beads of sweat had formed on my forehead and quickly dripped down as I strained to overcome the sharp pain. "What the hell line of work are you in, anyway? Torture?"

Nurse Brooks gave me a long, cold look, but didn't reply.

Oh shit.

From there, the process — and the pain — got worse. "I will be separating this segment of your skin, containing both epidermis and dermis, for remote evaluation," she said. Then, using the scalpel and a pair of tweezers, she pulled up the newly sliced section of my skin and cut it away from the underlying tissue. After what seemed like an eternity of me crying out in pain, Nurse Brooks held up a four-inch-by-one-inch rectangular section of my flesh, then quickly deposited it into a container on her cart.

My arm bled like a stuck pig. Or a stuck person, for that matter. What sort of creature wouldn't bleed when stuck, or in my case, sliced up? For a moment, I imagined my dad, from the times when he'd prepare fish for dinner. He would lay the fish down on a board, then use a really sharp knife to separate the skin from the meat. Nurse Brooks was prepping me for dinner like a rainbow trout fillet.

Except, unlike a fish dinner, I wouldn't stop bleeding, having a heart still actively working inside my chest — at least for the moment. She picked up a pad of gauze from her cart and dabbed at my arm. I can't say that felt terribly pleasant. Finally, she produced some sort of spray that was oddly cool. Hell, maybe she froze my arm. All I know is that next, she covered the location with more gauze and a large bandage, then wrapped it with tape.

I panted, disbelieving the government would subject me to such experiments, but relieved that at least it was done.

Then she turned back to me with the scalpel.

"Well, that's one," she said.

I shuddered. *One?* The spray she used continued to tingle under my bandage, and felt weirdly soothing given the insanity I'd just been through. Maybe it was laced with some sort of heavy topical drugs, too. All I knew was that, at that moment, the pain dissipated, and did so quickly.

— Inner arm, check. Next up, chest. Then thigh. Then onto the internal tissue collection agenda —

I snapped to attention, squinting at Nurse Brooks. *Wait a minute... those weren't* my *thoughts. Can I read her mind?* I tried to send a tendril into her head, as if I actually had power.

— About another hour here, then onto the girl's room —

Holy crap! I could! I could read Nurse Brooks mind. And if I could do that...

There was a buzz and a click and the door to my room pushed open. And there in the hallway was my sister, Holly.

No, that's not right. It was her, but she glowed with power, hovering in that lunatic way she did, jet-black hair falling into her face, wearing an expression like doom had come.

And it had.

Just not for *me*.

Shadow Ghost had come to save me.

6

I ran beside my sister, down a corridor marked by regular pools of fluorescent light. I didn't want to dwell on what had happened in the room. In my room. In my *cell*. Where they had been holding me. Holly had unleashed some fury. I didn't want to believe that some of those people might have died, but, honestly, I couldn't say for sure.

If Barry Wilk ever got the chance to experiment on me again, I doubted he'd be so apologetic about it.

For the record, I took the slab of flesh they had cut off my arm, container and all. I wasn't leaving that behind to find out later that the government cloned me or something. Running, I ripped off the bandage and closed my almost healed wound with my own rectangle of skin. I had to hold it there for a few moments, but after that, it was like the time Pip put her arm back together — everything became one happy whole again.

News of our escape was circulating. As we passed through a room filled with cubicles, I saw several people — government agents in unimaginatively plain government-approved attire — backing away from us, seeking a way to put distance between themselves and the dangerous superhumans.

I pushed my mind into the thoughts of a female agent as we passed. *Samples. From us, from the superhumans. Where would they be kept?*

Searching the woman's mind for an answer, I concentrated until words appeared silently in my head like a neon sign flicking on: *U2, north wing.*

"Holly! We need to head to U2, north wing!" I said, still running beside my hovering sister.

Why, John?

To get back what they took from us, I replied. I sent her the mental image of the skin sample Nurse Brooks had peeled away from my arm, and Holly cringed. She was lucky enough to have been second on the nurse's list, so she hadn't experienced the joy of dissection like I had. *And Holly... Where's Mom?*

She kept going the same direction, not worried about *U2, north wing* for the moment. *That's where I was taking you.*

* * *

We arrived at what seemed like the central security office — video feeds showed the wreckage of my cell, as well as several other cells I assumed were Holly's and Mom's. On screen I saw movement in my room and gave a sigh of relief. Although I had killed more people than I cared to admit, for some reason I wanted Holly to avoid the same fate. Of course, she had created the giant Gorgol monsters and they had slaughtered untold masses of people, so I guess trying to protect her from killing was a bit of a moot point.

"John, thank God you're okay," Mom said, standing up from behind a bank of computer monitors. She stepped forward and the three of us shared a hug. I don't think I ever hugged Holly in floating, standing-up position before that moment. It was a little weird, but also kinda normal. Probably the strangest part was that I hadn't hugged Holly standing up in a very long time.

Stepping back, I took a deep breath. "All right, somebody clue me in. How did you do it, Holly? How'd you get free of Naima's influence and get us out of there?"

My sister just shook her head. *It wasn't me.*

"They forgot about me," Mom said with a strange expression that was part sly grin and part embarrassment. "Or, more likely, they never really knew about me in the first place. If I knew how to use these... *powers*... better, I would have gotten you two out much sooner. It took me time to figure out how to influence the guard, get him to do what I wanted. But I've felt power since the moment they put me in my room."

"Which means they didn't house you close to Naima," I said. "Only Holly and I got that special treatment. That means the government doesn't know what you can do. Good."

"Well, I think they know now," she said.

"All right, that advantage is gone." I nodded.

Mom pointed toward a nearby monitor. "Look at this."

On screen was a list, unlabeled, but completely clear nonetheless. A list of people with power. Or, from Barry Wilk's point of view, *targets*.

That probably explained the letter before each number in his list.

T1 Jose do Branco, aka Sol
T2 Phillipa "Pip" Siva, aka Red Hope
T3 John Black, aka Black Sword
T4 Bobby Graden, aka Yellow Fury, deceased
T5 Jake Weissman, aka Ranger, whereabouts unknown
T6 Margrethe Vit
T7 Dr. Naima Ramadi, TGA
T8 Holly Black, aka Shadow Ghost
T9 Green Fire, rumored, real name unknown

Of course the list was all too familiar to me, although T9 had me scratching my head. *Green Fire? Who the hell is that?* Well, it did only say *rumored*. Maybe rumors were just rumors. I had to figure many people were out there falsely claiming to have power in order to make a buck — like the brothers who had once pretended to be me and Bobby on national TV. So maybe Wilk's target list wasn't foolproof. Besides, Petrus and Walter Ivory weren't listed, and they didn't seem willing to accept that Ranger *became* Sol. *Oh Wilk. This is shoddy work, sir.*

Still the one that hit me the hardest was T4, Bobby Graden. *Deceased.* The word echoed in my mind. Seeing it in writing somehow made the truth more real.

"I'm pretty sure I know who will be *T10* on this list very soon," Mom said, pulling my attention from that single word beside Bobby's name. "The government might not have known about me before, but I won't catch that break twice. None of us will."

It made sense. Naima had been present when I saved my mother's life with my blood, but she'd no reason to assume that transferring *blood* also transferred *power*. Another break that none of us would catch twice. After reviewing what had just happened, the government would quickly figure out that our blood was important. And that meant I absolutely had to get to *U2, north wing*. To take back what they had taken from me. From us. "Is there a map of the building somewhere?" I asked.

Mom shook her head. "Not a map, but these monitors have feeds from all over. We're underground, or so I'd assume, from the complete lack of windows." That also made sense. It was pretty unlikely the government would keep us out in the open, in some nondescript but far too obvious downtown building. Dangerous subjects were best kept in remote locations, underground when possible.

It dawned on me that I had seen a number over and over again while running through the halls. *Five.*

"We're on level five?" I asked, and Mom nodded. "Then that probably means *U5*. We've got to go up three levels. To *U2*." I explained about my blood.

"They never even tried to take a sample from me," Mom said. And that was a good thing. If they had, and failed, the agents would have realized their mistake.

What about you? I asked Holly.

They did. I didn't like it. If I'd had my powers then...

I didn't want to think about the words that might complete that sentence.

In the end, we stomped up staircases and found level U2, then made our way to the north wing. The cold storage was locked, but that was hardly a problem for us. We tore off the doors and discovered the blood samples and saliva swabs — conveniently, the government had them well marked — and we smashed them all onto the ground, then turned off the refrigeration and left the door open. It would have to do, because the only other thing I could think of would have been to drink my own blood. Ew. No, having watched a thorn trying to escape a dying cell, I figured the floor would be sufficient. And less gross.

A quick flight of stairs up from U1 had to be the ground floor, right? And the ground floor had to be the way out. It made sense, until we found out the U not only meant "Underground," it meant *way* underground.

7

Unexpectedly, the stairs ended at U1, so we looked for alternate ways up — a different staircase or an elevator. The main structure of the building was a basic rectangle, bisected by a long central hallway. At least we assumed what we were in was a "building," because we assumed a significant portion of it stood above ground. That was where we were wrong.

The place was completely deserted by the time we emerged from the storage area, so we figured agents and staff had been warned to high tail it out of there. Considering where we were — an underground holding facility for superhumans — evacuation protocols were probably drilled into the heads of rookie staff from day one.

At the far end of the long hall, there was a wider section, like an atrium, and from there the hall continued straight ahead, apparently with no deviations or intersections. In fact, it led off an unknown distance into utter darkness.

Thankfully, we had a Shadow Ghost.

Holly floated ahead of us and began to radiate light. It was a power that she had somehow figured out that none of the rest of us could muster. But in this case, it was pretty handy. Don't have a flashlight? Just use your sister.

With Holly leading the way, we followed the hallway straight for what seemed like an hour. It was probably only a couple of minutes, but when you're in an underground government prison/laboratory walking down a spooky corridor in the dark, with the only available light emanating from your superhero sibling, well, time seems different. Finally, we reached another atrium, this one with polished marble floors that reflected Holly's light. On the far side were four sets of double-doors painted an industrial blue: elevators, one of them sitting open and waiting. From inside, the dull glow of lit-up buttons made me believe it was fully functional.

Suddenly, fluorescent lights flickered overhead and turned on with a dull static hum. In one high corner, a closed-circuit monitor came to life, showing the grainy black-and-white image of a familiar face. Deputy Director Barry Wilk. "John, I'm going to need you and your family to stop where you are and go back to your rooms." His voice seemed tinny and small, but it echoed through the open space.

I laughed out loud. "That's not going to happen."

"You're going to want to reconsider that position, I'm afraid," Wilk said.

"And exactly why would I want to do something as ridiculous as go back to that prison cell?"

"Because you're trapped either way. In that *prison cell*, as you call it, at least you have a chance. Let us finish our work, and then we can talk about next steps. But if you try to go up those elevators, you're done."

My internal fire kicked in. Power flowed through me. I had fought monsters and villains. Barry Wilk was just a normal man, and while he had the might of the government backing him, that also meant he was constrained by laws. What could he really do to me? I admit I was arrogant, posturing before the video monitor and taunting Wilk. "Please explain," I said with cocky grin.

Wilk paused, rubbing his eyes. Was it all an act? Or did he actually give a damn what happened to me, to my family? "John, you and your mother and sister are not in some *basement* in the suburbs. You're in a highly classified government bunker, two kilometers underground, buried underneath a whole lot of solid rock. There's only one way in or out — those elevators in front of you. My team has already completely evacuated while you were off destroying our sample collection." He must have been watching everything we did on closed-circuit cameras. "And by the way, John, if there is a next time for me to get blood samples, I won't be so cavalier with them. Clearly they're important to you. Oh, and of course we now realize your mother has superpowers, too. Not sure if that's a new thing, or if you're just really good at hiding them, but congratulations, Ms. Black." Wilk nodded toward her on the screen. Mom looked away, embarrassed. "Anyway, you're down there *deep*. And we have a safety net. If you even attempt to get on an elevator, I'll blow the shaft and you three are trapped down there, permanently. There's a generator, so you'll have power for a while. But that'll eventually run out. So will the oxygen."

The threat hung in the air like a toxic cloud.

"I don't believe you," I said.

"John, wait—," Mom interrupted.

I held up a hand toward her. "I mean it. I don't believe you. You might have the elevator shaft lined with explosives — that I wouldn't put past you — but you're not going to blow it up and trap us down here."

"I wouldn't be so sure, John," Wilk replied.

"No, really," I said. "If you trap us down here, then who's left out there to face down Sol? Who stops the bad guys in this scenario?"

Wilk shrugged. "We'd still have Red Hope." Crap. Good point, Deputy Director. I felt stupid. Of course Pip was still out there, and unlike with the rest of us, the government had constant reminders of what side Pip was on — she was always out doing good in the city. Maybe they really didn't need us after all.

Maybe Wilk really would trap us two kilometers underground. But I couldn't let him know I was thinking that.

"Sure, but Red Hope would be by herself," I said. "Plus, if she finds out you trapped us — or worse, trapped us and let us die — she isn't going to be too happy with you. So go ahead, blow everything up if you need to, but we're getting on the elevator." I began to walk toward the open doors. Holly floated after me, and even Mom came along. I was glad there was no debate. If we were going to be trapped, might as well show solidarity in the face of it, right?

"Have it your way," Wilk said with an exasperated sigh, just before the monitor flicked off.

I stepped into the elevator and scanned the glowing buttons, as Holly and Mom joined me. There were 10 numbered buttons that began with the letter U, obviously all subterranean floors, and only one that had no number. I pushed the button marked B, all the way at the top of the bunch, figuring it stood for basement. And that meant we had a long way to go before we even came close to the surface. But was my assumption right? Was it *basement*? Maybe *B* stood for something else. *Building*? *Bungalow*? *Butcher shop*? *Banana stand*? I had no idea, but the doors closed and we started to go up. It was slow at first, but soon I could tell the elevator car was moving at a rapidly increasing rate. I guess if you have to go up several kilometers in an elevator, you gotta get a move on unless you want to be riding all day long.

We were zipping along, each of us holding our breath, each of us practically thrumming with our power, waiting for something.

Nothing eventful happened after that for, oh, I'd say maybe 20 seconds.

And then we were hit by a wall of sound and force that rang against the elevator car like the fist of an angry god, pounding downward.

Suddenly we were in free fall, inside an elevator car cut loose from any support, and plummeting down some unseen great distance toward a crash landing that probably wouldn't kill us, but certainly wasn't going to feel very good. And after that we'd be trapped underground until the air ran out and we died.

So I guess my day wasn't turning out so great after all.

8

Shield her! Holly shouted with her mind, the words forming real sound we all could hear.

We were falling, gaining speed, and Mom was screaming, her feet lifting off the floor of the elevator car as we dropped. Mom had superpowers, but she'd hardly used them. There was no way her mind could comprehend what would happen when we hit the bottom.

John! Listen to me! Shield Mom from the fall — she's never done anything like this before!

"Neither have I!" I yelled back, not bothering with telepathy.

But you know how to make a shield — you did it around her before, in the empty warehouse that I blew up.

Right, oh yeah. Nearly forgot about that. But, no time to dwell on such memories. Our time was going to be up any millisecond. I made a spherical bubble of power to encircle my mother, then for good measure, enlarged it to include both Holly and me. "What are you going to do?" I asked my sister.

You know how to make shields, she said with a strange look in her eye. *And I know how to move the earth.*

Oh crap, I thought. "Mom, you better hold on to something, too."

Holly focused her attention upward. There was no way for her to see outside the elevator, but I don't think her goal was overly specific at that moment. Broad brush strokes first. Move however many tons of stone stood above us. And get us *out*.

Suddenly she closed her eyes and we abruptly stopped falling. Mom and I crashed to the floor, and I almost lost hold of the force shield surrounding us. Holly simply floated, like nothing had changed.

Then the elevator car shook like it had been struck by a giant boulder. Because I'm pretty sure that's what happened. Or maybe it was an iron girder. Or half a building. Anyway, it was something big and really heavy.

Holly pushed toward the ceiling with both hands, and the elevator car rose. I stood up and looked toward my mother, allowing myself to smile. *Go to hell, Barry Wilk!* I thought. *The superpowered Black family is getting the heck outta here!*

That's when the wall on the far side of the elevator was ripped open by something large, rough-edged, and dark — another boulder or whatever, trying to crush us.

Make the shield bigger! Holly shouted. *I can push us up, and try to move the earth out of the way, but I'm going to miss some of the things falling. I can't promise I'll only miss the small ones!*

"I'm on it!" I tried to grow the bubble, but at first nothing changed. I imagined wrapping the entire metal box we were in with power. Still nothing.

John, hurry up — I'm breaking through now!

I realized I was scared. Maybe not so much for me, even if I was trapped underground. I was scared a little for Holly, and a whole lot for Mom.

That pissed me off.

And suddenly, the fire within burst forth and the shielding sphere of energy I had made became a cube that extended outside the elevator car. Almost immediately, I could feel things of all sizes bouncing off of it. The smaller ones could be easily tolerated. The medium-sized ones got my attention, made me concentrate. And the big ones were a struggle.

I once tried to stop a Gorgol with the power of my mind, and failed. This was like that. The things falling down, ramming into us, were huge. Chunks of rock that Holly was blasting apart, keeping us moving upward. I had to wonder at our speed. It felt slow, labored. How long would it take to make it two kilometers? Would Holly and I even have the strength to last that long? I strongly suspected one or both of us were going to need reinforcements, so I looked once again toward my mother. "Mom, have you tried flying yet?"

Mom blinked, confused. "What? No, I wouldn't even know where to begin. I don't even *want* to try."

"Well, you might not have the luxury of that decision soon. You're probably going to need to help us. Or else..." There was no real need to spell it out. We all knew that crashing to the floor of the shaft, crushed in rubble, left to die when our oxygen depleted... Well, that would be sorta crappy. To top it off, Mom was staring at the prospect of not one but both of her kids dying with her. I didn't need to cajole her any further.

"Fine, tell me what to do," she said, standing up slowly as we continued to ascend and shockwaves repeatedly jolted the car.

I tried to think about how to describe the process, then remembered what Bobby had once told me. I could hear his voice clearly in my head, and I realized that would be the only way I'd hear his voice ever again. The pain of his death was real and urgent, but I had to move past it and use his words to help my mother. "Try this: Look at your shoes. Don't think of them as *your* shoes on *your* feet. Just think of them as shoes. Just try to slowly pick those shoes up, with your mind."

Mom glared at me. "That's your advice? Pick up my shoes as if they aren't mine?" Mom didn't know it, but she was pretty much repeating my thoughts when Bobby gave me the same direction. "But, John, all this stuff with… *powers*. I have no clue how to do the things you do, even if supposedly I can."

Another massive object bounced off my shield, and I staggered under the force of it, although nothing had actually touched me. Yet. "Just try, Mom, please?"

Next to us, Holly's entire body began to quiver from the strain. She was carrying us upward at the same time that she was breaking a path through who knew how much rock and debris. And there was still so far to go.

Mom didn't speak, she just stared at her shoes. Nothing happened. Nothing at all.

I had an idea. "Get pissed about it, Mom. If you can't do this, we all die. Doesn't that make you mad?"

She looked toward me, the strain evident in her face. "No! It makes me scared!"

I hated to push my mother to such unpleasant depths, but it had to be done. "And if you die — if we all die — because you were too scared to do something, won't that make you angry until the second your life ends?" It was rude and harsh, but it was the best I could do.

Mom tilted her head back and screamed through hot tears. Fear and anger. Fuel for power.

She lifted a few inches off the floor of the elevator.

And immediately the surprise of doing so broke her concentration. She thudded back down, looking at me in amazement.

I smiled. "Good. Now do that again, but this time lift the entire car. I'll help, too, but I can only divert a little of my power away from the shield without risking us getting crushed. Don't worry that you have to do it all yourself. Just, you know, *help*."

Mom nodded. Then she screamed again and combined her power with mine and Holly's.

And we soared toward the surface, blasting through anything in our way, a strange blue metal box rising up through stone like an alien from out of time.

9

I'd love to tell you that we broke through to the surface and soared into the bright light of day, but I'd be lying. When we made it past the main blast zone — still at a depth of perhaps 500 meters — the rest of the tunnel seemed to be clear. But even rising quickly, we had a couple of minutes with nothing to do but wait as Holly lifted us to the surface. Let me tell you, when your adrenaline is pumping, even one minute of waiting around seems like *eternity*.

I tried to redirect my power to bolster Holly's (and, to a much lesser extent, Mom's) and get us topside faster, but my sister shot me such a look of *Chill out, I've got this* that I immediately stopped. And waited. And waited.

To occupy myself, I kept the shield around the elevator car humming and ready, which was good, because when we finally did hit something, we hit it hard. I suspect that we probably hadn't been moving upward in a perfectly straight line. That resulted in us sort of careening diagonally into a wall before slamming against the underside of whatever capped the giant shaft.

Sorry, Holly said sheepishly. *I stopped pushing through things when there stopped being things to push though.*

I made a slight waving gesture with one hand to tell her it was okay. Mom nodded in agreement. Compared to death by crushing or asphyxiation, a little abrupt stop was acceptable.

Holly once again focused her efforts overhead, and soon more debris was raining down on us. It slid off my shield without so much as touching the elevator, and Holly floated us up.

After a few seconds, Holly pushed us horizontally forward for a brief time, then dropped us down a few inches, the elevator car coming to rest with a thud on some flat plane.

Holly grinned. *We're here.*

With that, the blue-painted doors of the elevator flew open to reveal a large, sterile atrium, not terribly unlike the one we'd left so far down below. This one, however, was infinitely brighter, with high rectangular windows that allowed blessed rays of sunshine to cast beams of gold on the floor and walls.

We stepped out. Well, Holly floated out, but, you know.

There was even a dark monitor hanging high in one corner, and not unexpectedly it buzzed to life, showing us, once again, the balding head of Deputy Director Barry Wilk. "So you made it out. I guess we underestimated you."

"Yeah, I guess you did," I said. "Sorry about that, Deputy Director."

"Well, John, all I can say is that I won't make the same mistakes twice. And all you three really have done is gone ahead and forced me to post an update in each of your dossiers. Red tab, white letters. E.O.S."

The three of us exchanged glances, but it was clear we were all in the dark. "What does E.O.S. mean?" Mom finally asked.

"*Enemy of the State,*" Wilk replied ominously.

I paused, frowning. "Wait, wouldn't that be *E.O.T.S.?*"

Deputy Director Barry Wilk didn't respond.

Mom tilted her head downward, but I could see she was hiding a smile.

I had to keep going. "Or maybe, if you're cutting out the shorter words, just *E.S.*?" My mother made a sound like a suppressed cough, but I knew she wasn't coughing.

On screen, Wilk cleared his throat. "All right, John. We could sit here debating the semantics of acronyms all day if you like, but it won't change a thing. You three have been labeled enemies now, and that means you'll get treated a whole lot differently."

That pissed me off. I walked over to where the most obvious camera was and stared straight into it. "You know what, Wilk? You and the rest of the stupid government are going to regret this. I don't mean putting us in your underground lair, or trying to dissect us, or even calling us enemies of the state. What I mean is, you're going to regret you didn't just trust us. We're the only people holding back the bad guys." I let that sink in a moment. "Where do you think you'd be right now if there was no one to stand up to Sol? Did you think he was just going to settle for a city? A state? Or even this country? He's a maniac. He wants everything and everyone to bow down before him."

"We're not talking about Sol right now, we're talking about you all," Wilk said.

"Sorry, but no," I replied. "There's no way to take the two apart. And if it wasn't for the good guys like us, I think I know where you'd be someday soon, Deputy Director."

Wilk smiled, but it was a smile of uncertainty. Even on the crappy black-and-white government-issue monitor, I could see that. "And where's that, John?"

I leaned even closer toward the camera. "One of two places. Either executed for disobedience, or bending over backwards to please your master. Maybe shining the Italian leather loafers of your new fearless leader, Sol."

Through the tinny speakers, I heard Barry Wilk bark a short laugh, but it sounded forced and unsure. "Listen, now, all of you," he said. "We've had our eyes on you. Mostly John, of course, but once you declared yourself Shadow Ghost, Holly, we've been tracking you, too. Ms. Black, congratulations. You now make the list as well. Let me know when you choose a code name. We'll be sure to add it to your file. And so far, given your track record, what are we supposed to think of you people? John, we have video of you cutting off Red Hope's arm, and several clips of you where you seem to be indiscriminately murdering people. Are we supposed to just trust you, based on that? Based on what you *tell* me versus what we see you *do*? Then, of course, we have today's escapades, where each of you is responsible for harming government agents and, to put it mildly, an awful lot of wanton destruction of government property. You tell me that Sol's the bad guy here, but you've got to look at this from my point of view. From where I sit, I can't tell who's good and who's bad, at least not clearly. You know that old phrase, *power corrupts, absolute power corrupts absolutely*, right? Maybe Sol is just a diversion from the rest of you. Or maybe he is the worst of the bunch, but still, he's not the whole story. In the grand scheme of things, I think you give that man too much credit."

"No, Barry," I said, seething at his blatant allegations. "I think you don't give him enough."

10

Once the monitor went dark, it was surprisingly easy to escape. Can you call it an escape when all we did was turn a corner or two, then walk out the front door? Sure, let's call that an escape. Sounds cooler.

We exited a drab four-story building surrounded by cracked pavement. Farther out, I could see a high chain-link fence, topped with barbed wire. Signs dotted the fence in regular intervals, but they faced outward, so I had no idea what they said. I'm going to guess "Government Property. Keep Out." Beyond the fence? Not a lot. Dusty hills and scrub brush, in every direction.

Other than a vaguely suspicious vibe, there wasn't much to give away the fact that this installation hid a bunker two kilometers underground. Correction: *Used to* hide a bunker.

A hundred yards or so from the front door, I turned and looked back. Was Barry Wilk somewhere up in that building? Were his agents? For that matter, was Naima? And if they were all there, why didn't they put up a fight, or at least try to position Naima to take away our powers once more? "Spread out," I said, a little too quickly, a little too nervously.

"What's the matter, John?" Mom said, her expression revealing how exhausted she was. Holly and I had been using our powers for a long time. Mom was a newbie. The large and stressful task of keeping us all from dying took a lot out of her.

John's worried they'll come after us with her *again*, Holly said to

Mom. *He doesn't want us close enough together that they can get us all at the same time, like they did at home.*

Mom nodded, and we all separated. It was ironic that the only way our family could save itself was by working as a team but not remaining close together. "How do we get out of here?" Mom asked. "And for that matter, where do we go once we leave? And for that matter, where the hell are we anyway?"

I could tell just by looking at her that she wouldn't be able to walk far. She was spent. Outside the fence there was nothing, possibly for miles. Hell, if I were the government, *I'd* put my secret bunker miles away from everything, too. But there was no way Mom would be able to escape on foot. Maybe Wilk thought of that. Maybe he was just waiting.

"Screw that. Hold on a minute." I started to circle the building, and before long I found what I was looking for. On the far side, there was a parking lot with easily two dozen cars, each more bureaucratically plain than the last. I gestured for Mom and Holly to follow, then began to walk the rows of cars, scanning inside.

It was pointless.

But not in the way you're probably thinking.

I was looking for a car with the keys still inside — which seemed like an awfully large dose of wishful thinking. I didn't expect to find one.

Imagine my surprise when I saw they *all* had the keys in the ignition. I guess when you run a secret government bunker, surrounded by a fenced perimeter, you handled vehicle security different than other folks.

We chose a car at random. Holly took over the back, and I plopped down in the front passenger seat. That's when I noticed my mom slumped against another car nearby, barely awake. She was in no condition to drive, and I didn't think Holly would be a good pick for our second string. So I got out and carefully guided Mom to where I had been sitting, then walked around to the driver's seat.

And that, friends, is how I got to drive a car for the very first time. Not picking up a loaf of bread or carton of milk at the corner store while my parents stood by the front door waiting and nervously biting their nails. No, we do things a bit differently in the Black household. We go big.

In a stolen vehicle used to escape government detention. That's how my first time driving will be labeled forevermore.

As I twisted the key and heard the engine turn over, I couldn't help smiling. And sweating. It was exhilarating and terrifying at the same time.

Ten and two, John. Use your turn signals. Easy on the gas. Be ready with the break. I'd never taken driver's ed, so I was mostly reciting concepts I'd seen on TV. "Everybody set?" I asked no one. Mom was sound asleep already, and in the back, Holly seemed to have dozed off, too.

I was telling myself all the right things, and, you know, maybe I would have done a decent job with my first driving attempt. Except that about 30 seconds after it began I realized I was going to need to ram through the chain-link gate, and once you do something like that, well, all the normal rules of the road seem adorably quaint.

Mom and Holly briefly roused, looking around confused as the metal gate rattled off the hood of the car. I did a quick inventory. *We seem fine. The car seems fine. I can do this!*

So I stomped on the gas and we roared down a dirt road, with no idea what direction we were going, what we might stumble on, or even where we were meaning to go in the first place.

11

There are many stories of first-time drivers who crash their car. So forgive me if I'm one of them.

I'm sure most of those drivers would say "It wasn't my fault!" I won't bother. You be the judge. But, you know, it wasn't my fault. All right, fine, Your Honor, I'm leading the witness. Or the jury. Whatever. I'm not a lawyer.

As my grandmother used to say, *You ain't gonna bleed this.* When pressed, she would swear the word was *bleed*, too, and not *believe* being slurred down to one syllable.

Granny was an odd bird.

Anyway, *you ain't gonna bleed this.*

There I was, driving a large, ugly, beige, government-issue sedan down a perfectly straight bit of dusty tarmac. Inconsequential hills of dirt and rugged brush scrolled by like the repeating background in a cheaply-made old cartoon. The sun had set behind us, which meant we were heading approximately east, unless the government had actually abducted us to another dimension where things were upside down or something. That seemed unlikely, so I held to the idea that we were moving east. The light slowly seeped out of the world, blue leaving the sky like water going down an unseen drain. Ahead there was a rise, long and gentle, although bigger than most of the hills we had encountered since leaving the bunker compound. I started us up the hill without a care, knowing that, as my family slept, I was guiding them to safety.

Then the engine started to rev.

At first it made no sense. I hadn't increased pressure on the gas pedal or shifted gears (the car was an automatic, anyway). Then I realized the slow climb up the hill wasn't ending, nor was it curving back down the gentle opposite side of the oscillating sine wave that should naturally have been there. No, we kept going up and only up.

Through the front windshield, I saw nothing but darkened sky, so I turned my head to the side. There, I watched as the rolling hills dropped away.

At that moment, a song popped into my head. The one about the fine four-fendered friend...

What the hell is going on?

Then a voice spoke, close behind me. From the back seat. Not Holly's mental projection of a young girl's voice. No, this was deeper, older, accented. Familiar.

"Hello, John. Oh, the many ways we seem to meet each other, my old friend."

I stomped on the brakes and jerked the wheel hard to the side. On the pavement, we would have crashed into a ditch or at least done a bitchin' power slide. Up in the air, it had no effect whatsoever.

There was a chuckle from the back seat and my blood went cold. The voice spoke again. "Did I startle you, John?"

Against my better judgement, I glanced at the rear-view mirror.

He was there. It wasn't just the dream of a tired kid driving through the night in a silent car. He was there. I swear it.

Sitting in the back seat, looking as perfectly manicured as ever in a sleek button-up shirt, the same one I recognized from our last meeting atop Babilu Tower, he was there. In the flesh.

Sol.

I panicked, trying again to slam the wheel left then right. Nothing mattered. We kept rising into the sky.

Hindered by the seatbelt, I twisted to face him. As I moved, I saw Mom still sound asleep beside me. Then I was looking over the front seat into the face of my enemy. I scanned the back seat, up, down, left, right.

Holly was nowhere to be found.

"What did you do to my sister, you bastard?"

Again Sol chuckled. "What have *I* done to her, John? No, the better question might be, what has *she* done to *me*? But this is a matter we can discuss at some other time. Right now, I have a question for you." Sol smiled, those perfect, gleaming teeth of his like points of light in the surrounding dimness.

"What do you want from me? Can't you just stay dead?"

Sol grimaced. "Oh, I am far from dead, John. And believe me, I have become a bit of an expert on the topic, having been dead before."

I balled up my fists in anger, the fire inside me immediately blazing, my power an almost physical force, ready to break free from my body and unleash itself upon Sol. "Then what are you? How is it that you're here?"

Raising his eyebrows, Sol nodded toward me. "I have you to thank for that," he said. "And, of course, your terribly charming mother. Oh, and Holly, too. Holly most of all."

I seethed. "I swear to you, if you've hurt Holly, I will rip you to shreds."

Nonchalantly, Sol crossed his legs. Government-issue sedans apparently come with significant legroom. "Relax, John. Save your energies. Now is not the time for such anxieties. Allow me my one question."

Dipping my chin, I glared at him with open hatred. "You can ask it, but I'm not guaranteeing anything after that."

"Fair enough," Sol said. "Here's my question." He smiled, but it was flat, an expression that didn't reach his eyes. In that moment, I recall thinking that Sol's smile looked more like a mask than a human face, and behind that mask was something probably too terrible to look upon. "You have lost people dear to you, John. Bobby, of course, but I know about your father, too. You must miss them both terribly." Sol's words struck me, almost physically.

Bobby.

Dad.

In many ways, the days since their deaths felt like echoes. Not like real days. Shadows of days, markers of passing time, but fake. A simulation of a life. Like the facade of a building that promises something grand but inside is dark and hollow.

The fire inside me wavered. "Ask your question or leave," I muttered.

Sol nodded. "If you could create life — or in the case of Bobby, or your father, perhaps *recreate* life — would you bring them back?"

I scoffed, starting to protest. "That's imposs—" But then, the reality of Sol sitting before me, a Sol who had been *dead* himself, sunk in. We were superhumans, and our lives had been completely changed. Maybe our deaths had been as well. No, maybe it wasn't simply our lives and deaths that had changed. Perhaps the very ideas of life and death were different, because of us.

Bring back Bobby? Bring back Dad? I thought. *No way. Well, maybe*

Bobby, since he had powers. But Dad? How?

Sol watched me, analyzing how the question filtered into my being, got dissected. He waited for the process to run its course, for me to find a solution that fit me. Under his staring eyes, I felt naked and powerless.

Feebly, I argued with myself.

Don't even think such things — Dad and Bobby are dead! Bringing them back would be, I don't know, unnatural!

As unnatural as the powers I now use so casually? I counter-argued. *The same powers that Bobby had, that Holly has, that Mom now has, too? Unnatural like that?*

You can't do anything about the powers. They're part of you now. But bringing someone back from the dead? That *would be a conscious choice.* That *would be immoral.*

What's immoral about giving someone their life back? Especially if that life was ripped away from them? Dad didn't die of natural causes. Bobby didn't die of natural causes.

And that's about when I realized that, by arguing with myself, I *wanted* to do it. I wanted them back. I couldn't even believe myself.

And still Sol watched, fascinated. Maybe he heard my internal struggles — maybe he had tapped into my mind when I was distracted, or before I even knew he was there. Quickly, I scanned myself, pulsing power through my own head, looking for invaders. But there was no trace of Sol that I could find.

No, I could never do something like that.

But...

Stop it! Even if you could bring them back, what would it do to them*? What would you do, dig up Bobby's body, dig up Dad's, and say,*

"Welcome home!" Like nothing ever happened?

Why not?

Why not? Can you imagine what that might do to them mentally? To know they had been dead, and then returned? It might just break them. And wouldn't that be worse than them being dead? To see them alive again, but broken?

I sat, silently, thinking.

And Sol still watched. It was as if his eyes rolled across my skin, leaving a trail of slimy residue like a slug. It started to itch. Then it started to burn.

The very idea of Sol looking at me turned my stomach.

And I got mad all over again.

"Stop looking at me," I said in a low growl.

Again Sol smiled. Again he laughed. "John, I am merely waiting for your answer. What is it? Would you bring your father back from the dead? Or Bobby, your friend? Your *best* friend."

"No," I said. I'm not sure if I really meant it at that moment. I'm pretty sure it was a lie, but a necessary one. Sol was tempting me, and I knew the truth. Did I want my father back? Did I want my friend back?

Yes.

But when the word came out, it was a relief. Perhaps I had passed the test. "No," I said again, as if trying hold myself to the answer.

With a sudden intensity, Sol leaned forward and grabbed the driver's seat, pulling himself toward me, his face just inches from mine. "Well, *I would*," he said through clenched teeth. "You disappoint me, once again, John Black. But no matter. *Your* choice is your own affair." Sol fell back into his seat again, satisfied and smug.

"What does *that* mean?" I asked.

"Only that others might have a different opinion," Sol said with a vicious grin. "Others like Pip. *She* might not share your desire to leave Bobby Graden rotting in the ground."

"Leave Pip alone."

Sol *tsked* me. "John, John... Even in this very car, opinions may differ." Twisting my head around, I saw Mom, still asleep. Holly was nowhere to be seen. And outside the windows? Nothing but sky. How high up were we, anyway?

"You've asked your question," I said. "Now go."

"As you wish, old friend. I'm in no hurry, not now. I can ask Holly whenever I like. And this wonderful news about your mother — that she has joined our collegial ranks, so to speak. Well, I'm simply thrilled that the entire *remaining* Black family has power. But that's sort of the issue at hand, now, isn't it, John? Your family is fractured, your father is gone. Did you ever think your mother might *resent* what you did? Even if she says she's forgiven you, she might still blame you for your father's death. And she might want her husband back." With that, the evil bastard began to laugh in my face. Not a simple chuckle. No, this was him guffawing at me. Mocking me.

My rage exploded and so did my power. "I said *go!*" I raised one hand violently and a thrust of sheer force rammed into Sol...

...but, after only a moment, it was met with resistance. Energy pulsed and flared, obscuring Sol from my view, although I persisted with my assault. "Go!" I repeated.

I doubled the force behind my attack, wanting to expel Sol, or at least rain fury upon him.

But my power was repelled. And then I heard a different voice.

John! What the hell's the matter with you? What are you doing? Stop it!

"Holly?" I said, stammering. Behind the glowing energy of my attack I saw her, sitting in the back seat where Sol had just been, one hand raised in mirror image of my own, turning back the force I was aiming directly at her.

I remember thinking one thing: *She has so much power.*

And that's when the car began to drop out of the sky, plummeting toward the unforgiving ground somewhere below.

Which is how I crashed the first car I ever drove. I told you, you ain't gonna bleed this.

12

Had I not attacked my sister, had her appearance not startled me, we probably would have been able to stop the car from crashing to the ground. But those two things did happen, so we were distracted, just long enough.

We must have slowed our descent at least a little, though, because rather than imploding on impact, the car landed on its tires and bottomed out on the pavement before bouncing back up. Foolishly, I still had my right foot jammed down on the gas pedal, which at first caused an intense screeching sound as the rubber spun wildly on the road before catching. When it did catch, we were sent careening out of control and into a low, wide ditch. The car jumped the front edge of the ditch before slamming into the other side. Air bags blasted forth from unseen compartments, but we didn't really need them. Inside the car, as supports buckled and glass broke, all three of our bodies sluiced and slid, out of harm's way.

I realized in the microsecond that it was happening that Mom had never experienced anything quite like this before. Plus, she had been asleep; waking up in a car crash was just about the worst alarm clock imaginable. She was gonna be freaked out. *Mental note: Calm Mom down first.*

The car lurched and bounced again, threatening to jump the other side of the ditch before I thought to lift my foot off the gas. Instead of speeding forward, the car achieved a sort of equilibrium atop the far side of the ditch. Then we started to drift backward, rocking up and down the curved walls of the ditch until we finally came to rest at the bottom.

I turned toward my mother and found her looking like a wild animal. Her hair went in every direction, her fingernails dug like claws into the dashboard, and her eyes were wide and feral. "Mom, it's okay. That's just how we survive things like this. You're... fine... okay? Just breathe." Slowly, Mom nodded, still not looking at me. I turned around to face Holly, who sat in the back as if nothing had happened. "You good?" I said.

Holly nodded, then raised her eyebrows while looking at Mom, but I waived it off. *John?* she said aloud with her mind.

"Yeah, Hol?"

What's that smell?

I sniffed at the air, not noticing anything. After a moment it came to me, faint at first, probably because of the adrenaline, then more clearly, growing stronger. "Gas," I said. "I smell gas."

That doesn't seem like a good thing.

"No, it's not," I replied. "Everybody out of the car! Now!" I grabbed the handle to open the driver's door, but pulling at it did nothing. The crash had apparently crumpled too much metal to let the door open, so I opted for Plan B. I kicked at the door, focusing my power, and it blasted off its hinges and flew a dozen feet before burying itself into the side of the ditch like a giant ninja's throwing star.

Leaping out, I saw that Holly had opened her door and was floating away. Mom, however, was still sitting, just the way she had been when I talked to her. "Mom! Come on! Get out of the car — it's leaking gas!" Nothing. She was frozen.

I ran to her door and tugged at the handle, but hers, too, had been bent and jammed shut, its edges twisted and jutting. Reaching out with both hands, I took hold of the sides of the door and pulled, augmented by my abilities. Like an echo of Margrethe from so long ago, I tore the door off the car and tossed it aside. "Mom! You need to get out." I gestured wildly, and she shook her head. Slowly she pulled her fingers from the dash one at a time, leaving ten little holes behind. Then I grabbed at her arm, pulling to try to hurry her. Sure, she probably wasn't really in any sort of actual danger, but given her reaction to the car crash, I didn't want to subject her to any more trauma. "Come on, Mom." Finally, she stood, and we staggered away from the car, with her leaning into me, still in shock.

We met Holly a couple hundred feet later, where she was floating above the tarmac.

Then the gas caught on something and the car exploded behind us, making a startling pop and boom. Bits of metal, glass, and burning plastic rained down. The only good news was that the blaze gave us a little bit of light to see, since it was now fully dark.

I hung my head, embarrassed. Obviously my first attempt to drive had not gone as well as I hoped.

Now what? Holly asked to anyone who might be listening. Given our mother's state, and my dejection, she probably thought she was talking to herself. But Mom answered.

"Look," she said, pointing down the road.

In unison, we turned away from the blinding bright fire burning next to us and looked into the dark distance. At first, I could make out nothing, my eyes incapable of adjusting so quickly. Then... dots appeared. Mostly yellow-white, blue-white. Some red. A few green.

City lights.

"Come on," Mom said, and began walking down the road.

Holly and I followed. "What city is it? Can you tell?" I asked.

Mom walked wearily, almost dragging one foot. "Not sure. Maybe the capital. We could be approaching the far western side."

The capital? I thought. That meant one thing and one thing only to me.

Pip.

13

"You all look like crap," Pip said with a wry grin, holding open the door to her condo. We'd snuck in the back way Pip had shown me long ago, leaving behind the constant, oddly reassuring noise and commotion that only a large city could maintain after the cloak of darkness had fallen.

"Thanks," I replied. "Nice to see you, too." She gave me a long, hard stare, then wrapped her arms around me in a hug. I figured that living in her condo alone those past few weeks had been lonely, so I held on until she was ready to let go. When she finally did, it was my turn to give her a long look. "How are you holding up, Pip?"

"Fine," she said, turning away. "It's just... *different*." Still, I thought I saw something about her expression, her eyes. The word that came to mind was *hollow*. I wanted to do something, to help Pip fill the void, but I knew the truth. I carried the same void, an empty space inside once occupied by my best friend Bobby, and I didn't know how to fill it now that he was gone. How could I help Pip?

We told her everything — how we were taken in the middle of the night, how they kept us, what they did to us, and what we did back to them. And, of course, we told her about Naima.

"Really? After all I *did* for her?" Pip muttered. "That *bitch*."

Mom raised her eyebrows and glanced toward Holly, who was sitting casually on the large couch. For her part, Holly glared back, clearly annoyed at Mom's coddling. Holly seemed quiet, almost brooding. I think it was the first time I ever felt a single home might not be big enough to contain the three of us together. It certainly wasn't the last. Not by a long shot.

"As crazy as this sounds, I can understand what Naima did," Mom said.

"Really?" Pip said.

"She's protecting her family, the only way she knows how. I can *definitely* relate to that. So, what now?" Mom asked. She was clearly unfamiliar with the superhuman lifestyle — you know, the lifestyle where every day began with "So, what now?"

Pip smiled. "I have an idea."

* * *

Looking out over the main avenue in front of Pip's condo building, I was surprised. "Where is everyone?"

"That's it," she said. "That's all there is these days."

I took a quick count. "What? Maybe five people looking for a photo of you to make a buck, and a dozen or so fans?"

"Yep. Not like it used to be."

"Is that actually a bad thing?" I asked.

"For peace and quiet, heck no," Pip said. "For what we need, yes. Absolutely yes."

We retreated to Pip's kitchen to brainstorm.

Mom presented us with a dilemma. Nothing major, really, but still one of those issues you felt you had to get *right*. Once we did something, it would essentially be set in stone, so there would be no second chances. The problem was simple, really. The world knew all of our names, but chose to call us Black Sword, Red Hope, and Shadow Ghost. Mom needed a name. Supermom simply wasn't going to cut it.

"This is the silliest conversation I've ever had," she said, as Pip and I threw options back and forth. Holly remained silent on the couch.

I groaned. "I get that, Mom, but we need *something*. We need this to be big news. The world, and those reporters — the ones that are left — they're going to want to have something people can sink their teeth into. If it's just about us, it might be *ho hum, no big deal*. But you? You're our ticket to renewed attention, and that's just what we need now."

"Fine, but these *names* — I mean, I just can't see myself being called any of these things." Mom pointed to a paper in front of me where dramatically angular letters spelled out the name *Matriarcher*. "*Especially* this one. Looks like a heavy-metal band. *And* I don't even know how to use a bow and arrow."

"Really?" I said, crestfallen. "Dang. I kinda liked that one." I didn't really mean it. Honest. But the logo was cool. Note to self: *Get a cool logo.*

Mom threw up her hands and began to pace.

"Don't forget, you'll need an outfit, too," Pip added. "The blouse and mom jeans aren't going to work."

Mom stopped and glared. "You're not helping. And these aren't *mom jeans*. Good lord, is there anywhere I can get some fresh air around here?"

"Of course," Pip said, opening a drawer and pulling out a key fob. "Tap this on the pad in the elevator and then press R. The rooftop is private. Well, *usually* private. Unless there are helicopters today, but I don't hear any. Come to think of it, I can't recall the last time there were helicopters. Besides, it's dark now, and they prefer well-lit, daytime video." Mom swiped the fob dramatically from Pip's hand and left.

"Sorry, Pip," I said. "She just isn't comfortable with any of this stuff yet."

"Of course she isn't. Are you? I'm not, and I've been doing this for a while."

Over the next 40 minutes or so, Pip and I debated names. We ended up with two we liked, but felt Mom should make the final decision, so we went to look for her on the rooftop terrace.

Outside, it was dark, but only in the way cities get dark, where you can still see most everything if you try. The glare of too much light pollution brightened our way, dull golden hues thrown by countless streetlights below, while the moon shone brightly above, adding its own blue tint. Scanning the terrace, I found no sign of my mother, and immediately became concerned. "Pip? Is there some other way down?"

Pip shook her head.

"You don't think she —?"

"She's *your* mother," Pip said with a shrug.

The roof was a decent-sized rectangle, with a little pop-up structure in the middle housing the elevator and stairs, but it didn't seem big enough to get lost. Still, we scoured its four corners but found it to be deserted. We even separated in case Mom was circling the middle structure opposite us, trying to avoid us for some reason.

Finally, we met near the middle, beside the door leading back inside. "Do you think your mom just bailed on us?" Pip asked, confused.

"With *both* of her kids here?" I said. "That seems unlikely." At least I hoped it was unlikely. Mom didn't seem too comfortable in her own skin now that she had power of her own.

"Okay, then," Pip said. "Where is she?"

"She wouldn't leave. It must be that —"

"What, that your buddies in the government tracked you here and snatched her off the roof?" Pip grimaced. It was a joke, yet it wasn't. "Well, I certainly think they could have tracked you here. In fact, this seems like the most likely place you *would* go. But as for snatching her off the roof? How?"

I shook my head. "I don't know — maybe Naima in a helicopter, close enough to shut down Mom's power? Then agents drop down on those ropes, with machine guns strapped to their backs, and *blammo*. Mom's back in custody."

Pip tilted her head slightly, eyeing me. "You have a very active imagination."

"Please! It's completely possible! They came for us at night, busting down our doors."

"All right, fine. Let's say it happened — that your Mom was picked up and taken away by your buddy — what did you say his name was again?"

"Wilk. Barry Wilk. *Deputy Director* Barry Wilk."

"Sure, okay," Pip said. "Wilk and his gun-toting agents swooped in. Now what? We have no idea where they'd take your mom this time, since you said you kinda demolished their old underground bunker."

I started to sweat. "She could be *anywhere*. They could've taken her *anywhere*."

"Don't be ridiculous, I'm right here." Mom's voice floated down to us from the thin air of the night sky above, and I nearly jumped off the roof in anxious surprise.

Looking up, I couldn't find her. I could only see the bright glare of the moon's round face. Then I realized my mother was hovering there, a silhouette dimming one portion of the moon's luminescence. "Mom? You're... flying?" I don't know what shocked me more: Mom's sudden appearance, or the fact that, against every expectation, she was using her abilities.

Beside me, Pip gazed up at my mother with a broad smile.

"Well, you *taught* me how to do this flying thing, remember?" Mom said. "I just wanted to try it out, you know, when we *aren't* all in eminent danger."

The dark form of my mother started to descend, edged in blue by the light of the moon. "That's it!" Pip said enthusiastically.

"What's it? What are you talking about?" I asked as Mom's feet settled down next to ours and she released her power with a sigh.

"Your name, Mrs. Black," Pip said. "I think I know what you can use for your name."

Mom looked skeptical. "And what's that?"

"*Luna Blue*," Pip said, her smile growing wider. "We can even get you a blue outfit — you know, so I'm red, John's black, Holly's white, and you're blue."

Mom waggled a hand and grimaced. "I'm not so sure about the whole color-coding business, but the name has promise."

"Awesome," Pip said. "So that's set!"

"No," Mom replied. "Not *set*, not yet."

"What? I thought we had it." Pip's expression mirrored the disappointment I felt. We had to act soon, and, as crazy as it seemed, I agreed with Pip that we should create a splash by announcing Mom by a new name.

Mom looked back and forth between Pip and me. "No, it isn't quite right yet. Not *Luna Blue*. If I'm going to take one of these hero names, I want it to mean something to *me*. And *Blue* doesn't mean much to me at all. But *Luna*? That, I like."

"*Luna*," I repeated. "Just that?"

Mom nodded, pointing one thumb at herself. "Just that. If *Sol* can simply be the sun, then *this* Luna will chase him around the world until the end of time, if need be."

How could I not be proud of my mom at that moment? Sol had done everything possible to set up a conflict that was simply *him* and *me*. It helped to know someone else was on my side. Plus, Mom sounded completely geeky talking about the moon chasing the sun. I loved it.

"*Luna*," Pip said, nodding, and that sealed the deal, then and forever. Like I said, with this kind of thing, there really aren't second chances.

14

"All right, we can start," Pip said into a microphone, punctuated by a brief high-pitched squeal. Despite the similarities, the production was notably less polished than Sol's had been back in the city, outside his Babuli Tower stronghold. Sol had swagger, stage presence. In front of an audience, he seemed to get bigger. Pip just seemed nervous. We all did. Mom especially.

Twenty-four hours had passed since we'd announced there would be an announcement — does that even make sense? I don't think it does, but apparently that's how superhero PR works: You announce when you'll have an announcement. Once again the city was dark. We stood in a semicircular area outside of Pip's condo building, a space quickly arranged by the few reporters left, setup with a mic and lights. Others came in when they heard there was going to be news, although we still delayed the start twice, hoping more cameras would show up. In the end, there were eight. That's it. Eight cameras to take our message to the world. Plus the several dozen people who were milling around. The crowd had thickened noticeably, but it was hard to tell if this was really a gathering of fans, or just a random collection of folks who happened to be nearby and were bitten by the curiosity bug.

One of the reporters, a woman in a crisp grey business jacket and skirt, tried to jumpstart the proceedings. "What is it? What's the big announcement?"

Pip — or, I should say, *Red Hope* — held up one hand, urging patience. In her head-to-toe red outfit, complete with mask, she looked every bit like a superhero. Like the leader I'd foolishly believed I could be. What did I know about being a leader? I stood behind her to one side, all in black, once again feeling more than a little silly for wearing tight spandex in public. Sorry, Bobby. I mean *elastane*. Oh, who did I think I was kidding? It amounted to the same thing.

Meanwhile, on the other side of Pip, Holly sat in a brand-new wheelchair — one of two packages that had arrived fewer than 90 minutes before we walked out the front door. From her expression, Holly seemed disinterested at best. Or possibly pissed off. It might have been the fact that she was back in a chair, but honestly, we did ask, and she did tell us that keeping up the floating routine got tiring. Still, one person's assistance can be another person's prison.

"Um, thank you all for coming," Pip began, sounding a little uncomfortable with having her voice amplified and bounced off the facades of the buildings across the street. For the record, I think Pip could have just spoken loudly and reached everyone in attendance without a mic, but that wouldn't have looked terribly official, would it? "It's been a pretty quiet few weeks in the city, as you all know. I've helped out where I could —"

"The Landsberg Building fire!" someone shouted from the ring of onlookers. "Thank you!" I scanned the crowd, but in the glare of the camera lights I couldn't locate the source. What I did detect was a strange feeling. At first, I had no name for it. Something about the crowd was off. I don't recall feeling that way before — like some kind of internal alarm was ringing. Not loud, a warning of fire or doom, but a low buzz. Just enough for me to realize it was there.

Beside me, Pip blushed. "Yes, thank you. The Landsberg Building fire. I didn't mean to say *nothing* had been happening…"

"You saved my cousin!" the voice yelled back. "We love you, Red Hope!" All right, at least one guy in the crowd was a true fan.

A new light popped on, over to my left side, catching my attention. Another cameraman had arrived, with a mic-wielding reporter rushing to catch up. Seconds later another light flared on the right, and I caught a murmur. "…they're really all together…" Apparently Pip's initial broadcast hadn't made it clear enough that we'd all be there, and the word was spreading at the last minute. Behind the cameras, people were joining the crowd.

Under the mask, I realized I was smiling. The people had come out for us, after all. Then my mood suddenly changed.

"Bring out Yellow Fury!" a woman's voice called out, followed by tittering laughter. Another woman echoed the sentiment with an enthusiastic "Yeah!" I realized that Bobby had become a heartthrob, an insane compliment he would never know. That alone was enough to undo my composure. I was glad the mask hid my expression.

I glanced at Pip, but her head was down. For a moment, I thought I'd need to take over the mic, but she rubbed at the back of her neck and cleared her throat. "Yellow Fury — our friend, our beloved friend, Bobby Graden — is dead."

The crowd gasped in unison, even the reporters. "So you're confirming the reports?" asked one woman holding a microphone.

"Confirming?" Pip replied, confused.

The woman nodded grimly. "Bobby Graden's parents have come forward saying their son is dead, but they couldn't really offer much in the way of detail, and, well…"

…*And even this reporter realizes that Bobby's parents are money-grubbing assholes*, I thought, finishing her sentence. *Unbelievable.* Even after their son died, the Gradens were trying to make a buck off of him. If Bobby's mom had appeared in the crowd at that moment, I'm not sure I could have kept myself from killing her over what she had done.

Pip was silent, struggling with the same emotions, or, really, a more specific variety. And hers were tinged with a healthy dose of regret. Cameras rolled and people stared. Still, Pip was silent, so I stepped forward and pulled the microphone toward myself gently, one hand on Pip's shoulder. It was a small gesture, but the best I could do.

"Yes," I said, and again the speakers squawked loudly with hideous feedback. I winced and pushed the mic away. When the sound abated, I carefully tried again. "Yes, Bobby — our friend, Yellow Fury. He died saving the life of a child. When we confronted Sol in the city."

"Where is Sol now?" another voice called out.

Under the black mask I wore, my eyes flitted to one side. "I — we're not sure. But we don't think you have to worry about him now." Boy, was I wrong. Let me just say, if you ever have the chance to go on the record about pretty much anything, do like the politicians do. Don't say anything concrete. I hadn't learned that lesson. Yet. "But that's not why we're here. We have two very important announcements." At that, Pip tapped my arm and nodded, ready to take over the mic once more. I stepped back.

"We want to introduce you to a *new* superhuman," Pip said abruptly, and a gasp went up from the crowd. "This is *Luna!*"

There was a moment of stunned silence, then the crowd just beyond the cameras began to applaud. Behind us, the lobby doors to Pip's condo building opened and Mom strode out, all in blue, a costume that had arrived in the second package we received that day. She tried to walk confidently, but I could see little giveaways. Quick glances to each side, a slight stutter to her stride. Mom was nervous all right. But she did it. She walked right up next to us and waved to the crowd, which only served to egg on their applause, and garner some hoots as well. I scanned the crowd and once more felt that tingle, like something — or someone — was there.

The reporters, however, weren't in a cheering mood. They flung questions at us all at once, from every direction.

"Is she really?"

"What can she do?"

"How did she become superhuman?"

"What's her real name?"

"Can she show us something?"

Pip waved both hands, trying to calm the crowd. Then, without a word, she turned toward my mother.

We had talked about the next moment, agreed on it, even somewhat rehearsed it. But still, I wondered if Mom would go through with it.

She looked at the ground, and I thought we were done for. I thought she had decided enough was enough. Then her heels lifted up.

I remembered what I'd told her. My directions. *She's not looking at the ground, she's looking at her feet. "Look at your shoes. Don't think of them as your shoes on your feet. Just think of them as shoes. Just try to slowly pick those shoes up, with your mind."*

She raised her arms up like an eagle taking flight and her toes came off the ground. Then, as if she'd come unstuck from terra firma, Mom soared into the sky, a hundred feet at least.

Camera lights swung to catch up, to capture video of the newest superhuman. Inside my mask, I smiled. Mom was having her moment. In midair she hovered, then with a little flourish she spun around and began to descend, with circles of light following her down. When she reached the ground, she did her best to make a gentle landing, to look polished. I saw the tiniest of jitter to her movements, but I didn't think it would mean much to anyone else.

Finally, we turned back to the crowd, four figures, red, black, blue, and white. In the back of my mind, I heard Bobby's voice. *You're gonna need a name. Not the Triangle Gang or Trio Supremo anymore. You need something new.* I wanted to tell Bobby to be quiet, that we didn't need a name, but the memories of my friend were strong. *The Fierce Four? No. All Four One? No, even I think that's lame. Wait! I've got it! Quattro Phantasmo!* I almost laughed out loud. I knew the words in my head were all my own, just a pale remnant of Bobby lodged in a corner of my mind, but it was *so him. Bobby*, I replied to my own false Bobby-thoughts, *why do all your team names sound like pizza specials?*

"So," a female reporter directly in front of us began, with an expression that could only be described as disappointment. "What's the other announcement?"

And with that, the world seemed to yawn, to collectively dismiss my mother. Maybe the reporter didn't mean it that way. Maybe she was just anxious for whatever else we had to say. But that's how it felt. Like superhumans were already old news.

It made me angry. Mom didn't deserve to be ignored like that. Beside me, she turned away. "I told you this wasn't right for me," she muttered before heading back inside. Even turning her tail and running, she seemed to have more dignity than I could ever muster.

15

"The other thing we came to say is this," Pip said, maybe too loud for the microphone, the sound of her voice distorting through the speakers as she tried to bring the crowd back to order. "We need your help."

Thankfully, the world hadn't become completely jaded to us, despite the reporters' reactions.

"Anything!" a man yelled.

"Yeah, tell us what you need!" a woman added.

"Thank you all," Pip said. "There's a small segment of our government called the Task Force on Superhuman Affairs. Their deputy director is a man named Barry Wilk."

We had done some research. The task force — and Wilk himself — didn't show up at all when we searched online. That gave us all a pretty certain feeling they were a shadow group. Nonetheless, they were out now. I imagined Wilk in some hidden command center, seeing us on a live feed and seething at the announcement.

Pip continued, telling the tale of how Mom, Holly, and I had been taken from our homes, imprisoned. Sure, she wasn't telling a first-hand story, but she was the voice the city trusted the most. As she spoke, I scanned the crowd for a reaction.

Movement caught my eye.

Someone was pushing forward.

I realized simultaneously that the strange feeling I had was growing, and I tensed. Power rose in my body. If someone was going to try something, here and now against the three of us, they were going to regret it. Of that, I was sure.

Then the person pushed into the front, just beside one of the cameras with its bright lights. I couldn't make out the face, but the person was short, slight, and was pulling a backpack off one shoulder.

"Hey! You!" I shouted, pointing a finger trembling with latent power, ready to strike down whoever it was before they could attack.

Camera lights, following my gesture, turned and illuminated long curls of red hair. The young woman blinked in the sudden glare, raising a hand to shield her eyes.

Immediately, the power in me faded. When I spoke, my tone changed back to my regular old John Black voice. You know, tinged with uncertainty and anxiety. My nerd voice. "Carrie?"

"Hi, John," she said, still trying to block the light.

A microphone was shoved in front of her. "Carrie? You're a friend of Black Sword?" a man in a blue suit and red tie asked.

No, no, that's not why we're here! I thought. *Leave her alone!*

"Um, yeah, well, sort of. I'm friends with John Black," she said, smiling her radiant smile. That got the attention of even more cameras.

We were probably seconds away from the whole press conference crashing and burning. I had to do something. "Carrie?" I said, trying to reconnect with a more authoritative voice. "Would you mind going inside? My mother — I mean, *Luna* — wants to speak with you."

The cameras swung back. "Luna's your mother?" a reporter asked, suddenly interested again.

"It makes sense," someone in the crowd said.

"Remember the whole kidnapping business?" said another voice.

"Yeah! Must have been a cover up."

Opinions began to pop up everywhere, bubbles rising to the surface, bursting randomly. In my head, I heard the voice of my grandmother saying *All you get is a lot of cluckin' noise.* It was a phrase she liked to use, and I don't think it ever dawned on her how close to vulgar the statement was. She always claimed it was an old farmer's expression: *Put one chicken in the coop and you can sleep at night. Add more, and all you get is a lot of cluckin' noise.*

I'm pretty sure no old farmer ever used that expression. What good is a chicken coop with one chicken? Granny was strange, no doubt.

Thankfully, Carrie understood my intent, recognizing that the throng might soon turn back to her. She slipped past me, squeezing my hand quickly before heading inside.

It was time to bring things back to order. I slid up next to Pip. "Mind if I say something?" She shook her head, moving aside so I could reach the mic. "Everyone! Please!" My voice boomed from the amplification. Again I scanned the crowd, noting the people most engaged in individual conversation and sending a tiny tendril into their heads. *Pay attention. This is important.* "What Red Hope said is right! The Task Force on Superhuman Affairs abducted me and my family, and they were about to perform experiments on our bodies. Their goal seems to be to get rid of us. I want you to think about that, especially here." A few more conversations lingered, so I sent a few more tendrils. Soon, every eye was on me. "Do you want to go back to a city where Red Hope can't help you?" Low murmurs indicated no, but they weren't strong enough for my liking. I found the guy who had shouted at Pip earlier. "You, sir. You said Red Hope saved your cousin. What if *your* building catches fire? Would you rather see the government put her in prison?"

"Hell no!" he yelled back at me, riling up the people around him.

That's more like it, I thought. *Thank you, sir.*

"We're all here to help you, just like Red Hope. Just like Yellow Fury did, before…"

"We love you!" a woman shouted.

Even better. "Thank you," I said. "Red Hope said we needed your help. I want to tell you what you can do. The government might show up here any time, at any hour of day or night, trying to yank us out of here. If they do that, you might never see us again. And then, when there's a robbery or a fire or an accident or whatever — we won't be here to help. Can you good people help us by keeping an eye out for Barry Wilk and his task force? All you have to do, if you see them coming, is make noise. Can you do that? Can you make a lot of noise?"

The crowd erupted in a wall of sound that nearly staggered me. *Yes, indeed, they can make noise! Can I get an amen?*

"But why?" a voice called out. "Why does the government want to take you away?"

I started to answer, but a hush fell.

Directly beside me, a man chuckled.

What—? I started to turn.

When the man spoke, his deep voice and accent were all too familiar. *Sol.* "I can answer that last question," he said. "Simply put, the government wishes to capture *every* superhuman — Red Hope, or even this new *Luna* — because in their eyes, *they* are no different than *me.*"

That's when someone screamed and the crowd panicked, with so many bodies running in so many directions, seeking nothing more than to get away.

16

I jumped.

Come on. You would have, too.

The major difference was that I jumped about 50 feet into the air. And, as you might expect, Sol followed.

Below us, the crowd scattered. Some kept running and didn't look back, but a good number stopped to stare at the spectacle. Cameras and lights turned upward to follow us, splashing their glow like we were enemy planes dogfighting above some war-torn city.

As I curved around to get my bearings, I saw Pip sprawled on the ground, right where she had last been standing, unconscious or worse.

What the hell happened? But there wasn't time to think.

I felt Sol getting close, so my body sluiced to one side, then immediately back, hoping to catch him off guard. No luck.

Sol stabbed at me viciously with his power, so I sent a shockwave of force directly toward him as I veered low and sideways. He avoided it easily, returning the favor with a shuddering bolt of energy directed at my head. I skidded hard right, fast enough to escape, but close enough that I felt the aftershock as it passed.

During it all, I realized we had never really *fought* this way before. Our previous encounters had been either weighted toward mental gymnastics or, when physical, over quickly.

"Daydreaming, John?" Sol said, adding his customary chuckle. "I suppose you don't find me much of a challenge, then. Is that so?"

We hovered, squaring off dozens of feet above the pavement. "I find you to be endlessly boring and utterly annoying," I said. "Oh, and your little laugh makes me want to rip your tongue out. That ought to count for something." I offered a mock smile.

Sol *tsked* me. "Such anger, once again, my friend. I'll be blunt and say it concerns me. For such a young man to have so much bottled rage. One might say you are at risk of losing your soul, John Black. Doesn't it concern you?"

Did it? Of course it did. He was hitting on a subject far too near and dear to me. My struggles against the fire inside. But I had beaten it, hadn't I? When I'd learned that the anger could augment my power?

Perhaps *beaten* was the wrong word. I knew how to use my fire, although I knew it still might one day get the best of me. Still, channeling rage made me stronger.

Which, at that particular moment, was an excellent reminder of what I could do, and gave me the perfect opportunity. I channeled my fire. And attacked.

Sol sighed. "I guess that such a construct as a soul means nothing to you, old friend," he said before shifting sideways to avoid me. As my blow missed, I realized that he'd moved only enough to evade harm, no farther. That pissed me off. I rounded on him, lightning quick, and stabbed my power directly at him again.

Once more, Sol skittered out of the way, only going as far as was absolutely necessary. So close, but just out of reach. So close that his malevolence was a physical presence, weighing on me. And there was something else, too, as if the air itself near Sol were tainted. It made me want to move back, desperate to fill my lungs with something clean. That, or he used a particularly pungent cologne.

But his lackadaisical movements irked me. He wasn't running from my attacks. *Is he... toying with me?* I thought incredulously.

"John, please, you really must stop this," Sol said with a lopsided, knowing grin.

He is!

I pushed toward him again, ducking to the right until I noticed him start to move, then pivoting left in the space between synapses. Sol realized the trick and his eyes grew wide, but again he slid aside.

At least that time I had his attention. I figured I'd just have to try harder.

"John, stop this madness," Sol said. "You cannot win."

I dove toward him, straight down the middle. But with an idea.

Listen, I only played soccer for 18 days or so when I was about nine years old. Coach put me in goal one day at practice, and after a dozen kids tried to take my head off with laser-accurate shots, well, you know me, that was my cue to look for other pastimes. But the one bit of coaching I retained from those milliseconds in goal was this: Make a choice and stick with it. Sometimes you'll be right.

It might take all day, picking directions and making random moves to disguise my intentions, but I figured eventually I should catch Sol in a mistake. The fact that we were flying through the air meant we weren't limited to just two dimensions, and that gave each of us a wealth of directional options. But eventually, my random choice and his dodge would have to intersect, right? So I juked left, then slid down and right, until I finally went in the direction I'd decided from the beginning — straight up.

Just above me, Sol grunted and his body twisted, and again I missed, but I felt... *closer*. I tumbled through the air, coming briefly to a stop.

"John, stop," Sol said again, his voice edging up into a higher register. He seemed to be getting concerned. *Good.*

Meanwhile, my fire blazed inside, intoxicating me with possibilities. I no longer thought I had a slim chance. I *knew* I could strike Sol. I didn't even believe it would take that many attempts to trip him up. I thrust forward again, a feint, a hiccup, then down and left.

Using my fist as a focal point, I drove toward Sol, and with malicious glee I saw his error. In only my second attempt, already Sol's evasion and my attack were fatefully heading in the same direction. A wall of force flowed from me, funneling through my hand, which was about to be slammed into Sol.

I knew it wouldn't kill him. Wouldn't even hurt him, most likely. But I needed to land a blow so I could begin to smother him, to make my thorn-filled cells work harder and faster than his, powered by the rage inside me, and wrap him up like I had done before.

My fist rammed toward him, and our collision became inevitable.

"*John, stop!*" Sol yelled, his voice straining even higher.

And I was diverted.

Sol didn't move — there was no time for that, really — and my energy wasn't diminished. But, like a river twists to wrap around a mountain, I was diverted.

Suddenly I found myself blasting down with nothing but a city street full of onlookers below me. I struggled to quickly smother my power, to slow my momentum, but there was no time.

I didn't slow. In fact, I sped up.

Sol pushed me from behind, leveraging the aftereffects of his sideways thrust that had sent me off target, wrapping around and shoving me even as I tried to stop myself. Still angled downward, I saw the crowd before me as I streaked toward an inevitable crash landing, like a human meteor.

People were going to get hurt.

My fire blazed, and I willed myself not to stop but to *bounce* backward in the air, to avoid the hapless souls who had only come out to see us and now stood with their lives in my hands.

But nothing worked.

My mind slowed the moment down. Four or five people stood directly in my path. One of them, a middle-aged woman, smartly dressed, pushed against those around her to get away, but a younger man gawked at me, unmoving, blocking her escape. In fact, several people simply stared, like they were watching me on TV. I had a millisecond to wonder if our consumer culture had dulled people's awareness of reality, even in the face of imminent danger. There's a spectrum for this sort of thing, I think, ranging from "Normal Human Mode" through "Deer Mode" and down to "Squirrel Mode." I've capitalized each of these because I'm considering trademarking them.

I know. You're thinking I've lost my mind. Hear me out.

"Normal Human Mode" is our ingrained instinct of fight or flight. Bad shit is going down, so it's time to either raise your fists or hightail it. And those options make sense. Dull that response down and you get "Deer Mode," which basically means you don't choose either option. You stand to face whatever's coming for you and make absolutely no decision whatsoever. Many Bambis died to bring us this information. The final and, in my opinion, worst option is "Squirrel Mode." Your typical squirrel will look at the oncoming grill of a car that outweighs it by about 4,000 percent and think, *I've got this*. What happens next is the most pathetic form of kamikaze attack possible, usually resulting in nothing but an unsightly stain on the vehicle.

Thankfully, the people below me hadn't been reduced to "Squirrel Mode," but many of them did seem utterly deadlocked in "Deer Mode." I had to do something.

Given that there was no time to stage workshops and educational seminars in an attempt to change our global culture, I opted for something simpler. I sent my powers forward like a battering ram to push people out of the path of my fall, trying my best to be gentle about it. You know, as gentle as a battering ram can be. And, like bowling pins with stunned expressions painted on, the people below me were knocked back, toppled onto each other, and swept aside.

I crashed into the newly vacant slab of pavement with a powerful force that split the surface and dug into the ground below, eventually coming to rest in a smoldering human-sized pit. Thankfully, the only thing injured was my pride.

I stood. Slowly, the people above and around me did as well.

One man pointed a finger at me angrily. "What the hell was that? You could've killed us!"

I blinked, surprised. "Sorry. Uh, I had no choice." Honestly, I felt he was being a little ungrateful. I could have just crashed into them all. Would they have preferred that?

Above, Sol chuckled.

That was enough to stir me back to action. I leaped into the air, once more dodging and sliding in an attempt to confuse my ultimate direction. I think Sol just sat back and watched me, because when I finally switched to my chosen attack angle, he was nowhere to be found.

"Well, this is amusing to see," Sol said.

I attacked once more, closer this time, forcing him to do *something*. But the result was the same, though. Another miss.

Dauntless, I went in again. Twice more. Three times. Four. We were doing a sort of aerial dance in which each of us ended up in our own spot in the sky, never intersecting.

I tried again, missed again, and came to rest slightly below Sol. "I suppose we could do this all day, John, but I'm really beginning to tire of it all." And with that, he went on the offensive.

I dodged. It wasn't enough.

Sol's force slammed me downward, once more plummeting toward the street below. There wasn't even time for me to clear a path. I simply had to hope that those in "Deer Mode" had finally come to their senses and run away. Again, I cracked the pavement with my body, tossing up dust and debris in a huge cloud. Again, I came to rest in a large hole.

Dazed, I looked up to see a faded blue mailbox, and behind that, the upside-down facade of Pip's condo building. Then, I saw a face. And curls of red hair.

"Carrie?"

She still wore the backpack I had seen earlier, but quickly dipped one shoulder to slide the bag in front of her, then reached inside. "Take this, John," she said, leaning into the hole, holding out something with one hand. The object looked like a small coil, and at first I thought she was offering me a rope, trying to pull me back up to street level.

"Carrie, you need to run — to get out of here! It isn't safe!"

She ignored my warnings. "When I didn't hear from you and you didn't respond to my texts, I went to your house," she said. "It was pretty obvious someone had broken in — the front door was wide open. I figured you were either captured or on the run, and I was worried sick about you, John. Your mom and Holly, too. But at least I found this." The object in her hand uncoiled, and gravity drew one end down toward me. On it, I saw a metallic glint and realized what it was: a belt buckle.

Not just *a* belt buckle. *My* belt buckle.

I stood, reaching up to grasp the belt, locking eyes with Carrie. "Thank you. But *go!*" She nodded, and her face slipped out of view, heading back toward the condo building.

There was no time for me to follow her, to try to get her to safety, because once again the thorns in my cells buzzed in warning. Sol was approaching. Using both hands, I tugged on the belt in opposite directions, my special weapon, my gift from Pip.

The two sides pulled apart and I willed them into long, deadly sword-spears, as I turned to face my eternal enemy.

17

Leaping into the air, I felt invincible. Like extensions of my arms, the swords stabbed upward, left and right, and I was ready to change the nature of my conflict with Sol. Where I had been relying on patience and luck, I would now inject a little vengeance and will.

Streaming toward Sol, I didn't bother with subtleties. I aimed straight for his chest, slashing hard with both swords, going as fast as I could. Which, by the way, is pretty darned fast.

Sol lost his cool. "John, stop!"

I didn't.

As Sol dove to one side, I flew past him at incredible speed. But I didn't miss. With the sword-spears, there were... *options*. I spun both weapons in a devastating double-arc, each blade slicing into Sol as I went by.

Of course, his cells sluiced and he was fine, but I didn't wait for an invitation to try again.

Using my momentum, I curled in a tight circle, upward and around to come plummeting down on top of Sol. Once more, he dodged. Once more my swords cut through him.

Soon...

He slid away and was made whole again by the thorns that kept his body intact. But I persisted, coming around and slicing at his side. The blades went through his left arm, momentarily severing it from his body, and of course I thought of Pip. Despite myself, I felt a momentary pang of guilt. Like Pip's, Sol's arm reattached as soon as the two parts came back into contact.

While his body was occupied, I circled back. To the people below, I must have been no more than a strange blur orbiting Sol, a whirling electron around an indeterminate nucleus.

"John, stop!" Sol was sounding desperate.

Soon...

Again, I struck, two harsh slices through the lower back. Sol was flayed, but almost instantly sewn back together. I spun, I attacked, he was sliced and cut, he healed. It happened over and over and over.

"I hate those damn swords!" Sol cried.

The pattern repeated until there was nothing except the pattern. There was no before, no after, only the now of spin, slash, heal, repeat. I moved with such speed, there was no way to go faster. Sol responded to every attack with no margin for error, no time to think of anything else.

Now!

I spun, I lashed out with my swords...

And I willed them back to their original form, straps of pliable leather.

In that heartbeat, Sol blinked, his confusion registering on his face as clear as the brightest morning waking the world after days of storm. "John, stop!"

The straps of leather wrapped around his body, and I willed them together, an unbreakable circle. I pulled, and Sol slammed into me with an unexpected force. Switching my power from physical to mental, I dove into his mind with my fire blazing brighter than ever before, delving down into his psyche to shut him down.

A wail pierced through me. *STOP!*

So I did.

The sound consumed the world, obliterated my pathetic attempt to force my way into his thoughts. I was mentally and physically repelled, shoved violently away from Sol.

Time slowed to an infant's crawl as I tried to shake off the effects, to come back to reality. I was still floating in the air, but now facing downward and away from my foe. Below, people were pointing, yelling, tugging at my attention, piercing the grey fog I had suddenly found myself within.

"It's her!" one man shouted.

"His sister?" someone else added. "Shadow Ghost? But she's *him*?" someone else added.

Sister? What are these people talking about?

Still in slo-mo, I turned back. And saw Holly.

Hol? Where — ?

I couldn't form complete thoughts, but my mind raced to understand. Why had Holly interrupted us? Where had Sol gone?

Holly floated above me, the folds of her white dress riding the changing flows of air. She would have looked peaceful, if it weren't for her face. Holly's expression was complicated — fear and anger and exhaustion and surprise. Her eyes looked only at me, unmoving and harrowing.

Then she opened her mouth… and screamed.

I was propelled backward, a tiny leaf trapped in the heart of a hurricane. It felt like my head exploded, then the rest of me followed. I remembered when I'd shattered Sol into so many thousands of pieces. Was my own sister doing the same to me?

No, not quite. I remained whole, but her voice was a weapon that didn't care about direction, didn't have to juke or dodge or sidestep. Didn't have to spin and slice. It hit all of me at the same time, and I was swatted to the ground like an overstuffed black fly, slow and out-matched.

The cement of the sidewalk cracked where I landed, blasted apart with a shuddering force. For the third and final time that day, I slid to a halt, curled into a U-shape and coming to rest deep in a crater made by my own flesh and blood. Without even looking, I knew the back of my black outfit was tattered like an old flag.

The remaining crowd murmured, many voices coming from all around. "You saw that, right?"

"I don't know what I saw."

"Well, I do! She was *him*!"

"One minute, Sol was there. The next, Shadow Ghost."

"How can that happen?"

"They're the *same* — we're being tricked!"

What? No! Stop! What are you talking about? I asked, still too stunned to stand or speak out loud.

High above, Holly hovered, her eyes still focused on me with a clear malignancy. She bobbed slightly up and down, in time with her breath.

At least she had to put some effort into it, I thought, laughing at myself for how easily I was tossed aside.

Had Holly dispelled Sol with the same force that sent me sprawling? I wanted to believe that. I really did. But even before I saw it, I knew the truth. Hell, you do, too, right?

Holly's entire body *flickered*, like static on a screen, resolving into something completely new.

Sol.

But he appeared ragged and tired. *What's going on?*

The static blurred and flickered again, and Holly returned, intense and strong, but only for a moment. Sol returned, and once more he looked exhausted.

A voice in the crowd yelled out. "See? She's him! Shadow Ghost is Sol!"

No, I thought, my internal rage erupting at even the thought of it. *No! My sister is* not *Sol, and Sol is* not *her.* But I knew the history. I knew Sol had disappeared into Holly's spinning vortex. Where else could he have gone but inside her?

Just like Ranger…

Jake Weissman — Ranger — was consumed by Sol. I had no great love for Jake, but I knew one thing: He didn't deserve to be annihilated from within by the living will of Sol.

Would Holly end up the same? Would my sister cease to be and provide Sol with yet another life, yet another do-over?

No!

No. I had to believe one thing. Being *inside* Holly didn't mean that Sol *was* Holly.

There had to be a chance to fix things.

"If I have to rip you out with my bare hands," I said, "I will." Still holding the two sides of my belt, I inhaled deeply, drawing in energy. Then I leaped into the air, suddenly holding two deadly sword-spears. "We end this now!"

Sol was tired. The time was right. I knew I could do it. I flew at him, the points of my blades focused on him, ready to cut him out of my sister however I could.

Then he flickered, and Holly was back.

The force of my attack propelled me directly at her, although in my mind I faltered.

Suddenly aware of what was happening, Holly raised one hand to defend herself against me, and I knew if she screamed again, I would fail.

But that didn't happen.

Instead, something slammed into me from the side, deflecting my attack and sending me rolling past Holly. I slid to a stop in the air to face my new opponent.

And I saw my mother, hovering just next to my sister. "No, John. I can't let you hurt her. She's your *sister*!" Together, they started to descend toward the street below.

"Hurt her?" I said, incredulous, lowering myself to follow. "I was trying to *help* her."

Mom shook her head as her feet touched the pavement. "How? By attacking her with those..." She looked toward the dangling lines of my double-belt. "Those *things*?"

Suddenly I was eight years old again, being scolded by my mother. "Mom, come on!"

She stepped ahead of Holly, just a few inches. It was a futile gesture. I knew my mother had hardly spent any time practicing with her new abilities, and I believed that meant she'd be easy to defeat. She was no match for me. The real threat was my sister, pulsing with breath behind her, hovering just inches above the street. Still, it wasn't like I could attack my *mother*. I may be a raging lunatic sometimes, but I'm not a complete monster.

Mom put one arm around Holly and whispered something in her ear. Then, together, they withdrew, walking slowly away through a crowd that parted before them like they carried the bubonic plague.

"Where are you going?" I asked, still too whiny. Still a kid frustrated by his parent.

Mom barely turned back, only enough to toss a final comment my way. "We're getting away from all of this… *insanity*."

Then the crowd closed in behind them and my mother and sister disappeared from view. I stood there in a circle of humanity without a single ally — not friend, not family — and a hundred eyes looked toward me as if I had any idea what might come next.

II

1

This next part is embarrassing.

I slid my double belts back into place and went to check on Pip — I had to, of course — to make sure she was still alive. The good news is that she was. The bad news is, I couldn't get anywhere near her. Pip was unconscious and breathing shallow breaths, but I only heard that secondhand.

Her people wouldn't let me close.

That's right, Red Hope's fan club — the diehards who had been camped outside Pip's condo building for who knows how long, the ones who sometimes referred to themselves as the Way of Hope — made a ring around her as I approached.

"Don't come any closer!" one woman yelled at me.

"What are you doing?" I replied. "I'm trying to help!"

"Well, Red Hope doesn't need your sort of help any more than Shadow Ghost or Luna does," the woman said, holding me with a fierce stare. She even crossed her arms for good measure.

I froze. It was crazy. Somehow, somewhere along the way, I'd apparently been transported to an alternate universe. One that made no sense whatsoever.

One where, apparently, I was the bad guy.

Taking a moment to consider my situation, I made a laundry list of issues, things that weren't going my way.

Maybe my only true friend, Bobby, was gone.

Barry Wilk and the entire weight of the government were trying to capture and dissect me.

Sol mocked me from within my sister.

Holly and Mom had left me behind.

And now Pip was off limits.

Unless of course I wanted to plow through a couple dozen innocent civilians. Like I said, I'm not *that* big of a monster.

Well, this is just wonderful, I thought. My expression darkened, like a cloud that warned of an approaching storm, and I turned aside. Right on cue, it started to rain. I guess my expression wasn't the only stormy thing that day.

Perfect, I thought. *Just perfect.*

* * *

I walked the city streets. I knew there were people following me, but for at least a little while, I didn't care. Let them get their pictures. Black Sword's sad walk of shame, getting drenched in the rain. I needed to think.

It seemed Sol was embedded within my sister, although, now that I had time to think, that wasn't much of a surprise. Holly had opened a gateway to her soul, the one that let her create life, whether spider or Gorgol, and Sol had fallen into it. Originally, I wanted to believe he had been sent to his death or at least another dimension, when he was sucked into the swirling vortex she made on the rooftop of Babilu Tower, but clearly I was wrong. Sol was inside Holly herself.

But that wasn't all. If Sol had become a part of my sister when he was sucked into the portal she'd made, then so had Gorgol Alpha — the giant monster Holly created and then uncreated, just before I'd nearly killed myself trying to defeat the beast.

All I need to do... Did you ever notice how those words always precede something remarkably hard to do? Like, *All I need to do to win the lottery is buy every number combination. Simple!* Or, in my case, *All I need to do to defeat my enemies is hope that Gorgol Alpha and Sol have a fight to the death inside of my sister and they both lose.* See? That seemed improbable.

Given the excruciatingly small chance of me winning without lifting a finger, I had to make some sort of plan, and that plan started with getting Sol out of Holly. The problem was, I had absolutely no idea how to do that, short of simply asking Holly to open another gateway and send Sol flying out.

But let's say she did that. Then what? Sol was unlikely to appear, thank us for the jolly good time, and whistle a tune as he walked off into the sunset. No, he would come out fighting.

And there was one more thing. If Sol was a part of Holly, it made sense that Holly was also a part of Sol. Meaning that I had to assume Sol had learned how to do everything that Holly could do — make an earthquake, hover, glow, and, most of all, create life. That would mean he'd achieved his objective plus some. And that would mean he was more dangerous than ever before.

I couldn't just spring this new and improved Sol out of jail without some idea of what to do next. Even supposedly stuck in Holly's jail, Sol seemed to be able to pop out and say hello from time to time, so a plan seemed even more important. Maybe he got something else from my sister, too. The keys to escape. So how could I handle him, whether he was dragged out or popped out on his own?

Of course, I thought. *It has to be her. Naima.*

There was only one true way I could stop Sol, permanently, and that was to take away his power. Only Naima could do that.

Then what? I asked myself. It was a weird walk in the rain, okay? I was talking to myself, asking myself questions. Real existential shit.

Then, when Sol is just plain old Jose do Branco again, a regular human, I finally do what needs to be done. Take him on a little journey. Besides, it'll be like a homecoming for the thorns in Sol's cells, going back where they came from.

And when I get Sol there, he dies, once and for all, with no chance for him to come back ever again.

2

I finally got sick of people following me, sick of the fact that every angle of my sad trek through town most likely would be online or on the air in five minutes. I was about to fly away, to leave the day's mess somehow behind me, when I finally saw a friendly face.

"John! Wait!"

Oh thank God, I thought. *At least Carrie's still on my side.*

She jogged to catch up, pushing past the people with cameras who had been trailing me like a swarm of gnats in the summertime, an unwelcome blot of parasitic companions.

If I had stopped to think about it, I probably would have realized that I'd last seen Carrie only a few days prior, but it sure didn't feel like that. So much had happened. Who knows what she was thinking while I was a captive of the TFSA? It must have been serious, because the moment she caught up to me, she buried her face in my chest and wrapped her arms around me.

To say the gawkers were on overload trying to capture *that* moment would be understatement. I couldn't get past the insanity of 30 people holding out their phones or shouldering giant cameras, all for us. "Carrie..."

"John, I was so worried about you when I found your house empty."

"Carrie." I gently pushed her back, but she gave me a startled look, like I was shunning her affection. "It's nothing — I just..." My eyes scanned the crowd around us. "I don't like standing here, with them. It's too... *public*."

Carrie, her forehead wrinkled in thought, wiped a curl of hair over one ear. "Is there somewhere else we can go? Maybe Pip's —"

I shook my head once, sharply. "No. Not today. Not after what just happened."

"Then where?"

I checked the surrounding buildings and noticed a hotel across the street. "There." We headed toward it, the throng of followers trailing behind us, blocking traffic.

A man stood in a black jacket and tie stood to one side of the hotel doors. He had dark hair with wisps of grey at the temples, and a posture that told me he'd been working that door — or ones just like it — for a long time. I could see right away that he recognized me, based on the amount of white showing in his eyes. Of course, I was wearing my all-black hero outfit and it was notably tattered from my run-in with Sol, so I wasn't exactly going low key. The man awkwardly reached for a shiny brass handle, pulling the heavy glass door open and holding it as we passed. "Good evening, sir! And miss!" he said with too much excitement.

I paused. "Hey, thanks. Um, can you do me a favor?"

If it was possible, he eyes got even wider. "For you, Black Sword, just name it!"

I nodded, then hiked a thumb at the mob coming across the street behind us. "Can you keep those folks out? I mean, if they have a room here or something, you know, that's fine, but otherwise, no. Okay?"

He gave me a confident grin that showcased wrinkles at the corners of his eyes. "Yes, sir. Consider it done."

Both Carrie and I thanked him again, then entered the hotel lobby. Behind us, the doorman let the door silently close, then shifted to stand in front of it. Moments later, the first of the crowd reached the hotel and tried — unsuccessfully — to push past.

A few people were scattered throughout the lobby, mostly professional-looking types in business attire checking their messages or reading newspapers, with rolling suitcases at their feet. People all looking to be somewhere else, and soon. They glanced at us, then generally went back to what they were doing. Maybe one or two snuck a photo, but I could deal with that.

I led Carrie to a back corner, out of sight from the large glass windows that stretched across the front of the hotel, toward a plush couch edged by two ornate end tables. They were clones of other couches and end tables stationed throughout the huge lobby, and if it weren't for the random occupant sitting here and there to shake up the monotony of it all, you might have thought we were in a house of mirrors. By the looks of the decor, I was willing to bet the hotel didn't shop in bulk at the nearest Swedish furniture store. Which was just as well. Think of the junk drawer full of hex keys they'd end up with.

Carrie and I huddled close together, her once more folding her arms around me, and for a moment we simply stayed that way. There had been very few moments since the beginning that I wished would never end. This, most definitely, was one of them.

But eventually, I had a question. "How did you manage to show up when you did, Carrie?"

She pulled back enough to look into my eyes when she spoke. "You all made that announcement — the announcement that you were going to make an announcement? I'd held on to your belt, hoping it wasn't the last thing of yours I'd ever know. And as soon as I heard where to find you, I talked to my dad and he bought me a bus ticket. So here I am."

"Your dad was cool with that?" I asked, surprised.

Carrie gave me a conspiratorial look, then fluttered her eyelashes. My

101

heart skipped a beat, as usual. "You'd be amazed what a girl can get away with when it comes to her dad. Besides, he's pretty star struck by the whole Black Sword thing." Suddenly, her expression changed to concern. "So this *task force*... it's real?"

Involuntarily, I rubbed at my inner forearm, where Nurse Brooks had cut away my skin to take a sample for the government's enjoyment. "Oh, it's quite real. Unfortunately."

"What did they do to you, John?"

So I told her. No point in sugarcoating it. I told her the whole story, including how we got out. I even included the part about Sol showing up in my back seat, conveniently the same seat Holly had occupied.

"Then today's wasn't the first time he did that?" Carrie asked.

"No," I replied. "But it was the most clear. Now I know what I have to do."

"What?"

A prim-looking man in an impeccable suit popped into view, clearing his throat to get our attention. "Excuse me."

I raised one hand. "Listen, we need some time alone. And, *no pictures.*"

If possible, the man stood taller, pulled in his chin tighter, and succeeded in appearing even more stiff and formal than before. "Sir, I am not here to *take pictures.*"

I guess I'd offended him. Although I still wasn't in the mood to chit chat. "What is it you want, then?" I said, my irritation plain.

The man cleared his throat again. "Mr. Sword," he said. There were other words, but those two took me aback, so whatever else he said was lost to me.

Mr. Sword? MR. SWORD? This guy does not seriously think my real, given name is Black Sword, does he? Black Sword of the clan Sword? It was ludicrous.

"I'm sorry," I said, coming back to reality. "What did you say?"

"I said, I would kindly ask, on behalf of the management of this hotel, that the two of you vacate the premises. Immediately." He paused, then either remembered his manners or realized he was speaking to someone with superpowers. "Please."

"Why?" I asked. A simple question, wanting a simple answer. *Keep it simple, stupid.* That's what my grandmother would always say, although usually it was when my grandfather was knee deep in transformers and wires and solenoids. He was an electrical engineer by trade, and a tinkerer on all things electronic in his spare time. And he most definitely did not work simple.

"Why?" the man repeated. "Sir, while you have been engaged in private conversation, my staff has been *completely overrun!*" He pointed a bony finger toward the front door, and I leaned around the edge of the couch to see what had become of the rabid people following us.

The first thing I noticed was that there were more of them. A lot more. The next thing I noticed was that they had completely blocked access to the front of the hotel.

I leaned back toward Carrie. "I think it's time for us to go — but not that way." I glanced up at the man. "Okay with you if we use your back door?"

He nodded vigorously. Anything to get us out, I suppose.

3

Carrie and I ended up in an alley, and no, it wasn't secluded and romantic. It was more dingy and gross, with a scent I would love to say was only vaguely urine, but nah, it was straight up intense urine. With any luck, our back-door escape would have been the end of it, but of course, the zealots wanna... hold on. What do zealots do? The zealots wanna zeal? No, that makes no sense. Crap, I didn't think ahead on that turn of phrase.

What I mean is that there were a lot of people trying to get in the front door; a few of them were bound to seek out a back door. We bumped directly into one such person. Immediately, the phone camera came out and was shoved in our faces. At that moment, I wanted nothing more than to be rid of all these people and their cameras. Did they actually care about us? Not at all. They only cared about posting pictures and video online, showing their friends, or worse, selling what they captured.

I had an idea. A simple idea, but one that would require something very, very strange to happen. "Do you trust me?" I asked Carrie.

She smiled, but her forehead lined with sudden concern. "Of course, John. But, what?"

"Well," I started, putting one arm around her waist. "All I can say is, this is going to be weird." Carrie shot me a confused look, not necessarily for the old arm-around-the-waist maneuver, but probably for doing it in front of a stranger.

Without further explanation I lifted us off the ground, taking Carrie upward with me. Not surprisingly, she screamed, but it was just a short yelp that she quickly stifled, covering her mouth with one hand. She wrapped both arms tightly around me as we ascended, her eyes wide and trying to take in everything at once, but mostly looking at the ground as it receded. Thankfully, I remembered to rise slowly. I didn't want to give my girlfriend a heart attack, after all. Sadly, it also made for a much more dramatic video to be posted online moments later. So, random stranger who filmed us, you're welcome for the huge view count you racked up.

I felt I needed to explain, maybe ease Carrie's mind. "I've got us both, so you don't have to..." *Hold on*. That's what I was going to say. *You don't have to hold on so tightly. My power to lift you isn't based on touch.* Then I came to my senses. I didn't really *need* to tell her to unwrap her arms from around me, did I? No. No, I did not.

We floated up, toward the top of the hotel, soon breaking above some of the shorter surrounding buildings. I had done it countless times, so maybe I was a little jaded. Carrie, on the other hand, was awestruck. She tried to talk but couldn't catch her breath. "John —"

I stopped our ascent. I'm not sure that did wonders to calm her heart palpitations, since it only meant she could spend more time noticing the gaping chasm of nothingness beneath our feet. "Are you okay? Do you need to go back down?" I asked.

Carrie gripped me tighter and put both of her feet on top of mine. Funny how the human mind works, isn't it? Somehow she could get her head around being up in the sky, as long as she was supported by *something* — me — even if that something wasn't technically supported by anything else. "John, this — this is *incredible!*" Still holding on to me as hard as she could, she swiveled her head around, trying to take in the entire view.

And really, the city did look pretty from where we were. Not down in the smelly alley, not running from a throng of cameras. Just peacefully floating there, high above everything. For once, I paused to take it all in. For once, having powers didn't make me feel like I was 99 percent freak around Carrie. We stayed like that for a moment, our backs to the tall hotel, with the rest of the city splayed before us, a diorama of tiny lights and distant actions playing on repeat.

Carrie turned toward me, looking deep into my eyes, and the experience was magical. For the second time inside a half hour, we were having a moment I wished would never end. Until...

Something distracted Carrie, and I could feel her focus shift to a point over my shoulder. Still hovering, I spun us around to see what was the matter, and came face to face with a startled woman in a fluffy white hotel bath robe. The woman stood frozen in her room, looking out at us suspended in midair. She didn't even seem embarrassed by the fact that all she wore was the robe and a matching towel swirled around her head. A toothbrush hung limply from her gaping mouth.

Carrie smiled and gave a small wave, and I slowly floated us upward, leaving the stunned woman to watch us depart as a dollop of toothpaste foam dripped onto the carpet.

We crested above the cornice running along the top of the hotel, and I guided us gently to a spot on the roof, so Carrie could stand on something more firm than my shoe. She pulled back a step, once more taking in the view. "Well, John Black. *That* was new and different."

I laughed. "Yeah, sorry. It's easy for me to forget what that feels like the first time around."

"I don't think I'd ever get used to something like that," she said.

"You'd be surprised."

"So, we're really alone now. What was it?"

I shook my head. "Huh?"

"In the lobby, you said *Now I know what I have to do.* So, spill the beans."

There was no way to say it that wouldn't sound crazy. Then again, Carrie had just flown for the first time. If ever she was going to realize how bizarrely plausible my next words would be, it was this moment. I took a breath, and then let the insanity of my plot come out. "I need to get Sol out of my sister, but when I do that, he'll be incredibly strong. He'll know everything she knows. So I'll need to kill him almost immediately, before he has time to kill me. There's only one way I can think of to do that, and it's going to be really, really hard for me to make it happen by myself, but I have to. I'm going to take him into outer space where he can't survive and where there's no other life for his superpowered cells to dig into like parasites. There will be no way for him to come back to life."

Carrie thought for a moment, glancing up toward the dark sky. If I had to guess her thoughts, she was probably reasoning that if I could fly us to the top of the hotel, I could go farther, too. I imagine it was weird to think your boyfriend could fly into outer space, but that's probably the idea that was bouncing around in her brain at that moment. "Okay," she finally said. "Three things. First, will anyone help you? Holly? Your mom? Pip?"

"Holly seems to be part of the problem right now. I'm hoping that once Sol is out of her she changes, but we can't count on it. And my mom is trying to protect my sister, so she'll probably try to stop us, not to save Sol but to keep us from hurting Holly." That left one option. "As for Pip, who knows? She was out cold, and I have no idea how that happened, or why."

"Hmm," Carrie said with an index finger to her lips, like she was asking for quiet while she thought. "Then I guess we should consider outside help to be a bonus, but not something to be expected. Second question. How can you be sure Sol won't just use his powers to fly right back down to earth?"

"Naima," I replied. "I'll have to use Naima to take away Sol's powers first."

"Won't Naima just take away your powers, too? And Holly's for that matter? Won't all three of you end up in a position where that task force can just swoop in and get you all, a three-for-one sale? Four-for-one, if your mom's there, too."

"Maybe. But I have to try. Naima is the only way to make Sol powerless."

Surprisingly, Carrie didn't argue the point, didn't tell me my plan was useless and foolish. "Okay, well, that just adds another complication," Carrie said, "and you already mentioned this was going to be really hard to do by yourself. So that brings up my last point."

"Which is what?" I said.

Carrie smiled again, not a romantic smile. Not an endearing smile. A devious smile. "Naima takes away *your* powers, and that puts *you* at a disadvantage. But to me, Naima is harmless. While I don't bring superpowers to the table, I also don't lose them the moment she walks in the room. So, that decides it. You need my help."

Not to say I was your typical late-to-the-party teenage boy, but I sort of was. "I do?"

"Yep," Carrie said, smiling and nodding. Something about her changed, as suddenly as a sunny day could give way to a fierce storm. Carrie had become bold. No, not that. Not merely bold. She had become *fearless*. "But first, can we fly around a little bit more? That was *fun*."

4

"You can go faster, you know," Carrie said.

"I was worried you might scream or maybe pass out," I replied. We were a thousand feet above the ground, flying west, already beyond the suburbs that surrounded the city.

Only inches from my face, she batted her lashes at me and my heart did its old familiar flutter. "While I appreciate your concern, good sir knight, we have a long way to go. The only thing I'm likely to pass out from is boredom."

"Have it your way," I said, launching us ahead like a pair of bullets streaming through the sky. Carrie shrieked, and despite her words, I figured I'd gone too far and scared her half to death. A quick glance told me otherwise.

Carrie was grinning from ear to ear.

* * *

As we approached our target, I realized we'd lucked out. The rectangular area that included all of the government grounds, the parking lot, and the building itself was covered pretty thoroughly by a system of security cameras, but each one seemed to rely on height as its primary advantage. They dotted tall poles around the fence line and dangled from the corners of the building. But what they didn't do was look *up*. I was sure some updated edition of the TFSA Handbook would correct this oversight, but at the time, I was happy that capturing and experimenting on superhumans was still a relatively new line of work.

I landed us behind a couple of cars in the back of the parking lot, angling between camera eyes by feel. For several minutes we sat there, waiting for the alarms to blare, the agents to swarm out, but nothing happened. Either we'd descended into a gap in their surveillance or their surveillance was simply half-assed. As much as I'd love to pat myself on the back for a stellar landing, I'd have to guess option B was more accurate.

So, you might be thinking, why did we come back to the place where I'd so recently been a prisoner? To the building that sat atop the deep underground bunker where I'd been held? Because that was the best idea I had to find Naima. Although I never saw her in the building, I knew she was there, that she worked there. Either she was *still* there, or someone would know where she'd gone.

It wasn't long before a woman exited the building, walked into the parking lot, and pulled out a cigarette and lighter. Thanks for having a bad habit, lady.

Her hair was done up in a professional-looking bun, and she wore a white lab coat with an ID badge clipped to one lapel. I let her take a drag or two before I reached out with my mind. I knew the poor woman was about to spend some time in cold storage, and then might have a lot to answer for with her superiors. Might as well give her a couple of seconds of enjoyment first, right?

I sent a couple of simple commands and within moments the woman was standing before us. She had the sort of glazed look you might expect from someone who in about 30 minutes would never remember even seeing us.

"Do you know Dr. Naima Ramadi? Um..." I glanced at her ID badge for a name. *Julie Greene.* "Julie?"

"I only know Dr. Ramadi by name," she said. "Never met her. She's part of Investigations. I'm in Administration." I guess the distinction was supposed to mean something to me. It didn't.

"Any idea where she is?"

Julie shook her head. "Afraid not. You could ask around in her department, although the agents aren't usually the most talkative bunch. Or just query the system."

Query the system was definitely my preferred option. "Tell me how to do that."

In normal situations, people are reserved, hesitant. Certainly, people who work for secretive government organizations aren't known for wagging their tongues at the asking of any random question. Still, this wasn't a normal situation. Julie rattled off her username and password without a second thought, and told us exactly where to find personnel locator records on the computer network.

"You know what this means, right?" Carrie said to me.

"It means I need to get in there and get into their system," I replied.

Carrie looked down her nose at me. "You?"

I didn't understand her point, but I wasn't such an idiot that I didn't recognize when I had said *something* she thought was stupid. "What?"

Carrie rolled her eyes. "Every agent in this place probably has your entire life story memorized and your face tattooed on the back of their hand for easy reference. How exactly do you think *you* are going to get inside without causing a huge commotion?"

Julie barked a laugh and pointed at me. "Hey, yeah — you're John Black. We're all looking for you."

"My point exactly," Carrie said, crossing her arms.

I leaned toward Carrie. "Before you get too cocky, remember this. In a little while, Julie Greene will totally forget we were even here. I can do the same thing to everyone inside. *Push, push.* Whoever sees me, ignores me, then forgets me."

"You can do that?" Julie asked.

Surprised by the comment, I turned to Julie and nodded. "Yeah, I can."

"Neat," she said. "Except they record *everything.*"

"Huh?" I said. Always the intellectual, that's me.

Julie pointed up. "Cameras — they're everywhere inside. All the video gets stored on banks of computers locked up on the lower level. Even if you make everyone forget, the cameras will remember. Unless you think you can pass for me." She laughed. Yep, despite the fact that I was pushing her mind to obey and respond to us, Julie Greene still had the ability to mock me.

I didn't want to look at Carrie. I could feel the heat of her eyes on me. I knew what it meant, and I didn't want to admit it.

Still, after 45 seconds of complete silence, something had to be said. "Fine. Do it." I did *not* look at her. I did *not* see her stupid big annoying smile that was stupidly stupid and annoying.

"Julie," Carrie said, "I'm going to need the lab coat and ID."

"Carrie, I can't let you do this," I said.

Well, friends. That was a dumb thing to say, on several levels. Carrie whirled around at me, full of fire and purpose. "*Let* me?"

"You know what I mean."

She shook her head. "Yeah, I do. I think you mean well, and you're trying to protect me, but frankly, you can check that sexist bullshit at the door, John."

"What if they catch you? You could be a prisoner of the government."

IN THE BLACK VEINS OF THE EARTH

Carrie was already donning the lab coat and pulling back her hair in an attempt to mimic Julie Greene's style. "I hear the food is good," she said.

"That's not funny," I replied.

Carrie came to me, hair up, lab coat on, and ID hanging in its place. To me, it was Carrie, 100 percent. No way she looked like a government worker. Still, to a security camera positioned high in the corner of some hallway? Maybe. She looked deep into my eyes and I expected her to say something poignant, about how she had to do this, for me, and for justice. Instead, Carrie grinned. "Don't worry, John. If they catch me, I'll just tell them I brought them a present. *You.*" She turned and walked toward the building entrance.

"That's *really* not funny!" I shouted after her.

* * *

The entire 20 minutes Carrie was in the building, I was freaking out. When she finally reappeared, I couldn't believe how calmly she was walking. Not running, not being chased by agents with guns, just casually strolling out. She sauntered over like her job was no harder than mine had been — babysitting our short-term captive, Julie Greene.

"Did you get it?" I asked.

Carrie held up a small square of paper with some writing on it, wiggling it back and forth as she grinned. Then she turned to the woman next to me and started pulling off her disguise. "Here's your coat and badge," Carrie said. "Thanks."

In two minutes, I sent Julie Greene on her way with a final mental push to forget. "Okay, then, where to?" I asked.

"You fly," Carrie said. "I'll navigate."

5

It's one thing to know your way between point A and B when you're on the ground, following signs and landmarks, It's quite another to be flying overhead, looking for a place you've never been before. Thankfully, Carrie had her phone, and that phone had GPS. Once she punched in the address she'd found in the TFSA computer system, we were on our way.

At Carrie's urging, we flew at a good clip, fast enough to cover the distance in about an hour. Frankly, I had to ramp us back a little from what Carrie giddily preferred, simply because I couldn't hear a word she was saying when high-speed winds were ripping the sounds from her mouth.

I realized at some point slicing high above the hilly landscape that I was learning something new and unknown about Carrie. Once, I feared she might shun me if she knew what I was, what I could do. That she might look at my abilities and call me a freak. But now I was realizing she might find my superpowers much more fun than I did. And thankfully it wasn't in an obsessive or weird way. As strange as it seems, I'm glad I hid my powers from her originally. If we had started off flying through the air with her smiling ear to ear, I might have thought she only dated me for the thrill. Maybe we both lucked out. She accidentally found a boyfriend who could fly, and I... well, frankly, I just lucked out. Flying or not, I was still a nerd, and any reasonably sane person might question Carrie's judgment. I made a mental note never to bring the subject up with her. No sense in pointing out my faults. After all, what was a pretty girl like her doing with a dope like me in the first place? Actually, that's not fair. Carrie was certainly pretty, but that was hardly her defining characteristic. She was smart and bold, funny and insightful, caring and adventurous. All right, fine, none of that helped at all. It still made no sense that she picked me.

"That must be it," Carrie said finally, pointing toward a peculiar rectangle of fenced property tucked against the curve of a rising mountain. It stood out for all its strangeness — the area outside the fence seemed disorganized, uninteresting, and uninhabited. But inside the fence, it was like someone had set up a private botanical garden, with large trees and dense bushes arrayed in a sort of grid over an area that must have covered a couple of acres at least. "I don't see anyone guarding the perimeter, but that doesn't mean no one's looking. Maybe we should go around it and come in from the back — from the mountain?"

I nodded. Carrie clearly had the whole thing way more figured out than I did, so I simply followed her lead. Making a wide circle, we skirted the property before landing on the shoulder of the looming mountain, amid some dense pines. "Now what?"

Carrie shot me a good-natured but chiding look. "Aren't you the one who does this superhero stuff all the time? You already know what's next. This is like second nature to you, right?"

"You might be surprised how much of superheroing is just winging it," I said. I wish I was kidding. "Besides, there's the slight problem that as soon as I get close to Naima, my powers will be gone. I know I have to do this. I need to try to get her help. But, you, Carrie — you don't need to go any farther. Once I'm in there, I won't be able to just fly us away to safety."

"So what you're saying is, once you're inside these walls, you're just a regular human?" Carrie asked.

"Yeah, exactly that."

She came closer to me, just inches away. "Is there something *wrong* with being just a regular human?" Her nose slid against mine, her breath all I could smell.

Let that be a lesson to us all. If your girlfriend asks you a question, most likely she already knows your answer, and she's already several steps ahead. I stammered. "No, no, it's not that! It's just —"

"Follow me," she said, giving me a wry grin before turning and carefully making her way down the slope toward the fence.

Lesson number two: Don't complain. Just follow.

I did.

As fences go, this one was significant. More of a wall than a fence, really. It was high — probably 12 feet or more — and solid. Stone or brick or block, covered smooth with a layer of hard plaster. No picket fence here. Instead, it was a structure that said, *Hey you — buzz off!* And I respected that about it. I almost felt like saluting that wall and heading home. If only, huh? For a moment I wondered why all my opponents couldn't be as respectable and straightforward as that fence. Sad, but true.

"Okay, let's go. Fly us over it," Carrie said with a cavalier attitude. She actually made a scooping gesture with one hand, like *Come on and lift us up — get this thing done!*

"Hold on a minute," I whispered. "We have no idea who or what is on the other side."

"Right," she said, "and we won't until you get us over there."

"No, *wrong*," I said, and Carrie balked. Maybe she was getting a little power-mad, telling the superhuman what to do. I deserved it, I know, but I had to be smart about things if I was going to risk both of our lives. "Let me check first. Wait." I put a hand to the side of my head, concentrating, trying to push my mind past the boundary of the fence. At first, it wasn't very effective. I had to get angry — I had to start a fire.

Closing my eyes and reaching inside, I lit the flame that was never really all the way out. It felt like acid burning away in my stomach, leeching into the rest of my organs and filling me with rage. Then, I channeled that rage forward, through the wall.

Suddenly, I could see shapes in my mind — the trunk of a tree a few feet past the inside of the wall, a row of plants, the rough texture of mulch — but nothing glowing with warmth. Nothing moving. At least not human-sized. My awareness was so acute that small dots of color became apparent, flittering between the flatter, cooler shapes of leaves. I realized they were bugs. I could see bugs in my mind. There's a joke in there somewhere.

Anyway, there were no people. No guards. I reached farther, scanning left and right, creating a sort of mental map of the pathways in this garden I couldn't actually see. In the far distance, diagonally to our right, I saw hints of a blocky structure that I assumed was a house, so I focused my attention in that direction. It had to be our destination. I scanned toward it and through it, and finally the warmer shapes of people emerged, but they were distant, as distant as the far walls, past even the house by a good amount.

Satisfied, I let the power go and the tendrils of my awareness dissipated. I opened my eyes. "There's no one on the other side, at least not very close by."

Carrie reached for me and pulled me close, and, to be frank, I thought she might suddenly be having ideas that were much different than invading someone's garden. Oh jeez. Forget I said that. That sounds almost dirty. And I don't mean topsoil. Wow. Forget I said that, too. *Stick to the story, John.*

Carrie put her arms around me, and just as I thought she was going to say something amorous, she surprised me once more. By being all business. "Then hop to it, flyboy. Get us over this wall."

6

Silently, we touched down, toes first on the perfectly manicured bright-green grass of the garden, just feet inside the wall. Around us, rows of dense shrubs and tall grasses, along with trees ranging from spindly to massive, made it feel like we'd entered a small enclosed room rather than a wide-open space outdoors. My nose filled with the scent of conifers and an almost cloying mixture of sweet flowers. Beneath it all floated the rich, damp smell of mulch.

The pathways I had seen in my mind were suddenly real and staring me in the face. Recalling my vision, I pointed. "This way to the house," I whispered, thinking it was Carrie's turn to follow.

Which turns out to be sort of a good thing, because with her behind me, I was saved from failing before things even started. A couple of steps down the path, Carrie reached out and grabbed my elbow, sharply but without saying a word.

I was about to ask her what was the matter when I saw one finger pressed to her lips. Then she pointed that finger back over her right shoulder.

Well, crap.

There, between fronds and leaves and tree branches, stood two large men dressed in dark navy blue. Luckily, they had their backs to us, facing themselves down the long path. Carrie dipped her chin and raised her eyebrows in a way that I assumed meant something along the lines of "You're really spectacular at this superhero business, John.

Remind me to thank you for keeping us both safe."

Okay, fine, I missed them. I'd gotten distracted trying to find Naima. But now the two guards — invariably agents from Barry Wilk's little club — were in my sights, and I was more than capable of taking care of things on my terms. I nodded reassuringly to Carrie and gestured for her to watch.

Reaching out with my mind, I pushed the agents, nearly simultaneously, to do two things. First, they walked down the main path then behind a large, thick-trunked tree. Second, they each chose a spot, almost carefully, and sat down. In seconds, the two agents fell into a long, deep sleep.

I'm sure Carrie knew I could do stuff like that, but still she seemed amazed. So at least I did that part right.

"All right, shall we go?" I asked with a grin.

Carrie gave me a look that put me back in my place instantly. "Of course. Though I think I'll keep my eyes peeled for other agents you might have overlooked. If I find any, you can handle their naptime arrangements."

As we walked down rows of arranged vegetation, I had the strange feeling of strolling through the enchanted forest of some Shakespearean play, or hurrying to take tea with the Mad Hatter. Although nothing particularly unusual happened over the next few minutes, simply moving through that space was surreal. I kept expecting to see a disembodied smile hovering near the tree branches above us.

We hit a main intersection and had to make a choice: left or right. The house was still basically dead ahead, but unless we wanted to push straight through dense brush, probably drawing all sorts of attention in the process, we had to divert. Still keeping quiet, I gestured for Carrie to decide. She picked left.

Rounding the large shrubbery, we saw the looming form of the house just ahead, poking above the last few rows of plants. I had a millisecond to realize that we might be too cavalier about this whole thing, that we could stumble upon something unexpected at any moment. And then we did.

Carrie pulled up close behind me, whispering sharply in my ear: "*John. Look.*" And for the second time since we arrived in the garden, I almost screwed up. Directly in front of us, there was a person.

Sharif.

Naima's son was wandering the garden rows with his nose down in a handheld gaming device. Part of me was pretty sure we could have walked right past him and he would never have known — hell, I doubt I would have at his age. I even knew the game he was playing, by the slightly tinny loop of music emanating from the device. It was a *Force of Will* game, the theme song immediately recognizable from its dramatic cadence and stirring rhythm. Given the shiny new quality of the device Sharif held, I assumed he was playing the latest game in the series, *Ultra Blue Assassins*. Personally, I don't think any *Force of Will* game will ever eclipse *Nova Star*, but I couldn't fault the kid. At least he was in the right ballpark.

Nevertheless, I couldn't exactly let him walk away scot free. Some kind of careful alert procedures almost certainly had been drilled into the kid's head by Wilk's agents. It wouldn't take him long to raise the alarm. Which meant I either had to push his mind and send him on his way, or… take him hostage.

Then, at that exact moment, Sharif stopped dead in his tracks, only a few feet away. He stared up at us, mouth dropping open in a silent, startled O shape, the game bleeping but forgotten in his hands.

Might as well break the ice. "Hi, Sharif. How are you?" He was motionless and silent, but with kids you can tell. It wasn't the kind of silence you see out of Buddhist monks. It was the kind of kid silence that ends quickly, with a complete eruption of sound. Sharif sucked in a long breath, getting ready to yell. "Don't do that, okay?" I said. "If you scream, I'll have to stop you. And you've seen I can do all sorts of things, so stopping you from yelling is going to be pretty easy, but you probably won't like it, so... you know. Just *don't.*" I hoped really hard that the kid couldn't tell I was lying.

For a second, he was confused. He had just inhaled deeply, and now his lungs were full of air that needed a release. Needed for him to yell the one word nearly every kid was excellent at yelling: *Mom!*

I eyed him carefully, trying to look calm. Hell, trying to *be* calm. I didn't want to hurt the kid, or even the guards for that matter. And I certainly didn't want to hurt Naima. I wanted her to help me hurt Sol, and for that I could be a little bit patient. I pointed at the handheld game system. "You like that game? *Ultra Blue Assassins*? I think it's really good, although I prefer *Nova Star* myself. Ever play that one?"

The change in subject worked. It both piqued his interest and confused the heck out of him. "You — you know this game?" I nodded. "Yeah, it's cool," Sharif said. "I mean, some of the boss battles are too easy, and others seem super hard. I only have this *Force of Will* game and *Warriors of Light*. Never played *Nova Star*, but everybody says that one's awesome."

"It is, trust me," I said. "You should get it."

"What are you guys doing here?" Sharif asked.

Ah, no avoiding that topic, is there? "I need to talk to your mom, Sharif."

"Talk?" he asked, wrinkling his brow, and I nodded. "Just talk?" Again I nodded. "But Mr. Wilk says not to trust you. He says we can never tell what you might do next."

I sighed. Despite the fact that I'd already stopped Sol once before and defeated giant monsters, I knew it only took a few skeptical minds to start turning people against me. Against any of us with power. "Sharif, you've seen me before. You know I'm one of the people trying to *stop* the bad guys. I just want to talk to your mom. I need her help."

"You're not going to hurt her?"

"Of course not," I said. "How about this? I know you could run and find an agent, or just yell for help. And that would be bad for me. But I'm not going to stop you. In fact, I'm going to ask you to run back to that house and find your mom, then ask her to come out and talk to me. Once you turn around and head back, it's up to you what you do next — turn us in or help us out. What do you say?" I daresay that my offer sounded downright magnanimous. As long as my tone of voice didn't give away what my mind and body could no longer deny. Walking through the garden, approaching the house, I had been feeling a strange, growing sensation, and I knew what it meant. Now, with the house near, I doubted I had enough power to flick an ant off a rose petal. I just couldn't let anyone else know I was powerless. Not yet.

The kid thought about it, longer than I expected. But in the end, he agreed. "I'll go find my mom," he said.

"Thanks, Sharif," I replied, hoping the bead of sweat on my upper lip was hard to spot.

He turned around, took two or three steps, and stopped. "Oh, hi, Mom. These guys are looking for you," he said, thumbing in our direction over one shoulder.

And just like that, we stood face to face with the power-killing force of Dr. Naima Ramadi. In one hand she held a walkie-talkie, her thumb over the button, presumably ready to call in the agents. At that moment, not only did I feel foolishly cavalier, I felt scared. I'd be caught, but more importantly, Carrie would be caught. What would they do to her?

But when I glanced up at Naima, I saw she wore an expression that took me a moment to understand.

It looked an awful lot like gratitude.

7

"Why did you do that?" Naima asked, still holding the walkie-talkie at the ready. "Why did you let my son go?"

I shrugged. "Because I came here to see you."

Carrie stood close behind me, most likely unaware I was completely powerless. She knew it would happen, of course. That Naima canceled out everything super about me — with the possible exception of my superior sense of humor and boyish good looks, but I digress. Still, nothing *visible* had changed. Carrie might have easily thought I was capable of flying us to safety, which I most certainly was not.

"And now that you see me, your powers are gone," Naima said, matter-of-factly. "I can tell just by the look on your face." I guess she was getting comfortable with her strange talent. Oh, and I guess that whole issue was out of the bag. Carrie seemed to pull back, just slightly. "The smart thing for you to do would have been to gain leverage. You missed a golden opportunity."

"Well, maybe so," I said. "But I don't want to play games like that. I'm not going to hold your son hostage to force you to help me. If I can't convince you on my own, then I've failed. Sharif has nothing to do with it."

There was a long, anxious pause, and then Naima lowered the walkie-talkie, allowing her thumb to slide off the button. "You always seem to be full of surprises, John Black. Where's Pip? How come she's not with you?"

I considered telling her about Pip getting knocked unconscious, and her fan club shunning me, but just thinking about it gave me a headache, and I doubted we had long before an agent checked on Naima, anyway. I needed to cut to the chase. "It's a long story. But I'm here, and I need your help to stop Sol, once and for all."

"Who's she?" Naima asked, gesturing past me.

"Carrie MacGregor, ma'am. I'm John's girlfriend."

"Powers?" An abrupt question, but worth asking, and understood by all.

"No, not me," Carrie said.

Naima wrinkled up her face. "Then why are you here?"

I interjected. "I'm pretty much down to my last friend," I said. "Once you get to that point, you don't ask that friend to juggle or do card tricks. You just take what you get."

"Hey!" Carrie said, punching me in the shoulder. A shoulder that didn't sluice out of the way. "That's pretty insulting to me, don't you think?"

"Oh. Maybe. Sorry." I gave her an apologetic smile. "I just meant that powers aren't what's important right now. In fact, getting *rid* of powers — that's what's really important."

"And you expect me to trust you? To join you?" Naima was quickly folding into a protective shell. Her hand tightened on the walkie. "People with inhuman powers simply can't be trusted."

"Naima, you know me," I said. "And you know what Sol can do. Help me stop him. When the time comes, help me by taking away his power, so I can finally end this. Please."

She changed the subject. "Do you have any idea how traumatizing it was for my son to be *flung* off a building? Off a huge *skyscraper?*" Her thumb twitched, too close to the button. "For him, and for me."

"No," I said. "I don't. I couldn't know. It was something unimaginable and I hope it doesn't give him nightmares. For that matter, I hope it doesn't affect you like that either, although I have to think it does, in some way. But remember, *that was Sol*. He tried to throw away Sharif — your son — like he was a crumpled-up piece of paper."

"We almost died!" she shouted.

I had to keep my cool. It was our only chance. One more outburst like that and we'd be up to our ears in agents. "My friend Bobby *did* die," I said. "To save you both. That's what he was about. That's what *I'm* about. Sol is the enemy, and he needs to be stopped. If you don't help because I'm asking, or because the world needs you, can you do it for Bobby? For my friend who died to save you and your son?"

She stared at me, and her lip quivered. Moments passed when I couldn't tell what she was thinking. A tear welled up in one of her eyes and I tried hard not to follow suit. Just bringing up Bobby's name started me thinking. Started me feeling things again.

"Sol is inside of John's sister, Holly," Carrie said, breaking the tension of the moment with her calm voice. "We think he's doing bad things to her, like a slow poison. But it's not that, exactly. He isn't a toxin that will kill her. It's his *mind*, or his *spirit*, some part of *him*. But we think it's changing her. If we don't do something, Sol won't be the only evil superhuman in the world."

After another silent moment, Naima nodded. Then she stepped forward and came toward me, standing just inches away. She seemed like such a normal person, the corners of her eyes betraying her age. Her hair showing individual lines of grey amid the dark. But, more importantly, she was just *human*. She didn't seem like so many of the other people I'd met and who had affected my life since the dawning of my powers. She wasn't someone who was driven by an angle they wanted to play, or a perversion to rule the world. She just seemed like anyone. For a moment, I wondered if Naima and my mom might make good friends.

Unexpectedly, she reached out with her free hand, and gently touched my left forearm. She looked deep into my eyes, and I saw conflict. She wanted to do what was right. The question was, right from whose point of view?

I knew the answer. She had to do what was right for her son. He was the most important thing. She wanted a world where he could be safe.

And so I wasn't even surprised when she gave her answer. What else could she do?

Blinking away tears, Naima stepped back and her hand dropped to her side once more. "No," she said. "I won't do it. I can't. I'm sorry, John."

And then she pressed the button on her walkie and a whole lot of shit went down really fast.

8

"Run!" I said, turning away from Naima and her son.

"Run?" Carrie repeated, head titled.

Naima's effect on me wasn't visible; I can imagine it was hard for Carrie to understand I had no power, even though it had been stated plainly. "Well," I said, "it's the best plan we've got right now — come on!"

From over my shoulder, I heard shouting men approaching, barking out orders, and the fuzzy snaps of walkie-talkies cutting in and out, punctuating their words. The agents would have the place locked down soon. Too soon.

Leading the way, I took the longest, straightest path to the far side of the surrounding wall. We might find a gate or something we could climb over, but I didn't want to count on that kind of luck. No, we needed distance — enough space between us and Naima that I could get my powers back, quick. And for that, the only solution was to run.

Nothing is ever easy, so why should we have expected that dodging government agents in some maze of a giant garden would be any different? Our straight route hit a dead end, forcing us left. My only goal was not to double back, to keep gaining distance. The wall seemed so far away, though. Really it was only an idea, a mystical oasis that may or may not have existed. Through all the damn bushes, there was no way I could really see it. I just picked a direction that wasn't *toward* Naima and tried to stick to it.

On our left, something dark ran down a parallel row. An agent. "Freeze! On the ground, now!"

Not a chance, pal, I thought. Then I heard the click. The agent was armed, of course. In my state, bullets could not only hurt me, they could *kill* me. Worse, they could kill Carrie. "This way!" I yelled, grabbing Carrie's arm and ducking down a row that led us away from the agent and his gun.

Fear for Carrie's life roiled my insides. And stoked a fire. But… the fire seemed like a solitary match in a hurricane, too easy to blow out.

We turned again, this time down a row of dense, tall shrubs, tightly planted together, forming a wall of green.

It was right about then that something strange happened. I felt a tingle on my right side, like a foot that's fallen asleep.

As I ran, I tried to stoke my fire and found that it was strangely difficult, as if I was trying to throw a ball around a corner. You ever try to throw a ball around a corner? Good luck on that. The strange effects of being near Naima continued to confound me.

"That's far enough!" a voice shouted, this time on our right. They were converging on us. Time was running out. If agents suddenly appeared in front of us, we were done for.

I grimaced, struggling inside, trying to fuel the flames, trying to reclaim my power, and there was a sudden, lopsided burst within me. It was strange and clouded my head so that I almost fell sideways into a group of thorny plants, but I shook it off and kept going. *Okay, okay! Come on! Come back to me, baby!*

Still we ran.

"John? Are you okay?" Carrie asked, breathlessly. I guess she noticed my little sideways hiccup.

"Yeah, I'm fine," I said, probably not sounding fine.

"Is this far enough? Do you have your abilities back?"

I reached inside again, and another weird one-sided *blurp* almost had me reeling again. "Not quite — keep running!"

We broke right, then left, then left and right again. For those of you keeping tabs at home, that's boxing out something we had to go around. A real time waster. People were catching up.

Why didn't you bring a gun, John? The thought just popped into my head. *Why didn't you bring a gun?* I mean, it made a lot of sense... I would still be without my power, but Naima couldn't do jack to a loaded pistol. I could've used it to coerce her to help me, or to hold her hostage so the agents wouldn't take me. *You mean all the stuff you promised her you'd never do?*

Yeah. Yeah, that stuff, me. Thanks for bringing that up. Point taken.

A long straightaway opened before us and, blessedly, like some divine providence, the far wall was there at the end. Bonus points: There was a gate. The only problem was distance. It was still some ways in front of us. But distance was good, right? More distance meant more likelihood that my powers would return.

But, say. Wasn't that strange? How long had I been running? Shouldn't I have had my power back already? Had Naima grown *that* strong? I certainly hoped not. If her circle of influence kept growing, where would we end up? Could Naima one day eradicate superpowers from the face of the earth simply by existing? That would be weird, huh?

I tried again. There definitely was *something* there. A partial burst happened again, which I still couldn't explain. Imagine if there was something stuck in your throat and you tried really hard to spit it out, but whatever came out exited through your elbow. It was that level of bizarre.

Carrie and I got closer to the gate at the far wall. Still running, I looked back and she gave me a smile. We were going to make it. Get the hell out of this place and hightail it to somewhere these government goons couldn't find us.

You know that's bullshit, right?

As soon as you think you've won, *that's* when you are right and truly screwed.

I turned back toward the gate and saw an agent casually step in front of us, raising a gun. It was like something from a movie. An *Oh shit* moment of the nth degree.

Then, as if they'd been teasing us all along, four or five more agents joined him, arraying themselves on each side. We thought we were running to freedom, and we ended up running right into a phalanx of the enemy.

They'll experiment on her, too, you know, I thought.

And that was that.

It was one thing for me to jeopardize myself. It was quite another to allow Carrie to come to harm. I couldn't. I just couldn't.

The fire blazed, still sideways, still weird, but blazing. My right side felt like maybe I could use it, maybe I could attack. But my left…

Still, if I had to burn through the agents using my right side only, so be it.

No, too risky. When I really concentrated, the strange bursts of sideways energy nearly crippled me. I couldn't be sure whether I would lash out at the agents or Carrie.

I had to do something. Now.

And that, friends, that *really* pissed me off.

Still, it was too late. We got within 20 feet of the agents, and one of them pulled the trigger. Not on a gun, or not the kind you might be thinking. No, this was even more special than that. They tased me.

Without my usual powers, getting zapped with electricity was, let's just say, an electrifying experience. I don't advise it.

But it was just enough to pull something out of me that I didn't think was possible at that moment.

My voice exploded outward, making the commotion of agents gathering to stop us sound like old ladies at tea in comparison. I didn't even mean to copy my sister, I swear, but that's what happened. I shouted with all my force and power, and I was amplified and bolstered. My sound became something tangible, smashing the air with a deafening roar.

And every agent dropped down, unconscious.

I had done it. I had won.

Slight problem. Well, two.

First, I was writhing on the ground from the electrical charge of the taser. And second, Carrie was out cold, too. My knockout roar didn't discriminate, apparently.

I wish someone had taken a picture. All of us laying on the ground, with only me twitching.

9

There was a great race.

With all of us splayed about like dirty laundry on my bedroom floor, it was the dumbest of all races: simply to see who could get up first.

I had a head start by virtue of being the only one conscious, but my handicap was the fact that every muscle in my body was spastically convulsing. Let me tell you, the amount of coordinated internal effort it takes to simply get up off the ground is probably more than you'd think — even on a good day. You know, like the kind of day when you haven't been tased. Muscles, bones, connective tissues, all balancing and working in tandem. Luckily for me, the thorns in my cells like to heal quickly. In under a minute, I could sit up. I was standing — though wobbly — before two minutes went by. I swatted the two electric probes from the taser out of my body like you'd wave off dive-bombing mosquitoes.

The agent sprawled directly in front of the gate groaned. Another, to my left, began to slowly flex the fingers of one hand. Time was running out.

I shook my head, trying to clear it, but the after effects of electric shock held on. My powers remained strangely dimmed, from Naima I assumed. Even at such a distance. It was incredible and terrifying at the same time.

Carrie wasn't moving, not at all, and that spurred me. Crouching down and ignoring the way my muscles complained, I touched her neck. Her pulse was there, a rhythmic beat. *Phew*. But she was still out cold, and we needed to be long gone before our friends from the government regained their senses.

Gently, I pulled Carrie into a seated position, then leaned my shoulder into her stomach and wrapped my arms around her. Just as I was wondering how I was possibly going to go from that awkward configuration to standing, it dawned on me that I didn't need to rely on brute strength alone to pick her up. Powers to the rescue.

Willing her to rise as I got to my feet, it probably looked like I lifted her with ease. Which, technically, I suppose I did.

Around us, almost every one of the agents was starting to wake up, moaning and twitching back to life. But I had won the race.

"Later, tater," I said, even though no one likely heard me. I launched myself into the air with Carrie over one shoulder, and soon we were no more than a speck in the sky.

I thought at first it was Carrie's presence that made me fly so off-balance, but that wasn't it. She hadn't had that sort of effect when we were flying toward Naima's hideaway, so why should she be dragging me down as we left?

No, something else was afoot.

* * *

I went as far as I could, flying like a wounded duck, listing heavily to one side. I went deep into the mountains until I found a wide, remote plateau, devoid of houses or roads. Toward the back of the space was an overhang of rock that formed a cave of sorts. There, I landed as gently as I could, which wasn't very gently.

"Okay, okay, I'm awake!" Carrie said as we bounced to a stop.

"Sorry," I said. "Wasn't doing that to wake you. I'm just not feeling 100 percent."

She gave me a long, hard look, concerned. "From Naima? Still? Is she here?" Carrie looked around, trying to make some sense of where we were.

"Nope. She's miles away, back where we left her."

"And she still affects you? This far away?"

I shrugged. "Yeah, I can't explain it. But that doesn't make it not true. It feels like, I don't know... I'm only partly working. Like half of me is the way I'm used to, with my weirdo abilities, but the other half is sort of *numb*." I almost said *plain* before realizing how insulting that might be to someone like Carrie. Who was, you know, *plain*, but only in the sense of not having strange powers.

"Has this ever happened before?"

"Nope." And with that poignant thought, I said everything there was to be said on the topic. But it got me thinking. Something was wrong with me, most likely because of something Naima had done. With my powers, I wasn't worried about scuffles with the government, and I was willing to take on Sol. *Without* my powers? Different story. Yet that was how Carrie was *all the time* — normal, human. She couldn't rely on magical thorn thingies to save her ass if she landed in harm's way. And I couldn't let her get hurt. "I need to take you home, Carrie," I said, out of the blue. "You shouldn't be messed up in all of this just for me. You could get shot. Hell, you could get killed." I crossed my arms, a pose that seemed serious to me and that I felt would convey my unwavering position. How I would not be taking no for an answer.

"No way," she said, without so much as raising her voice. See how well my stern gesture worked?

"I mean it. This is no place for..."

"What? A *woman*? Were you going to say that? Please tell me you weren't going to say that."

Thankfully, I wasn't. I'm not a *complete* idiot, thank you very much. "No, not *a woman*. It's not a place for someone without these crazy superpowers. I mean, as it is, Bobby had them and he died. I don't want to expose you to that." I paused, not sure if I would say the next sentence. "I care about you too much for that." Okay, so I said it.

Carrie stared into my eyes, for what seemed like an hour. My heart fluttered, and, if I were admitting things to myself just then, I would have had to admit in that moment I would have let her do anything she wanted. "John, you're not *making* me do anything, and, well, damn it, this isn't even about just you. You need to stop being so self-centered."

So, you know, *that* was surprising for her to say. "Huh?"

She punched my shoulder, my left one, and it didn't even try to sluice out of the way. If there was a service shop for superpowers, I needed to make an appointment.

"This struggle — this battle to rid the world of Sol. That's not just *you*, struggling against your personal demons. That's the *world's* fight. If Sol wins, we all lose. He's a megalomaniacal asshole who wants to be the ruler of the world and a total self-centered tyrannical despot. No offense, John, but even if I didn't know you, *I* would want to be a part of the resistance to *that*."

She made sense, of course, but there were dangers in resisting. Real, tangible dangers. I was thinking about all those possible dangers when I realized Carrie's nose was mere millimeters from mine. "But..." I began.

And then my next lame argument was cut short by her lips on mine.

I probably had something I was going to say. It may even have been a sensible, cogent thought. Didn't matter. Carrie's kiss became my world, filling me with warmth from head to toe.

At some point it started to rain, but I was focused only on her. Carrie's left hand wrapped around my neck, her fingers burying themselves into my hair.

After a moment that felt like a year and a too-short second, all at the same time, she pulled back and lifted her head. Droplets of water splashed onto her forehead and cheeks, running in rivulets down her perfect skin.

"Damn. It's raining. Sorry, we should maybe get under that overhang," I said, nodding toward the shadows behind us.

Carrie smiled, and the water flowing down her face shifted paths, little rivers she diverted with ease, mirroring the effect she had on me. "It's just water, John. The human body is, what, 60 percent water? So who cares? Let it rain a little bit."

I barked a little laugh. "And my body is like 90 percent super-thorns." My own words startled me back to reality.

The thorns. In my cells. *All* of my cells, even the saliva in my mouth, although sure, less common there than in blood or skin cells, since so much of saliva is just water.

But didn't that mean every kiss was like playing Russian roulette? A chance — even if a slight one — that I'd pass my superpowers to Carrie?

Shit.

I mean, don't get me wrong. I absolutely, definitely wanted to kiss her. But I couldn't, right? It was too risky. It could *change* her.

I stepped back from Carrie and the look on my face must have killed the moment. Her smile faded. "What is it? What's wrong?"

How exactly should I have answered that? Should I have told her that I couldn't kiss her because she might be infected by the same superpowered curse that was inside me? Or should I have told her I jealously wanted to keep my powers to myself?

For that matter, which one was the truth?

10

We slept together.

In the cave.

Literally slept, you perv.

I know, I know, before your dirty mind starts going all over the place, remember that (a) I was feeling out of sorts and exhausted, and (b) I was deeply concerned about spreading superpowers around like Johnny Appleseed. That sounds gross. Sigh. Whatever.

Our evening was platonic. Sorry to disappoint.

I woke up hoping to feel good as new, which is to say, superpowered through and through.

I didn't.

My left side still felt, I don't know, *asleep*. Something was very, very wrong with me. And I couldn't even pin it on Naima — she was nowhere around, and besides, she had more of a light-switch effect. Off or on, all powers or none. This was different.

Maybe it was finally ending. Maybe the thorns in my cells were dying out. Hell, they came out of nowhere. I suppose it shouldn't surprise me that they might leave without warning.

Carrie had her arms wrapped around me as we slept, so it probably would have taken a nuclear strike to make me willingly abandon that. Instead, lying there, I took the time to mentally assess what was going on in my body.

My left side felt almost dull in comparison to the right. Is this what the powers had done to me? Did they make me *have* to have them? If I lost them, would I live the rest of my days feeling incomplete? *For you the blind who once could see…*

Carrie must have sensed I was awake and felt my growing distress. "Hey," she said sleepily. "Feeling any better this morning?" I shook my head, just barely. She came wide awake at that. "How can Naima reach you this far away?"

"I don't know," I said. "Maybe it's not her. Maybe I'm just… I don't know… *losing* it. In more ways than one. I mean, I might be losing my powers, or my mind, or both. You remember old Walter Ivory — how he was driven insane by these powers. And Sol. Probably the same story. Why *shouldn't* I be losing my mind?"

We both sat up. "I don't believe that," Carrie said. "You're as sane as I am."

"Well, then, why is *this* happening?" I said, reaching around on the rocky ground to find something I needed. Something sharp. I found an arrowhead-shaped stone with a ragged edge that looked like it would do the trick. I held it in my left hand, then tried dragging the edge across the flesh of my right hand. And nothing happened. My skin simply sluiced out of the way of harm.

Switching hands, I repeated the test, scraping across the back of my left hand. And I bled.

Even knowing what I would see, I couldn't believe it. No powers on my left side.

Of course this had to happen to me. The only person in the world with *half* superpowers. As if my story could get crazier. Now I would be forever known as the guy who flew in circles or could avoid bullets on one side only. God, how would that even work? Was it a perfect split, down the middle? What if something crazy happened, like getting stabbed in the heart? Was my heart half full of power and half normal? Would I heal? Or would I die? I didn't really want to find out.

Carrie sat wide-eyed. "Can you get it back?"

"Don't know," I said with a shrug. "No one gave me a user manual. I wish there was some way to, you know, *reset* myself."

"How?"

"Again, don't know."

Her brow furrowed as she thought. "There has to be a way, John. Has to be."

"I'm all ears if you have suggestions."

Carrie started to look downright perturbed. But suddenly, her expression changed. "What about Holly? Or your mom?"

"What about them?"

"*They* have powers. They should be able to help you. Me, I just feel helpless in this case. I barely understand what you can do, so how could I tell you how to change anything about it?"

"It's not a bad thought, but there's a slight problem."

"What's that?" Carrie asked.

"Well, if we go to my sister and mother, we're also going back to Sol. The last time I saw Holly, Sol popped out of her and tried to kill me. That was when I had a hundred percent of my powers. Now I'm down to half, give or take. I seriously doubt that would be enough to fend off another attack. I mean, I don't have a better suggestion. But even if we want to go find them, there's this other problem. I can't fly you around anymore. It's not safe. As I am right now, I'll fly in lame circles, like a rower with only one paddle. But what if we're a thousand feet in the sky, and the rest of my powers decide to give out?"

"*That* would be bad," Carrie said with a shiver.

"You can say that again. So we're sort of stuck here, it seems."

"Not exactly," she said, standing up and heading out of the cave.

* * *

Following Carrie, I climbed up the slope. "Where are we going?"

"Some place where I can *see*," she replied, huffing upward. After several more minutes of effort, we crested the rise, looking out over a wide valley. There below us, a road stretched across our view, from one side to the other. The roofs of houses peppered the dense green forest cover, and off to one side, a lone gas station rested inside a curve in the road. "There. Good." Without another word of explanation, Carrie started off down the far side of the hill.

"Now where are we going?" I said, hurrying to catch up.

"I'm sick and tired of you having to do everything," she said. "I'm not helpless."

"I never said you were. But what are you going to do?"

Carrie paused, turning back to me with a gleam in her eye. "We need to travel, and you can't fly us. But that doesn't mean I can't take over. I'm going to get us a car."

"How? Steal it?"

She grinned. "If I need to. Is that a problem?"

11

"Whatever you do, don't fiddle with anybody's mind, okay?" Carrie asked as we approached the gas station. There were four or five cars parked to one side, though whether they were in for service or belonged to the staff, I had no idea.

"Why?" I said. "What are you planning to do?"

Carrie grinned. "Take the easy way, if we can." She stopped in the middle of the station's paved lot and raised her hands above her head. "Hello?" she yelled.

I turned to her, confused. "This is your plan? Call for help?"

"Just shut up and watch."

All right, I thought. I had a moment to wonder if we were getting into some kind of strange spy-movie situation, where Carrie would concoct a wild story, perhaps even affecting a Russian accent, to see if she could talk her way into the use of a car. *This should be interesting, comrade.*

Carrie dropped one hand to point at me. "Anybody who can hear me, my friend here is John Black!"

"What the hell are you doing?" I muttered at her sideways.

Just then, the garage-bay door rolled up, and a middle-aged guy in a faded navy work shirt and matching pants stepped out. He had dark skin that shone at the top of his neatly shaved head, with beads of sweat glinting down the sides. Plus, he looked like he outweighed Carrie and me both by about a hundred pounds. Adding to his intimidating appearance, the guy carried a long metal bar with something that looked like a small, rubberized football near each end, held by hands covered in light-blue latex gloves stained with grease. His biceps bulged where he'd rolled up his sleeves. Whoever the guy was, he was tall, black, muscular, and adept with tools. In short, he was the anti-me.

I was about to apologize, tell him that my friend was just making a joke, when the giant man before us broke our strange silence. "Well, damn. So he is!" He smiled broadly and spoke affably, making me instantly like him. "What are you doing here, John Black? Come to give me some of your superpowers? If so, I'm ready! I'll just fly right out of here. Sick of this place, anyway."

I laughed. "No, sorry. Besides, I wouldn't know how to give you my powers even if I could." That, friends, is what we call little white lie. I had already made one superhuman — my mother — by tainting her blood with mine. And given my half-powered status at the moment, I most likely could have drummed up some blood from my left side to share.

Of course, maybe my left side blood didn't have powers any more. In that case, I could do a swell job of bleeding on him, nothing more.

Did blood choose sides of your body like that? It didn't seem logical at all.

The man in front of us stepped forward, echoing my laugh with a deep and resonant one of his own. "That's all right, it's a pleasure just to meet you. My wife isn't gonna believe this." He stripped the latex glove off his right hand and reached out for a shake. "The name's Derrick. Derrick Cawl, but you can call me Dee. My friends do, and I sure wouldn't mind calling a superhuman my friend."

We shook hands. For a moment, he eyed me sideways, like I might use my powers to crush his hand or fling him against the wall. And weirdly, I think he was kind of disappointed that I didn't. "Nice to meet you, Dee," I said.

"And what brings you around here?" He twisted his head, taking in the majesty of his surroundings. "This isn't exactly the capital, or even, you know, a real town. All we have here is me, the local mini mart, and a few houses up on the hill. Oh, and plenty of raccoons, if you like those. You can have 'em — they're always getting into the trash anyway. What are you all, lost or something?"

I answered defensively without even trying, always subconsciously needing to keep myself to myself. "No, of course not."

"Yes, we are," Carrie said, stepping forward with her hand extended, inserting herself into the conversation. "Hi, I'm Carrie MacGregor, and I'll put this simply. We're lost, and we need to get out of here. It's urgent and a lot of lives are probably at stake. Can we take one of your cars?"

Dee looked stunned, both at the request and at Carrie's boldness in asking, especially since he probably assumed I was the bold one. His expression flattened for a moment, then his big grin returned as he looked back at me and slapped forcefully at my shoulder. My *left* shoulder. "I *like* her, John. She says what she means, doesn't she?"

"Pretty much," I said, clutching my shoulder with a grimace. Of course he chose the left side.

* * *

"What a piece of junk!" I said as another pothole felt like it would reduce the car to nothing more than scraps of rubber and motes of dust.

Carrie smirked at me sideways from the driver's seat. "It's better than the car *you* got us."

Touché, Carrie. Touché.

The road out of the mountains was clearly in disrepair. Each time the tarmac gave way to scattered gravel or we hit another swimming-pool-sized pothole, I grabbed at the door handle, thinking I might need to keep the entire door from falling off. "Where did that guy say this car came from, again?"

"He said some old-timer just came by and left it, almost like a gift," Carrie replied, keeping her eyes on the road.

"Or a curse?" *That was a wise old-timer. Better to give this car to someone else than drive it and risk killing yourself.*

Carrie didn't laugh. Again, her junker car was many times better than my complete lack of one.

Although she had offered — no, demanded — to drive, her experience behind the wheel was maybe 15 minutes greater than my own. Which is to say that she'd probably driven a car fewer times than I had, oh, let's go with "escaped death." Getting out of this vehicular rust collection alive would be another notch added to that particular tally.

"Okay, so for now we're headed down out of these mountains, but then what?" Carrie asked. "I mean, once I hit an actual intersection, which way do I go? Do you have any idea where we can find your sister and mother?"

Inside, I was still feeling that awkward *halfness*, but even with just half my superpowers, I could find my sister. I raised my right hand and pointed, toward some distant place slightly to the right of our current forward track. "There," I said. "Right there."

Carrie scowled. "And what does that mean?"

"All of us with these powers emit a sort of sound, but it's not a sound. It's just in our heads. I call it our beacon. Holly's is loud as hell, as you might expect. But she's able to tamp it down quiet enough that I can't find it."

"Okay, so you're hearing — if that's the right word — a beacon, but it's *not* Holly?"

"Nope, it's my mom. She hasn't really figured out all the rules and all the norms yet. I can still find her beacon pretty easily."

Carrie pointed, generally toward where I had. "And you say they're over there somewhere?"

"Yeah, but don't worry. I'll be more exact as we get closer. For now, I need to concentrate on whatever the heck is happening inside me. If we hit an intersection, get my attention and I'll point again."

"This sounds like an efficient means of getting someplace," Carrie grumbled under her breath.

* * *

As we bumped along the country road, I pulled inward, trying to shut out everything around me. I had to dive inside myself, see what was happening. At one point, Carrie started to hum a pop song and I had to ask her to stop. I think she was offended. I told her it was me and that she sounded great. I was only half lying. Some of the notes were on key.

In my head, at first I saw nothing. I tried to follow the tunnels and pathways of my own brain, like I had done delving into other people. It's remarkably hard to do. In fact, I couldn't even figure out how to start, until I remembered what Bobby had once told me about flying. The same thing I told my mom when we needed her help. *Pick up your shoes as if they aren't yours.* Only I wasn't trying to fly, I was trying to figure out the inner workings of my mind, find out why I was only half good anymore. Still, if I could do it to someone else's mind, why not my own?

Dive into your mind as if it isn't yours.

Sounds simple, right?

And just like that, I was in. It was an out of body experience, I'll tell you. Actually, I guess it wasn't. Technically, it was an in-body experience, on top of an in-body experience, since I was in my body and also — nah. Never mind. That makes my brain hurt.

But there they were, the passageways of my mind. And, strangely, unlike anyone else's mind, if I concentrated on any of them, they *made sense* to me. Like I knew my own mind. Weird, right?

Sliding down dark tunnels, I passed through areas that called up memories — playing catch with my dad in the park. Laughing at a cartoon with Holly long before her first seizure. And Bobby. I saw Bobby, from so long ago. Not the Bobby who was my friend. The jerk Bobby, the bully. In my mind's eye, he sneered at me, a fist raised beside one ear. I had seen that particular pose many times. Strange how now I felt nostalgic about it, considering it was a memory of him beating me up. But I had things to do, so I let that image slide by as well.

Finally, I was in a sort of round, central network, with what seemed like pulses of energy whisking to and fro in a million directions at once. Maybe I was rendering it as a sort of visual hub to make sense of it to myself, but that what I was seeing.

And there before me were dots.

Hundreds, no thousands, no maybe millions of glowing dots. I pushed closer and saw even more detail. The dots formed strange arrays that interlocked and spread all around me.

Except on one side.

There, things were dark. I know, I know. The symbolism wasn't lost on me, either.

I needed to go to the dark side, but a sudden fear gripped me. Something about that darkness made the power within me afraid. Why?

I had to see.

As I moved closer, the glow of the dots receded and the darkness started to overwhelm me. Within it, I felt an almost physical revulsion. Something in me — the thorns, I presumed — did not want me going into the dark.

But I had to.

I went closer. And closer.

Until my... well, I was going to say, "My eyes adjusted," but that's not really right, is it? My real eyes were closed as I sat in the passenger seat of the car next to Carrie. My *mental* eyes, however, saw details emerge out of sheer blackness.

There were dots there, too.

Millions of dots that were even darker than the surrounding darkness. And, as if I was a satellite caught in a decaying orbit, those empty specks pulled me down to them, toward their nothingness of black.

Mentally I reached out, a single tendril toward a single dot of darkness.

And my tendril was sucked down into the black, like soap bubbles pulled down a drain.

The black dot tugged at me, threatening to pull me in, and every cell within me lurched in a fearful reaction, pulling back, trying to get away.

For a moment, nothing happened. The forward tug of the dot equaled the entire backward pull of *me* and all my powers.

Then, my mental tendril popped out of the darkness.

And a single little light turned on amid the utter black before me.

What in the holy hell is this? I thought, pausing just a moment...

...just before I dove into another dark dot and tugged, and then another dot, and another, and they began to blaze like brand new stars in an empty sky.

12

I admit it. I went nuts. For what seemed like an endless period of time, I tugged light out of darkness, turning on the stars in my mind. Then, I had a different idea. What would happen if I did the same to a dot that was already glowing?

I tried it.

And sure enough, the glowing dots went dark when I pulled at them.

Soon, I was throwing out mental tendrils by the hundreds, sweeping entire sections around me — first to light then to dark.

And then the car horn blared and scared the living crap out of me.

"John Black! Wake up!" Carrie yelled.

I startled worse than a timid kid blindsided by a jump scare in a horror movie. "I'm awake! I'm awake!" The car wasn't moving. I scanned, back and forth, looking for whatever danger Carrie had stumbled into. "What is it?"

She tilted her head to one side, giving me an exasperated look, then waved her hands at the windshield. "Which. Way. Do. I. Go?"

Oh, was that all? She really had me worried. I took a deep breath, then listened inside my head. My mother's beacon was off to the right, still there, though strangely quieter, like maybe she was moving away from us faster than we were moving toward her. I didn't want to think about how much of a pain in the neck that was going to be. We needed to keep moving. "This way," I said, allowing the urgency to seep into my inflection.

Carrie dropped the car back into gear and made the turn, the spinning tires spitting flecks of gravel behind us, like leaving memories behind.

* * *

I dove back in, once more sweeping across large fields of dots, turning them light then dark then light again. With effort, I sought to turn on all the lights, and I did. It gave me a strange and intoxicating feeling, this ability to throw switches in my mind.

Then, I tried turning them all off.

And… well, I couldn't.

Hold on. That's not totally right.

I think it's more accurate to say I *wouldn't*. Something inside me — had to be the thorns, right? — wouldn't let me turn off *all* of the dots. I didn't even get very close before a sort of revulsion came over me. If I wanted to pull the plug on *every single* dot, turn my whole mind dark, I would have to do it over the strenuous objection of every other fiber of my being.

"Are you scared, John?" a deep, resonant male voice said from the darkness around me, coming from all directions at once.

Sol.

He was echoed by a higher-pitched voice, one I was more used to hearing in my head. "Are you scared, John?"

Holly.

Then silence.

I sat in the darkness of my own mind, looking around, as it were, although such a thing technically speaking was impossible. Still, I looked around, ventured into my mind, looked for the source of the voices. In the deepness of black, with only a handful of lights left on, I tried to find them. Holly and Sol. Or find their shadows echoing through my thoughts.

I had to. Something compelled me. I had to find them.

Where are you...?

My heart raced as I dug deeper into the dark.

Where are you?

In a well of near-complete blackness, I paused, tense, seeking.

And the voices spoke again, Holly so close in my right ear, and Sol in my left. If this had been a real place, I would have felt the heat of their breath.

"Are you scared, John?" they said in unison.

I spun, finding nothing but more empty darkness.

"You should be."

And then Holly's high laugh rode across Sol's rumbling chuckle.

They mocked me.

Pain struck me, high, on my shoulder, once, twice.

"John! Come on already!"

The voice... it was female, so it wasn't Sol. But it wasn't the voice of my sister. It was...

I jumped awake again. "Carrie! What?"

She gestured forward, but there was little need. The world around us was turning violet with the coming of night, and I vaguely realized Carrie must have been driving all day. But, barring a miracle, she was done now. A dozen or more beige and navy vehicles blocked the road ahead at staggered angles, cars and large trucks. Around and on top of them were more government agents than I would have guessed existed in a hundred-mile radius. Their guns were drawn, pointed at us.

Our car was stopped just over the crest of a hill, meaning Carrie couldn't have seen the roadblock until it was far too late and we were far too close. The engine still idled, like the promise of escape, but we were only about five hundred yards away from Wilk's forces. Although their guns looked tiny from that distance, I had no desire to test the agents' range or accuracy.

"I can't let them take you," Carrie said softly. She reached for the shifter, ready to slide it into reverse and try her luck.

I put my hand over hers. "No," I said. "I can't let them *shoot* you. Taking me is temporary. You dying isn't."

Her eyes implored me. "Can you...?"

She didn't ask, but I knew what she meant. Could I take care of the agents, my way? Even if my way wasn't very fair, it was at least effective. When it worked, that is. I reached inside myself...

...and I found my powers barely there, much worse than before, sputtering like the engine of a dodgy old pickup that has spent one too many winters parked out behind the barn. Dejected, I shook my head. If I was lucky, I might be able to push the agents to say please and thank you while they arrested us. I doubted I could do more.

"I can't. So we have to give in here, see what happens. It's the only safe option."

She tried to pull her hand away, but I wouldn't let go. "You don't know what they'll do to you," she said, creasing her forehead in worry.

I thought back to Nurse Brooks and her little experiments, and I forced a smile. "On the contrary. I think I know *exactly* what they'll do to me." But there was no other way out, so, slowly, I released Carrie's hand, took off my seatbelt, opened my door, and got out. Standing beside the car, I gestured for Carrie to do the same, then put my hands over my head, palms facing the blockade of agents.

"We surrender! Please lower your weapons!" Hands still raised, I nodded toward Carrie. "Please — she's not a superhuman."

There was a crackle of static as an amplified voice replied. "But you are, of course, John. Keep your sights trained on him, everyone." I recognized the voice as Barry Wilk's right away, but didn't see him until he ducked out from behind one of the larger vehicles, carrying a megaphone.

I laughed. "I don't have *any* power at the moment. You can thank special agent Naima Ramadi for that."

Another crackle as the loudspeaker kicked in again. "Cut the bullshit, John. Naima isn't here. But I'm sure you already knew that."

"She isn't?" I muttered, too quiet for Wilk to hear. Confused. No, of course she wasn't. She hadn't been at the cave or in the car, either, but whatever she did to me back in her garden... it *lingered*.

Still, it seemed Wilk knew as little about Naima's possible *extended* aftereffects as I did. He seemed to think I had my powers, right then and there. His agents didn't flinch. Let me just tell you, without the luxury of knowing I couldn't be killed by their bullets, staring down the barrels of all those guns was enough to freeze my blood.

But Carrie... she was in real danger, too. I needed to separate from her, get her as far from the target of all those guns as possible. And that target was me. I started to walk away from the car, hands still up.

Immediately Wilk reacted. "Ah ah, that's far enough, kid. Stay where you are." Then he nodded toward a handful of agents near him and they broke ranks to run forward, coming for us. The two in front unclipped handcuffs from their belts.

He thinks I have power, but he thinks I won't use it because Carrie will be in jeopardy, I thought. *And that would be right, if I had power. The only problem is, Carrie isn't the only one that can die from a gunshot right now.*

As the agents closed the distance, I had time to consider what would come next. Carrie and I would be taken in. Separated? Definitely. Returned to someplace in proximity of Naima to squash my supposedly still-functioning powers? Yep.

Experimented upon? *Both* of us? I suspected that would be a *yes*, as well, and my blood went from ice to fire.

The agents were steps away, and I was hatching a plan to do something very, very stupid. Something that, without powers, would likely get me killed. I tensed, clenching both fists.

And that's when one of the agents in the far back — not someone approaching us, but one in the rear guard, behind the vehicles where I couldn't even see — went flying through the air and landed in a heap on the side of the road.

Shouts rose from the crowd of agents, and they turned away. Even the ones closest to us glanced back, trying to figure out what was going on. Wilk, in the middle of it all, got angry, shouting orders and dividing up his team. He turned the rear half of the group to face whatever was back there, while the remainder kept their guns trained on Carrie and me. The closest ones remained frozen, unsure of how to proceed.

A second agent was flung through the air like a rag doll, screaming through the high point of the arc, uttering a loud *oof* at the terminus, and then lying in the grass, moaning. It wasn't long before yet another agent turned this into a three-act performance.

Whatever — whoever — had come, it was someone with power. And yet my own powers escaped me. What was this strange new wrinkle?

The yelling continued, and I could see Wilk swiveling his head, trying to keep tabs on both me and what was happening toward the rear of his team.

Another agent flew, and another. Then a car, which landed, rolled several times, and burst into flames. At least that helped to illuminate the madness going on, as the hues of night deepened around us. Finally, one of the large trucks bounced and slid, skidding off the side of the road and into a ditch, leaving a gaping hole in the center of the blockade.

And there, standing in the middle of the road amid the hysteria and destruction of Wilk's government forces, was the Norse God of Vengeance, Margrethe.

Needless to say, she did not look happy.

13

"We need to go," I said sideways to Carrie. "Now!" There was no point. *She* had seen us. Or, probably more accurately, she had come specifically for us.

As the colors of the sky faded to black and the stars gradually came out, Margrethe stepped forward from the destruction, not gleeful from the wreck she'd made, but searching. She was only a dark silhouette against the bright fire of the burning car, but there was enough light that I could see a glint from her eyes as they slid dismissively over Barry Wilk's crew of government agents. She might have acknowledged the agents as living things, but they were just a blur in her eyes, with no individual worthy of too much of her time.

The coldness of Margrethe's gaze struck me. Mostly because when it landed on me the scanning stopped.

"There you are, John Black," Margrethe said, her voice deep and strong with resolution, although something in her tone sounded forced. Put on, like the required uniform you donned for your shift at the hot-dog stand.

She stomped toward us, and the agents scattered, even the ones who had been approaching Carrie and me with their handcuffs ready.

Behind Margrethe, walkie-talkies crackled and buzzed, echoing commands Wilk shouted to his team and they shouted back to him or to each other. "*...active engagement with both Tee-Three and Tee-Six...*" "*...need Special Agent Ramadi here now...*" "*...multiple agents* *down, med unit on site in 90 seconds…"*

The codes were familiar from my brief yet far too long stay at Wilk's Iron Bar Hotel and Skin Rejuvenation Spa. T3 was me; T6 was Margrethe. Funny how seeing Wilk's target list only once on a computer screen had burned it into my brain. And there was something else about it that I remembered. Something important.

"You're no different than me!" I shouted to Margrethe as she approached like an advancing tornado. Carrie huddled behind me, although in my current state, she might have been better off hiding behind a random tree, or perhaps some gauzy curtains or a dust bunny. I had about as much chance keeping her safe as any of those. Margrethe seemed to ignore my statement, so I shouted again. "I mean it! In the eyes of these agents, you, me, Sol, Holly. We're *all the same!*" That was the meaning of Barry Wilk's list of targets. None was any better or worse than the others. Pip was a target, just like Margrethe. I was a target, just like Sol.

Still the big blond woman pounded forward. "So what? These words will not be enough to pay back what you owe me, John Black."

And like that, she was upon me. I raised both hands in a futile defensive pose as Carrie smartly ducked to the side, behind the car. About a millisecond later, I was flying through the air; Margrethe had grabbed me by the neck and flung me aside, tossing me against an outcropping of rock beside the road. And she wasn't done. Before I could even shake away the stars in my vision or the ringing in my ears, she grabbed me again. For a second time, I sailed through the air, and like the agents she had handled before me, I ended up in a broken heap on the ground, letting loose a loud *oof*. Every bone in my body felt like it broke at the same time. My neck stung and tingled where she had grabbed it, my trachea nearly crushed. But I had to speak. To tell her one more thing. Sucking air into lungs that felt as useless as the rubber remains of a popped balloon, I tried to push sound from my ruined throat. *"Naima"* was all I could muster.

Reaching out to grab and throw me a third time, Margrethe paused. "What about her?" There was a tone to her voice. What was it?

Oh, I know.

Fear.

Of course Margrethe feared Naima — didn't we all? Naima could render us useless without raising a finger. What wasn't terrifying about that? "She works for them," I said, nodding toward the agents behind Margrethe. Somehow my voice was stronger, like my lungs had found a little more air somewhere deep inside. "And she'll be here, soon."

That got Margrethe's attention. "How soon?"

I had no idea, of course, but I wasn't about to let *her* know that. I didn't need any more broken body parts. "Ninety seconds. Probably less." The voice on the walkie had said medical help would be here in that time, so I borrowed the idea. Would Naima be traveling with the medics? Who knew? I only needed to keep Margrethe from killing me, so anything that stalled for time was a good idea.

"Then I kill you now, the agents next, and leave before she gets here," she said, her straw-colored braids swaying beside her head in dazzling contrast to the dark need for blood that was apparent on her face.

My little 90-second deadline was a bad idea. Rather than force her to decide not to kill me, I forced her to do it faster. It seemed rather fitting that my final achievement in life would be a mistake.

Way to go, John. Brilliant to the last.

I was thinking those words as Margrethe reached out for my head — ready to rip it from my body or crush it in her bare hands — and I sluiced away from her grip.

Wait. What? How did that happen?

Quickly, in the space of the next heartbeat, I ran internal diagnostics. Heart beating? Check. Lungs breathing? Check, and oddly better than anticipated. Trachea? Decidedly non-crushed. So... did I have my powers back? Um, that would be a most definite *check*. I stood up, and Margrethe staggered backward.

Still her hatred of me ran strong and true. She struck out, and again my body sluiced out of harm's way. Then again, and again.

As she attacked, I simply walked toward her, forcing her to step backward with each blow. "Stop, Margrethe. I don't want to hurt you. I never have," I said. "Petrus, either."

"Liar!" she screamed, swinging over and over as I continued to approach. All she could do was fall back.

"I'm not lying. If Petrus hadn't attacked me, I would never had done a thing to him. Really."

Margrethe hissed at me, seething rage. "All you do is lie, John Black! *You* are the evil in this world. *Only you!*"

More swings, more sluicing. Still I walked toward her, and she was forced to retreat. "How am I the evil? Sol wants to enslave whole cities, maybe the entire world, and rule by terror. All I want to do is…" I paused to think. Hmm. What did I want to do? I glanced sideways and saw Carrie huddled behind the car, peering cautiously over the hood to watch my duel with Margrethe. "All I want to do is hang out with my girlfriend."

Margrethe's attention shifted quickly, and I knew right away I had made another mistake. "Girlfriend?" Her eyes fell on Carrie, and a lopsided grin appeared on the Norse woman's face. "Perhaps I should take her from you, as you took my Petrus?" She danced sideways, and I found myself trying to keep my body between Margrethe and a clear route back to the car. Back to Carrie.

"I told you, I only hurt Petrus because he tried to kill me. I didn't want to do it."

"And what difference does that make, now? If you had meant to do it, would Petrus's mind be any less destroyed? Would his life now be any less meaningless? Would he have been given a second chance?"

Petrus is still alive. Of course he was. I hadn't killed him, only burned away his mind. If he was still alive, that meant someone, somewhere, was caring for him. *Margrethe? Is this what you do when you disappear? Is this where you go, to take care of him?* I felt guilt. Shame. A deep sense of sorrow for what I had put her through. And I knew there was no way I could ever make amends. I started to speak, to apologize, though I didn't know the words to use. More so, I knew there could be no words that would help. That, in some cases, apologies only made the problem worse. Sorrow is not the opposite of anger. Pity can't put out the fire of hate.

Behind Margrethe, in the blackened sky, I saw the lights of a helicopter leaning into the wind, running hard and fast to reach us. "She's coming, Margrethe. Naima. She'll be here in seconds, and then we're both out of time."

The tall blond woman hesitated. Although she didn't turn, she could hear the fast *whoosh-whoosh* of the chopper blades cutting the air, growing louder.

I was sure her hate would win out, that she would attack me even though it would mean we both got caught. *For hate's sake…*

Then she turned and with a sweeping gesture, she used the power of her mind to raise a government truck into the air and swipe it across the road like the world's noisiest and most destructive broom. Cars were crushed and agents tumbled and ran. Several more gas tanks ruptured and exploded.

By the time the helicopter swooped down, Margrethe Vit had faded into the surrounding landscape, and Carrie and I were flying south, fast, nothing more than a speck of black streaking high across the night sky.

14

Arrow-straight, I flew toward my mother's beacon, making infinitely better time than we had by car and giving Carrie her chance to be an idle passenger. She had certainly earned it, given that I spent most of her driving time adventuring inside my own head.

As we arced high above a land cloaked in darkness, the air was tinged with the fresh, rich, green smells of the forest below. Carrie was quiet and still. She may have been asleep, which is saying something. I was the one who could fly, and you wouldn't catch *me* asleep with nothing but hundreds of feet of empty air below. Carrie clearly had nerves of steel.

My powers had been fully restored, a fact that I pondered as we zipped toward the distant inaudible tone my mother had yet to learn how to silence.

What had brought my powers back? Imminent death? The presence of Margrethe? Naima approaching? Nothing made sense, and yet nothing seemed utterly implausible either. But I needed to know the answer, despite the fact that having my powers back was a very good thing, a gift. As we got closer to Holly and Mom, I not only looked that horse in the mouth, I was probing for cavities.

On the horizon, a large lake rolled into view, just as the sun was coming up behind us. The irregular shape of the water transformed from inky black to pale shades of blue as we neared, then turned to flames of orange and red, tinted with purple, as I lowered us toward the water's edge and the sun peeked above the surrounding trees.

"Is this it?" Carrie asked. "Are we... are *they* here?"

I nodded. "Pretty sure, yeah."

We followed the lake shore, closing the last few hundred yards toward the source of the beacon in my head, toward my mom. On a picturesque point of land that jutted into the calm waters, tucked amid a grove of tall conifers, a house sat. Across the water, a shadowy group of ducks flew, a few dark forms moving low and fast toward some unseen destination. Funny how, if you're like most people, you assume animals don't think — yet every single critter you've ever seen was probably going someplace on purpose. The ducks quacked and honked as they disappeared behind a small island near the opposite shore.

The house we approached was small but in a cozy-looking way, covered in wood siding painted the lightest tint of yellow imaginable, or maybe faded from some ancient vibrant version of its current self. Along the water's edge, a long screened porch dominated the structure but stood empty, white rocking chairs waiting for someone to sit with their morning coffee, watching the sun complete its daily ascent into the sky.

Only small windows pocked the slatted side walls that faced the gravel driveway to the north side of the house, where we landed with a faint crunch. Those windows were just big enough to let in light toward the back of the house. I knew the larger windows were on the other side, facing the wide expanse of water. That was, after all, the view that made people pay extra for houses like this.

Wait. I *knew* the bigger windows were on the other side. I wasn't simply making a guess based on my keen understanding of lakefront properties, since of course my knowledge of such matters ran about as deep as your average mud puddle.

No, it was because I knew the house. I recognized it.

The idea came to me suddenly, but I was sure of it. I gestured for Carrie to stay put. Then I reached out with my mind, scanning the building. With heightened senses, I heard the faintest crunching of gravel that I assumed to be Carrie next to me, but I pushed the sound from my thoughts and focused on the house.

Thin traces of two figures emerged in my mind, presumably my mother and sister. Then, to one side, a third person. No, a fourth? It was confusing. Human shapes seemed to blend, combining then separating. I had to know more, so I tapped into my fire.

Anger grew my powers like throwing gasoline on a barbecue grill. I focused on the fear and frustration of being chased, imprisoned, persecuted. Everything I'd been through. Then, big whoosh, lots of light. And with it, I could see detail.

The figures were grouped together in a central room and making gestures like they were talking. But they remained blurry — shadows that stood nearly side by side in one moment, then morphed into a single glowing blob in my head the next. Were there two people, or three, or four?

"What are you doing?" Carrie whispered, breaking my concentration. I realize that to her I must have looked like I had fallen into a trance or maybe just dozed off.

Coming back to myself, I pointed to the house. "I know this place," I said softly, trying not to announce our presence to whoever was indoors. "I've seen it before."

"Really? Whose house is it?"

"Mine," a male voice said from behind us. With a start, Carrie and I swung around, and there stood Marcos, my not-uncle, maybe-cousin, and definite part-time taekwondo instructor.

Without warning, he spun at me, kicking toward my head.

I was stunned. If it weren't for my powers, Marcos would have hit me right in the ear, and probably would have knocked me out. Thankfully, the thorns in my cells had something to say about it, and I fluidly sluiced, sliding around the kick before something in me responded more thoughtfully. I dropped into a fighting stance.

"Stop it!" Carrie yelled. "What are you doing?"

Marcos wasn't done. His high roundhouse was followed by a twisting low sweep kick, trying to take me off my feet. This time, superpowers only augmented what I was already doing. I dodged back, avoiding his blow by less than an inch. Marcos spun up into fighting stance and punched at my midsection, trying to catch me while I was distracted by his footwork. I saw it coming, just barely able to skitter to one side and out of the way, but he was back at it without pause. Another roundhouse flew, spiraling into a second one on the fly, trying to anticipate my location as I circled him, but I blocked both with raised forearms.

I was beginning to realize Marcos wasn't going to stop.

Unless I stopped him.

He dodged left but I had seen him do something similar before, in our training together. We only sparred once, but it was a good one, seeming to go on forever at that moment. With my heightened awareness, I was able to notice and memorize some of his tendencies more than most would.

Fighting Sol in the sky, I'd guessed at his attacks with much less to work on. This was different. Memories of squaring off with Marcos flooded back to me and I made an educated guess.

Feign left, duck, up and right, into a high, spinning back kick. That was my guess. So I met him at the end.

Palm outward, I slid under his spin and the forceful blow of his flying foot, striking him in the solar plexus just as his body turned toward me once more. Already airborne from the kick, Marcos's body simply changed direction, sailing awkwardly to the side.

Ten feet or more away, he hit the gravel and slid, grinding to a stop and kicking up dust.

When he didn't move for several seconds, I became concerned. "Marcos? Are you all right?" I took a step closer.

"John, wait — look," Carrie said.

Marcos slowly pushed himself up, then brushed flecks of gravel from his clothes. Deliberately he stood, facing away, tugging his clothes into place and wiping them clean until he was finally satisfied with his appearance. Then he turned toward me.

He bowed.

"Well done, John," he said, breaking into a smile. "That was almost as much fun as the first time."

Slowly, I dropped my guard. Was that it? Did he only want to spar once more? I started to laugh. "You're crazy, you know that? I could've killed you."

Marcos shrugged. "I suppose that's what made me do it. The knowledge that you could truly harm me, and the desire to see if you really would." He walked up and extended a hand, and we shook, bowing to each other, just the way he had taught me. "Carrie MacGregor, I presume?" he said, turning and gesturing toward her next. Marcos had never met her, but I'd most certainly said her name countless times.

Confused, Carrie shook his hand, even bowing a little when he did so. "Um, hi? Nice to meet you."

Marcos turned away, walking toward the house by the lake. "Come inside. They've been waiting for you."

"*That's* why this house looks familiar," I said, mostly to myself. "Holiday cards."

"Who the hell is that? What *was* that? And what are you talking about?" Carrie was trying to speak in a low voice and failing.

Marcos didn't even bother to turn back, instead calling out over one shoulder. "My name is Marcos, and this is my house. And yes, I've had a picture of this house on my holiday cards for about the last 10 years running, so I would hope it looks somewhat familiar to you, John. By the way, Carrie, don't let John lie to you and say I'm his uncle. I'm far too young and good-looking for that. I'm a cousin, on his mother's side. Now hurry up. I can make us all some food." He opened the door and went inside without another word.

What could we do but follow?

When we reached the house, I held the door open for Carrie, but she stopped. "No way. After that? I have no idea what's going on here, and I'm not going in there first."

"That's a good point," I said, walking in and holding the door behind me, so she could follow.

The house wasn't large, and the path wasn't hard to guess. I led Carrie down a straight hallway that ended in a wide sitting room, full of those large windows I knew would be there, showing the expanse of shimmering lake waters beyond.

But the picturesque view didn't get my attention. Neither, honestly, did my mother or sister.

No, my mental scan of the house had been accurate. There were three people. Four, if you wanted to count Sol trapped inside my sister.

Sitting beside my mother on the couch was Pip, all in red, with her sword casually leaning against the wall next to her. "Howdy, John," she said.

Holly, Mom, and Pip. Add me to the mix, and Barry Wilk would be in hog heaven, if he knew where to find us.

I blinked. "Can someone please explain what's going on here?"

Interlude

There is dark. There is light. At once, in the same place.

They are the same thing.

There is death. There is life. At once, in the same place.

They are the same thing.

But —

If I can discern light from the darkness...

If I can tell the living from the dead...

Then there is still hope.

III

1

Thrown back together, we four of the most powerful beings on Earth — yeah, yeah, five, if you counted Sol — did the only thing we could think of, the only thing we could agree we needed to do at that moment.

We ate breakfast.

Marcos whipped up some scrambled eggs, bacon, and toast, and after living on the road for a couple of days, Carrie and I gobbled it up like Labrador retrievers eating, well, anything. Labs eat like that, see? Oh, never mind. We were hungry.

Marcos even made coffee. Mom, Carrie, and Pip took some, although I noticed Carrie's sat untouched after her first sip. Marcos may have been a great taekwondo instructor and an all-around nice guy, but his coffee was shit.

As we ate, I felt like my mother did nothing but smile. At us. At me. It was weird.

I looked up, half a piece of bacon still poking out of my mouth. "What?"

"Nothing," she said. "Enjoy your food, John."

I froze, spitting the bacon onto my plate. "Oh my God. It's poisoned, or drugged, or something."

Carrie stopped eating in shock, but Marcos began to laugh a deep, hearty laugh.

"The only thing that will poison you here," Marcos said, "is my ability to cook."

I shook my head. "Then what? Mom? Why are you looking at me that way?"

"I'm just happy," she said, still smiling. "Happy to have my two kids here, and to have peace. Even if it's just for a little while."

"Peace?" I asked, incredulous. "What peace is that? Is Holly really at peace with Sol inside her like a virus?"

Yes, Holly said, with her mind but aloud for all to hear. *Sol is... manageable.*

"Really? Sol? *Manageable?* Are we talking about the same person?"

Someone sighed, loudly, but from their expressions, it could have been any of them — Pip, Mom, or Holly.

Holly broke the silence. *John, you need to stop trying to* solve *everything for me. For us. For everyone. All the time.*

"Why?" I asked. "Because it doesn't seem like everything is solved here, now."

"Then what?" Pip asked. "What would you do? Sol is *gone*. Yeah, we know his essence, or whatever you want to call it, is inside Holly, but she's strong, and we're here for her. Your sister, mom, and I came together to make this work."

"To make what work?" I asked.

Pip smiled. "To wipe Sol off the face of the earth, forever."

I shook my head. While I completely agreed with their goal, I didn't think my little sister was up to the task.

Sol had invaded Jake Weissman's body, and after a while, Jake ceased to exist. My sister would be no different. I couldn't sit by and just hope that she could manage.

"No," I said. "No way."

Oh, go to hell, John, Holly said.

"Holly, please," Mom said. "Watch the language, and let's try to be civil here."

Why? she retorted. *So he can continue to ignore my strength, belittle my power?*

I considered what Holly said carefully. They were not words I'd heard from her before. Not only was my sister growing up, she was becoming... *conceited*? God, I hoped not. An arrogant superhuman? That sounded an awful lot like Sol himself.

"Hol, listen. You are incredible. You can do amazing things. But you — like anyone — can be affected by Sol. He's a virus, an infection. The worst one ever. He makes smallpox look like the sniffles. He's inside you and he wants to either get out or take control of his situation. That means you either release him or you become him."

Or he becomes me, she said, unblinking.

"Is that really any better?" I asked, slamming my fork down with a loud clank, small bits of scrambled egg splattering the table.

"Of course it is," Mom said. "Holly can fight him, a little bit at a time, even though he's trying to hold on. Win the small battles and eventually win the war. We can help. All of us — by lending our strength."

Carrie spoke up. "What do you mean when you say he's *trying to hold on*?"

My mother deflated, suddenly more interested in her mug of Marcos's bad coffee than in continuing the conversation. "Nothing. Just that we can help Holly, that's all."

"We can *help* Holly by removing Sol from her before he does any more damage," I said.

"It's too late for that, John," Pip replied. "Listen, I get it. I thought the same as you, when I first met up with Holly and your mom. We had to get Sol *out*. But we can't, not anymore."

"Why?" I asked.

Mom finally looked up from the mug she now held tightly between her palms, like the object of a prayer. "Because he's everywhere inside her. She can feel it. And he's digging in. Tell him, Holly."

My sister looked like she'd rather eat dirt than explain. She really did have an arrogant streak. Admitting she was in trouble was admitting weakness, and she didn't like it one bit. *It's true. I can feel Sol in every part of my body. As long as he's holding on, the only thing I can do is fight him bit by bit.*

"Have you tried that?" I asked. "Does it work?"

Yes. I mean, it does, but there's no stopping once we really start — once we mean to do it for good.

"She can beat him if she's focused on a particular location, like her left hand," Pip said. "Getting rid of him there is like cleaning a room, but the problem is that he comes back. So the only way it's really going to work is if she does it bit by bit, all throughout her entire body, without stopping."

"But how?" I asked. "That sounds exhausting — how can she keep it up?"

"That's why your sister needs us," Mom said. "All of us. To feed her strength while she fights the fight. And now that you're here, I think we can start. We just need a plan for how we're going to keep it going — what order the three of us work in to keep her energy up."

I thought about it, and still the plan wasn't working for me. All it would take was a lapse by Holly, and Sol would come roaring back. We might work for hours on end, only to be right back in the same boat. Plus, after we made the attempt once, would Sol have new information on how to fight back? Maybe. "Why don't we use all of our combined powers to just *try* to remove him all at once?"

I'll tell you why, John, my sister said. *The truth is, I don't need any of you to get rid of Sol. If I wanted to expel him, I could do it all by myself, any time.*

"Then why haven't you?"

Haven't you been paying attention? Sol doesn't want to leave my body. If I pull him out, he'll slash and burn whatever he can on the way. He'll rip me apart as I rip him out. Then, once he's out, what's next? The end result is Sol, standing right in front of me, superpowers and all. I seriously doubt I'd be in any shape to fight him once I got him out. I don't even know if I'd still be sane after all that. But hey, you know Sol best. Maybe you can talk nicely to him and convince him to leave.

I shook my head in frustration. "Well, it sounds like you all have this figured out, like this is the only way possible. But I still don't like it one bit. What if you miss something? What if you wipe Sol out of every cell in your body but one? What if he hides? What if he comes back?"

"It's a risk we've got to take," Mom said. "The step-by-step solution is the safest way. The best way."

There's another problem with ripping Sol out of me, John, so you know.

"What's that?"

My sister's eyes blazed with some emotion that was part pride, but also part fear. *He knows everything I know now. Everything I know how to do.*

Immediately I knew what that meant. "The portal…"

Yep. If Sol comes out, he'll have the ability to make portals.

"And that means he could create life," Pip said. "He could make monsters, or a thousand clones of himself. It would be a disaster."

So either we left Sol in and hoped Holly could destroy him one bit at a time, or we yanked him out in a process that would break my sister and bring forth the most powerful evil force the world had ever known.

"*Well, if this isn't a pickle…,*" I said, reciting words I'd heard at a million family get togethers.

"*…then I'll make you a dill,*" Marcos said, completing the ridiculous phrase. "As my aunt — your Granny — used to say."

I shook my head, and despite the tension we all laughed. Granny really was an odd bird, but she could cut up a room.

2

Hours later, Carrie and I walked along the shore of the lake. The air felt damp, rich with the weirdly sharp, fresh scent of pine. A thick mat of brown needles muted our footsteps as we made our way, holding hands.

Marcos told us it was called Lake Fenice, which he explained was from the same origin as the word *phoenix*. A place of rebirth, although that rebirth might be by fire. Not sure if that was a good omen or not. I jokingly called it Lake Venice and asked Marcos if we could borrow a gondola. Carrie laughed. That's a win. Doesn't matter if anyone else laughs. Really.

Lake Fenice/Venice wasn't a vacation kind of place with swimming platforms and water skiers. No, it was simpler than all that. Just the occasional house and wide stretches where there was nothing but forest along the shoreline. Marcos explained that the home lots on the lake were larger than usual, generally several acres each. He liked that, for the additional privacy. It wasn't one of those waterfronts where they crammed as many docks as possible around the edge, and you risked diving onto your neighbor's outboard motor with every jump. It was more like a secluded swath of rippling blue and green, surround by tall pillars of green and brown. The sky above looked like it was painted in place, completing the effect of having nature in a nutshell. Natural colors, sounds, and smells were everywhere. Frogs croaked, the water gently lapped the shore. Even the smell of mud on the banks seemed fresher than most other things I could think of.

We saw a few large and impressive houses along the lake, but they seemed like an afterthought. So, what I'm saying is, we were pretty much completely alone.

We found a spot where the trees ran thick and an old log offered the perfect place for us to stop and sit. From our vantage point, we could see a couple of houses on the far side of the water, but nothing more that revealed other people might be near. And those houses we saw were so far away that a person could have been standing naked and waving their arms in the yard and we wouldn't have seen it. Which turns out to have been a good thing.

I'm describing the moment this way for a reason. Because you'd think, based on everything so far, this would be a lot like the hundred other times I had been with Carrie. But it wasn't.

"What's going through that head, John?" Carrie smiled at me, and even sort of batted her lashes, which still sent my heart racing.

But reality muted my excitement. "This whole situation with Holly. I can't stand it," I said. Just mentioning it got me worked up. The idea of doing nothing and hoping Sol would slowly be snuffed out, like waiting for fire to burn itself down… it seemed just wrong.

Carrie turned and leaned close. "I can't either," she said. How was it that we'd been on the road for days and slept in a cave, and she looked amazing and smelled faintly of flowers? I suspected I looked and smelled like last week's crumpled laundry. Or worse.

"I don't know how my mom does it," I said. "She's letting Holly try to tackle all this alone. It's way too risky. If all of this goes bad, if we don't try to get him out, I don't know what I'll do. My sister could be like Jake Weissman. One day very soon, she could just be *gone*." I was confused, both by the situation and by Carrie's nearness. Despite my worries, or maybe because of them, I fell into her arms as we sat together.

"You're a good person, John," Carrie said, her head leaning on my shoulder, arms around me. The warmth of her body was near and very present in my mind, as rational thought started to slide away. "Your mother and sister love you, and you love them. You're just trying to keep Holly safe. There are a lot of reasons why, but that's another one. Another reason why I love you."

I had reservations, you know I did. But we were both 17. At some point, clear thinking loses to something else. Passion. Yeah, I said passion. "I love you, too, Carrie," I said.

Carrie's skin was warm and soft, her hand sliding up to my cheek as she gently turned my head, my lips meeting hers. Just like back in the cave, I pulled away, my thoughts full of *what ifs*. Carrie held her hand beside my face momentarily, then started to let it drop, and that moment — that *losing her* moment — was enough. I caught her hand as it fell and returned it to my cheek, and we kissed again.

In time, the weight of it all struck Carrie, too, and she pulled back. I'll freely admit I was crushed, my heart a throbbing lump wedged in my throat, making it hard to breathe. Carrie sat looking out over the water, and I believed the moment had passed. I tried to focus my breath, return to normal, but the passion remained. And when Carrie turned back to me, I saw it in her eyes, too.

We were alone, in the wonder of nature, and we became natural with wonderment.

Look, I'm not going to kiss and tell. Well, I did that already. I'm not going to go beyond kissing and telling, but suffice to say we became something more that afternoon.

Images of red on pale white, against a backdrop of green and blue. These will forever be in my memory.

And it's a darn good thing the people in the other houses were too far away to see someone — or some two — naked by the lake.

3

I am an idiot.

I know. This isn't news to you.

I mean, you didn't read all the way to this page and then suddenly think of it just because I said it. You, no doubt, knew that I was an idiot long ago. You've been kind not to mention it, but I know you've been thinking it.

But now it was obvious even to me.

What exactly the hell did I think I was doing? Or had done?

Was I crazy, too? Or just immensely stupid?

I had been worried about *kissing*? And yet...

Let me stop. First off, like many firsts, it was both incredible and a certain kind of terrifying. There were awkward moments as well as unbelievable ones. But the sheer fact that *it happened* consumed my thoughts, allowing nothing else in. I burned through every possible option, every permutation, and with undeniable guilt, I realized my utter and complete stupidity.

One thing I had found out quite certainly was that I could, under the right circumstances, pass my powers to someone else. Using Naima to first allow me to cut myself, then switch my powers back on, I had used my blood to save my mother when she was nearly bled out. More than just bring her back from the edge of death, it turned her into something different — a superhuman.

And, foolishly, at that time at least, I assumed that was probably the *only* way I could make a superhuman.

I just forgot about the most obvious way — the way humans had been making humans since the dawn of time.

And I had just walked down that gilded path with Carrie.

I am an idiot.

Because, to put it simply, I had no clue how things would work out. Would Carrie become superhuman now? And if she did, had I just irrevocably changed the dynamic of our relationship? Why would an amazing, awesome, beautiful, intelligent, charismatic, and now *super* girl like her want to hang out with a total idiot nerd like me? I had just punched my own ticket to rejection and loneliness. You know, the place where I started.

Hey, John? Hi. It's me, you. Aren't you selling Carrie a little short by thinking she would dump you as soon as she gained power? Isn't the implication there that she's only with you because you have power? And so, like I said, isn't that selling her a little short?

In other words, don't you think you're being a little bit of a self-centered asshole?

Fine, me. Point taken.

But then there was this other thing… Oh my God. What if she got pregnant? Could she produce the first super baby? If nothing else, the fact that I just used the phrase *super baby* proves how much of an idiot I am. Carrie could become the mother of a new race.

Or maybe not. What if the baby was superhuman, but for some reason Carrie wasn't? Giving birth to that child would have huge ramifications. They might even make Carrie a saint, although technically it wouldn't be immaculate conception. Carrie would become almost a tragic figure of history, the mother of power who herself had no power.

Or... or... If the baby had power, would it even wait to be born? Geez, man, even *thinking* this is awful. I mean, there was simply no way of knowing, right? All of the rest of us got our powers after being born. Who knows what might go on otherwise. Would a superhuman baby burst forth from Carrie's abdomen like the creepiest crawly from some graphic horror film? Had I sentenced Carrie to *death*?

You can see my thoughts were all over the place.

No. No no no. Nononononono. Why was I even thinking like this? Carrie wasn't *pregnant*. There was no super baby. That's just crazy talk. I had absolutely no reason to think such things.

Except I totally did think such things, and the longer I did, the more I was certain. Even if we dodged a bullet and Carrie was her same normal self, not changed in one little bit and certainly not expecting a child, she *could* be. And that meant, for her sake if nothing else, I could *never* let it happen again. Ever.

That's what my mind was telling me.

The rest of me wasn't so sure.

I mean, Carrie was nearly an adult. She could decide on her own what risks she was willing to take, right? If she wanted to... After all, it's not like when it happened, it was terrible...

No, stop that. That's just you talking yourself into doing what you want to do, John. Pretending she could possibly grasp the ramifications in the same way.

But...

One thing remained. I did love Carrie. How could I possibly tell her all of this, and then keep her at arm's length or worse? How could I do that if I loved her?

Simple. I *had* to do it that way. *Especially* if I loved her.

I had to take a step back from Carrie. Or maybe a lot of steps. For her sake.

* * *

We returned to the lake house as these ideas were only beginning to swirl in my head. Trying to look nonchalant and failing miserably I suspect, I took the first moment to get away from Carrie. She went inside, saying she would see how the other women were doing, so I quickly looked for something to distract myself. Marcos was practicing taekwondo in the yard, and I made a beeline toward him. Not because I was in a sparring mood, but because I needed to roll through all the crazy things happening in my mind without Carrie's presence, but didn't want her to think I was ditching her.

Once the door clicked and Carrie was inside, I gave Marcos a quick, awkward wave and just kept going, right past him, into the woods, and beyond.

I circled the lake, all the way around. It took about two-and-a-half hours, total. When I finally returned to the house, the sun was beginning to set, casting long dark shadows on the western edge of the water while turning the rest of the surface rich hues of red and orange.

Carrie came outside as I approached the house. Marcos had apparently finished his practice and was presumably inside with the others. "Hey, John," Carrie said with a smile. A mischievous, knowing smile that still seemed fringed with worry. She knew something was up. I hadn't made it common practice to just disappear for hours. "You've been gone for a long time. Everything okay?"

"Yeah," I said, mostly out of habit, before clearing my throat harshly. "I mean, no." Carrie's smile fell, and with it, my heart. "I just... I just have to apologize, Carrie. For what I did. You know."

She shook her head and even gave a small laugh. "John, there's nothing to apologize for. What happened was... *mutual*."

"No, well, I mean, yeah, I think it was." It was at that moment that I realized those conniving thorns in my cells might have *used* me. What was it they were about, almost to the exclusion of anything else? Self preservation. And what could possibly preserve their species more than a little good old-fashioned self-replication? I realized at that instant the thorns might have not only influenced my behavior, they might have reached out to Carrie's mind and coerced her. Could they even do that, without my knowledge or approval? I didn't think so, and honestly I wanted to believe it wasn't possible, but once the idea hit me, I was terrified. "I don't know, really."

Her smile was swept away again. "What are you saying, John? Everything is *fine*, really." Her expression was forced, but earnest. "I love you."

I was quiet. I'd like to say it was my only sin at that moment, but it wasn't. I let those important words pass with only silence to see them go. Until I finally found something to say that was even worse than silence. "I can't let... *that*... happen again, Carrie. Not ever." I meant it for her own good, but she looked like I had just slapped her across the face. "I—" I wanted to explain, but the 50 ideas of what might happen swirled in my brain and my tongue was tied.

Carrie was tenacious. She crossed her arms. "What are you talking about, John? Tell me what's going on. Why are you acting like this?"

"Because I have to," I said, trying hard to be stern and sensible, cool-headed and realistic, in the face of such heated emotions. Everything, every stupid and awful and gigantic decision I had to make, was about me and these powers. Everything. My dad died because of me and my power. Bobby listened to me and got killed, too. Sol only chose me as his mortal enemy because of power. And now it was going to be what came between Carrie and me. "I just have to." I even crossed my arms and gave a little nod, sort of like some sitcom father dictating house rules to the kids.

That was not a wise stance to take.

Her faced reddened and she blinked, holding back tears. "You told me you loved me," she said, arms so tight across her body that her muscles might snap.

And I replied with the truth, but in a way that only the truest of idiots could. A way she didn't understand.

This is another of those moments that I'd like to take back, if I could. But even superhumans are powerless before time. Once something happens, it's done. There's no going back. Like the day with my father, like when Bobby jumped. This was one of those... moments when I wish I had a do-over.

"I can't love you any more," I said. "It's just that it's too dangerous."

What I *meant* was that I loved her so much, there was no way to love her more, and that I had to pull back because of the danger to her. The simple fact that I have to explain that sentence to you tells you why she didn't understand. She took it completely the opposite way. Like I was no longer *willing* to love her. Which those words in that order definitely *could* mean, too.

See? Idiot.

In the pressure cooker of the situation, Carrie stood like she'd been carved from ice, frozen cold and barely breathing. Her eyes flicked left and right, the only movement she made, trying to look at both of my eyes at the same time. Then, like ice, she melted.

I'll never forget the look in those eyes just before she turned away. It wasn't hatred or anything so simple. It was the worst look anyone you love could ever give you. It was utter and complete disappointment.

As the sun gave its final glint of light for the day and the world darkened, Carrie walked away toward the woods and I let her go. I gave her time alone to think.

I just didn't realize she wouldn't be coming back.

4

More than 30 minutes later, I was waiting for Carrie to return, pacing from one side of the house to the other to scan pools of brightness where Marcos had turned on his outdoor floodlights. Typically, he kept them off to let his eyes gently acclimate to the beauty of the lake at night, but I demanded he switch them on until Carrie got back.

So when there was movement on the south side of the house and the silhouette of a woman walked into view, I was more than relieved. Carrie and I could figure it all out, somehow. I would apologize, try to make up for how I had hurt her. We'd move on. We'd figure out some way to proceed without putting her at risk. We had to.

I crossed the living room toward the front door, watching her approach through the windows.

The female silhouette paused just inside one floodlit circle, and for a moment I froze. Shadows slanted sharply downward, obscuring her features. Except one.

Blond hair.

"Shit!" I jumped for the handle of the front door and rattled down the stairs to stand on the opposite side of the light from our new visitor. Our intruder.

Margrethe.

Apparently everyone in the house was on edge. We hadn't talked about any sort of plan if something bad were to happen, but it must have been in the back of everyone's mind. In seconds, Mom, Holly, Pip, and even Marcos stood behind me in a semicircle, five against Margrethe's one. Marcos clutched a baseball bat he'd grabbed from who knows where — I assumed it was his version of home security. Holly, of course, floated ominously and even began to emit a faint white light, using her unique ability.

With the five of us arrayed against her, Margrethe tensed, slipping down into a loose fighting pose before raising one hand, palm out. "Hold on," she said. "I'm not here to fight with you."

"How did you find this place?" Marcos asked with a tone that was part anger, part fear.

Margrethe simply pointed at my mother. "That one is loud."

I sighed. Of course. The same way I had tracked down my mother and sister, courtesy of Mom's inability to mute her beacon. I made a mental note to work on that with her. It could become a problem. Hell, it was already a problem.

Pip stepped forward, the hilt of her sword notably poking above her shoulders. "Why are you here, Margrethe?" she said. "Rematch? We can leave the others out of it." Pip had fought Margrethe one on one atop Sol's building, Babilu Tower. Given that they both were still alive, I'd say Round One would have to be called a draw.

Margrethe shook her head. "I said I wasn't here to fight. Believe it or not, there is one issue where we might see eye to eye."

"And what's that?" Pip asked.

"Sol," Margrethe said.

My mother scoffed. "You were Sol's highest lieutenant when he ruled the city, but we want to make sure Sol never comes back. How is that eye to eye?"

"He and I have been partners, yes, although our relationship was one of convenience only. I never bought into his whole ideological agenda. Ask John Black, he knows. I've also opposed Sol. Right?"

"You mean the time you and Petrus tried to kill me, even though Sol told you to bring me to him?" Just saying the name Petrus, the man who she loved, whose mind I had burned out, caused a momentary flash of hatred to darken Margrethe's expression. "I'd hardly say that instance gives me a lot of confidence that we're on the same side."

"You ripped the door off my sister's car!" Mom suddenly blurted out.

Margrethe looked perplexed for a second. "Sorry?" Pretty sure she ended that with a question mark. Although I'm not sure if it was because she wasn't sincere or she simply didn't have enough practice apologizing to make it sound right.

Holly's eerie mental voice suddenly boomed loudly all around us. *You worked with Sol to hold me captive. Twice. For that, I will never forgive you, and if you come closer to this house, I promise that I will kill you.* My sister seemed to pull in, consolidating power into herself. She was a star sucking inward before going supernova.

Holly was about to strike, and frankly, that was not likely to end well for Margrethe.

"Hold on!" Margrethe shouted, both palms now pointing at us, as if we were mugging some helpless woman in a back alley. "*That* is why we're on the same page — *her*."

"Explain," I said.

Margrethe spun toward me. "She's so powerful —"

Holly cut in. *Don't talk about me like I'm not here!*

"You — you're so powerful," Margrethe stammered. "If Sol could do what you can do, I don't think anyone's safe. You, me, it doesn't make a difference. I realize that now. John, when you said to me that the government thinks of us as all the same, that's when I realized it. So does Sol. He thinks of all of us like we're convenient tools for a purpose, but he'd rather just destroy us and prove to the world there is none better than him. And if he's inside you, Holly, he'll eat away at you. He's a cancer. You need to get him out of you before you *become* him. And that's not even what I'm really worried about. It's him becoming you. If he wins, he can do *anything*. Including destroy us all."

"You just want Sol free so you can go right back to being his second in command, don't you?" Mom spat.

"No," Margrethe said, dropping her hands and standing tall. "I'm done with him. I have no love for that man. He is only a danger to the world."

Love? Wait. Something was missing. I had to know what it was. "Why? What's changed?"

Margrethe stood stone faced, eyes blazing at me in the artificial light. "Petrus has... He's dead." At that moment, I actually admired Margrethe, the way she held herself, the way she spoke. She was strong. "He was with my mother while I was out trying to find you. She helped me, taking care of him when I couldn't be there. She called me and told me to come, that he was having uncontrollable spasms, violent ones that worried her."

I know what you're thinking, because I was thinking it, too. *Margrethe had a mother?*

No, what it meant was that I was right. There was something deep inside her that was better than Sol. We weren't all the same. We weren't all trapped in our fate. Sol was wrong, and so was Barry Wilk. And that meant Margrethe had more heart than I had ever given her credit for. "What happened?" It was the only question I could think of that wouldn't sound forced. While I had gained some new respect for Margrethe, I knew any words of sympathy I might offer wouldn't reach her ears the way I intended, given my responsibility for Petrus's fate.

Margrethe shrugged. "I returned to him and made a choice. And then I killed him." Around me, a collective gasp erupted. "What was left of him. He was never the same after what you did to him, John Black, but I realized two important things recently."

"Which are?"

"First, that Petrus deserved better than to live the way he was. So I released him." The offhand way she said that, talking about killing someone she supposedly loved, was surreal. "And second, that Petrus was right. Sol is not a man to follow. For Sol is not really on any man or woman's side except his own. Sol needs to be nullified, and that's just what I promised Petrus I would do before I killed him. My parting oath and solemn vow. Which is why I'm here."

"Okay," I said, blinking away my attempts to follow her logic. "I'm not sure I agree with your tactics, but if you're here to help us deal with Sol, that *is* something we can all agree on."

"John!" my mother said. "You can't possibly be willing to trust her."

"We need to get Sol out of Holly, Mom," I said flatly.

It was Pip's turn to interject. "We already told you we aren't doing that. We're here to help Holly, but she handles Sol herself. Her way."

"Holly needs our help, yes, but not to keep Sol inside," I said.

"I agree with him," Margrethe said, startling everyone. So at least I finally had an ally. Too bad it was someone of questionable moral fiber who had previously sworn to kill me.

"You need to leave, now," Pip said threateningly to Margrethe.

I couldn't believe the words I was about to say, but I said them anyway. "If she's here to help, she can stay."

"Are you crazy, John?" Mom said. "We have to protect Holly."

Since you can't stop talking about me like I'm not here, I'm going inside, Holly said, and floated away before anyone could even respond.

A light rain began to fall, and it seemed like we would stand there at an impasse until each of us was eventually drenched. Thankfully, a voice of reason was heard. "I know you all can do what you want, but I own this property," Marcos said, wiping raindrops off his forehead. "I say we call a truce until morning. Let's go inside."

"Inside?" Mom asked. "With *her*?"

Marcos seemed to understand immediately. Mom was just trying to protect her daughter. And possibly me as well. He nodded toward the single-car garage that stood at the end of the driveway, then looked to Margrethe. "You can stay dry in there. We can pick up this conversation when it's light out."

Believe it or not, that's what we did.

A short time later, I was back inside, hovering by the windows, waiting for Carrie once more. As the night grew long, I felt all I could do was wait, hoping for her sudden — and increasingly unexpected — return.

I should have gone out to find her when I had the chance, of course I should. It was the right thing to do. But how could I leave, now that we had a lion sleeping in the garage? Leaving would be the wrong thing to do.

I was stuck.

Mom walked into the darkened front room, the way only a mother can do, calmly and without judgment. I assumed she was coming to tell her son to get some rest, that we would have to look for Carrie in the morning, but no such luck. Instead she pressed a button and her phone sparked to life. On it, there were three simple lines, from Carrie:

No need to come looking for me.
I'm going home and I'm fine.
Take care, Mrs. Black.

5

Eventually, sleep found me, the way it does when you're so wound up that you're certain you'll never close your eyes, and then the next thing you know too much time has passed in an improbable instant. You startle back awake and try to convince yourself you were never asleep, but you know you were and in time your foggy mind admits defeat.

I blinked and the shadows all changed direction. Somewhere above, a fuzzy, cloud-covered moon gave off just enough light as it slid across the stormy night sky to send beams of eerie blue into Marcos's front room. In one moment, the shadows leaned to the left; in the next, to the right.

So I figured I must have been out for a few hours.

There in the dark, I began to make a plan for the next day, how I would handle my search for Carrie. I had to do something to apologize. That meant I would leave Margrethe to the others, although I didn't feel good about it at all.

Carrie would have to talk to me, if I found her. She'd have to listen to me. Right?

I wasn't trying to hurt her feelings. I was trying to *save* her. Not just her feelings, maybe her life. From me.

Something moved in the corner.

No, wait. Had I fallen asleep again? Was it just the moonlight, changing angles too quickly as I blinked an hour-long blink?

I froze.

And concentrated.

Then, in my sleep-deprived state, I realized something simple. *Use the powers, dummy.* I reached out.

There, in the corner, was something. Something that didn't want to be discovered. Which meant only one thing.

It was her.

I stood, filling myself with power. "Come out of the shadows," I said, in a quiet but forceful voice.

The darkness before me moved. "I just want to talk to you," Margrethe said.

A tendril of my mind sought to connect with hers, but she repelled it. Gotta say, that didn't fill me with confidence.

"I have an idea," she said. "Will you hear me out?"

I mean, what the hell was I going to do? Say no and start a war in Marcos's front room? He seemed to be more particular about the decor in his lake house than at his normal home. There were cute little vacation-themed tchotchkes all over, with pithy statements like "Lake House: No Rules Allowed" and "Gone Fishin'" and "Sunsets Are Better by the Water." If Margrethe and I went at it, we might break some of those, and I was pretty sure Marcos wouldn't like that. So I demurred. "Sure, go ahead."

"You and I can manage it together," she said. "I just need to know you'll back me up. It's the only way you can save your sister, if the rest of them won't see the truth."

"Why don't you pretend like I have no idea what you intend to do, and explain it in detail?" I asked. Because I had no idea what she intended to do and wanted her to explain it in detail. Sometimes you just gotta come out and say what you mean, you know?

"I didn't know if you'd want the specifics, really," Margrethe said. "Just figured I'd get your okay and we'd go from there." She waited, half in and half out of shadows.

"Sorry," I said. "I'm going to need a bit more information. She *is* my sister, remember? Otherwise, your first opponent is me." I crossed my arms.

Margrethe rolled her eyes. "I get it. You've got no reason to trust me, just like I have no reason to trust you. But I heard you earlier. You agreed with me. You and I are on the same side here. Sol needs to be pulled out of your sister, and it sounds like no one else wants to help you. I do. Back me up and we can do this."

I admit, I was anxious to agree. Beyond all sensibility, Margrethe, my mortal enemy, was the only person who was actually listening to me, actually agreeing with me. "What's your plan?"

"It's pretty simple, really," Margrethe said. "I will start a fight with your sister."

"No," I said, cutting her off.

"Calm down, John Black. I won't hurt her. I just need to get her to a point where she'll open a portal. That's where you come in."

I jumped ahead. "Let me guess. I zip in and pull Sol out through the portal?"

Margrethe shook her head. "No, I do that. He'd expect you. He won't be expecting me."

I sighed. "Did you forget something? Well, several somethings?"

"Pip? Your Mom? No, I didn't forget them. That's your job."

"And what exactly does that mean?"

"Simple," she said. "You keep them away from me while I do my part. And if you can't, or won't, we fail."

I scoffed. "Come on. What am I supposed to do? Fight them? Fight my own *mother*?"

Margrethe fidgeted, tugging at the long braid of her blond hair, flashing gold in the blue-tinted moonlight. "They won't understand, I know. But if you have to fight them, do it. It's the only way. And once Holly opens her portal, once I pull Sol out... once *he* is here in front of them all, they'll change. They'll help destroy him."

"What makes you so sure?"

"They want him gone, just like the rest of us. They're just too scared to do what has to be done. But once *you and I* do it, they'll help. Trust me."

I thought about it, listening to the crickets chirp their night song outside the house. "Trust you. That's pretty hard to do, you have to admit."

"Then don't do anything and watch your sister die."

"You know I won't do that," I said.

"Okay. If you don't trust me, trust yourself. Trust what you know to be right, that Sol needs to be taken out. And trust that they'll see the truth when the time comes, too."

"We need Naima," I said. "It's the only way we can really finish off Sol. His powers have to be eliminated."

"No, anything but that woman," Margrethe said. "Besides, she won't just take away his power. We'll all be useless."

"There has to be a way."

"There is," she said. "But not with Naima. She would just ruin everything. We need to pull out Sol, and then, between me, you, Holly, your mother, and Pip, we can do this. *We* can destroy Sol once and for all, his power and all." Margrethe leaned into the light and I saw a fire blazing behind her eyes.

The whole conversation was surreal. Speaking — no, conspiring — with Margrethe, a woman who'd tried on multiple occasions to kill me. But even if I couldn't trust her, as she said, I saw the point in what she was trying to do. Sure, I had misgivings about Naima. I thought we'd need her, but Margrethe was right that she would just make us all normal. Something could go drastically wrong, following that path. And that wouldn't get the job done. So Margrethe's way... made sense. I nodded.

"Then it's decided?" she asked. "Let's begin." Margrethe stood up taller, rolling her head around on her neck like a boxer preparing for a match.

"Hold on a second," I said. "I mean, I see the point, and I can't believe I'm saying this, but I agree with you. But give me time. Let me sleep on it."

Margrethe was conflicted. I could see she was as unused to working with someone like me as I was working with someone like her. "Every minute you wait, it'll be harder. He'll be more a part of her. Your sister is disappearing, John Black, moment by moment."

"Just — come on, just give me a *minute*," I said.

"Your choice. But make your peace quickly," Margrethe said, fading into darkness before slipping away.

I wish she hadn't taken my last words so literally. Maybe I would have ended up with less blood on my hands.

6

Having an unexpected ally gave me a resolute feeling that was oddly calming. It lulled me into a brief period of sleep. Morning had to be near, but still I dozed.

Until a deep, resonant sound like the horn of a freight ship tinged with electronic static shook the house. I knew the sound, although elements of it seemed to have changed. More disconcerting, it was accompanied by a wave of radiating power that literally knocked me off the couch where I had been asleep.

I knew two things immediately. Margrethe was done waiting. And Holly was fighting back.

"No! Stop!" I jumped up from the floor and ran down the hall toward the back room where all the windows overlooked the lake.

As I entered, I was struck by another deafening wave of sound, Holly's staggering beacon. At the same time, my vision was smothered by white light, the blinding light of a thousand suns. I stumbled to a halt, shielding my eyes with one arm, trying to discern what has happening.

In the center of the room, there was a smudge, like a stain in my vision. It was conflict, dark against light. The light tried to wrap the dark, smother it, destroy it, and the dark resisted.

I blinked, over and over, tears streaming down my cheeks involuntarily, until finally I could make out some detail. Margrethe and Holly faced each other, one standing, the other floating. Wave after wave of pulsating light emanated from my sister, a bizarre display that I couldn't comprehend and had no idea how to replicate, despite our similar powers. In the middle, Margrethe simply resisted. She tried to make a shell around herself, very much like the one we'd made in the city after we first met Naima and Holly collapsed that warehouse around us. Only Margrethe's shell wasn't holding up a falling roof. It was keeping herself from being obliterated by Holly's force. "Why didn't you wait?" I shouted to Margrethe, without thinking.

Another blast from Holly's beacon rocked the house. *What's going on here, John?* she asked. *Was this your idea?* From the center of the white glow, my sister turned her gaze toward me, her eyes trying to sear the truth out from me. I felt tendrils of her mind stab at me like a thousand needles, but I pushed them aside.

The back room wasn't huge, but it was tall, with something like nine-foot ceilings. Had there been no blinding radiance, we might have seen the first rays of the sun tint the lapping waters of the lake. Instead, in that open space, Holly ascended from the floor and hovered high above us, becoming our personal rising sun.

I held up an arm, trying to block out some of her glare. Without any conscious thought, my powers flowed. I guess the thorns knew a dicey situation when they saw one, and figured it was a reasonably good idea to start the engines. But for the moment, all of my power was latent.

Holly could sense it. Sense the coursing energies within me. She floated away from both me and Margrethe, and her light dimmed. Thanks to my flowing power and the simple basics of my returning vision, I realized my mother, Pip, and Marcos were behind me.

I was farther into the room than they were, and with Holly pulling back, the center of the large room was now notably occupied by just two people. Me and Margrethe. Yet, at least for the moment, Holly's waves of force only pounded on the Norse woman beside me. I was lucky enough to avoid that particular pleasure.

So, the two of you have been working together, Holly said. *You* attacked *me, while I slept.*

"No!" I waved my hands, denying it all. All right, perhaps my luck was running out.

Mom spoke from behind me. "Is this true, John? You've decided to ignore us and work with this... *woman?*"

"Not cool, dude," Pip added. It was subtle, but I could see her edge into the semblance of a fighting stance, the very type of preparation she had once taught me.

And there I was, stuck in the middle of giant freaking mess, with my sister, mother, friend, and cousin — or uncle or whatever Marcos was — arrayed against me, and only a mortal enemy as my ally.

We were doomed.

"He told me you could only do it once," Margrethe blurted, glaring at Holly as she strained to hold back the force waves of my sister's power.

What are you talking about? Holly said. *What did my brother tell you?*

Had I revealed something without thinking? What was Margrethe saying?

"Not your brother," Margrethe said with a sneer. "Sol."

Explain. Holly's expression turned smug. She was so commanding, so forceful, it was hard to reconcile her with the little girl I had known my entire life, or the girl in the wheelchair who never spoke. If it was possible, I loved Holly for it, and hated her. Admired her and feared her. Was drawn to her strength, yet repelled by it. More than any person alive, I should have known my sister, and I felt I did, but at the same time it seemed like I didn't understand the first thing about her. Because maybe she was more Shadow Ghost than Holly Black. *Explain!* she demanded again, shattering my thoughts.

Margrethe tried to seem unfazed, but she was putting every ounce of her power into holding off Holly's pulses of energy. The fact that she could even speak was amazing. "Sol said you could only do the portal once. That if he pushed you hard enough, you might do it, but after that, he thought you could never do it again."

A burst of energy rolled up my sister like curls of flame. *If Sol believes that*, she said, *he's even dumber than I thought.*

Margrethe shuddered, her knees buckling before she could catch herself and stand straight again. Everything she had was going into simply staying alive. Still she spoke, through gritted teeth. "I believe it, too. Obviously, you have power, but you're too wild. You can't control yourself enough to make a portal again."

To me, Margrethe's tactic seemed ham-handed and obvious. Goad Holly into making the portal? It would never work, not in a million years. I was sure of it. Why would it? How could it possibly benefit Holly to prove Margrethe wrong? Why would she even care?

And that was where I was supremely wrong. Where I proved once more that, despite knowing my sister well, I didn't know her at all. Or, why knows, maybe I did. Maybe she was still that little girl in the wheelchair, emotionally stunted, needing to prove herself.

Not only can I make as many portals as I want to, I can do it easily, Holly said, diverting part of her energies to focus on an empty section of the room, between her and the rest of us. Blackness began to swirl, a vortex like a vertical hurricane of clouds so dark they absorbed all light. Even Holly's blinding glare ceased to exist where it touched the blackness. The portal grew quickly, spiraling into an opening several feet tall in just seconds. Holly's smug expression grew as she demonstrated her power, showing off for no reason.

The flow enveloping Margrethe subsided as the portal got bigger, but only somewhat. Holly had enough strength to hold back Margrethe *and* make a portal, all at once. I stood dumbstruck.

The tall blonde continued to strain, just trying to keep from being blown back and knocked down, or worse. Still, she turned to me and shouted, "Now! You need to do it!"

I snapped to attention, staring into the impossible black of the swirling portal. *Me? I had to do it?*

"Now!"

I had an estimated three milliseconds to choose. As soon as Holly realized what Margrethe was urging me to do, she'd close the portal. It was time to act, even though I was supposed to be the one holding off Pip and my mom while Margrethe retrieved her old boss. That clearly wasn't going to happen, so I gathered my strength and prepared to dive in. I'd grab Sol with both hands and pull him out, that simple. Or at least I hoped it would be simple. It didn't really matter, though, because just before I made the leap, I did something very ill advised.

I looked into my sister's eyes.

And I hesitated.

The glare she gave me was brimming with hatred. It staggered me, maybe more than her powers were staggering Margrethe. In my instant of inaction, Holly released everything — not just the flow of energy emanating from her, threatening to crush Margrethe, but the portal itself, too. Light and dark disappeared, making the world so plain that it almost seemed to have faded into a dull grey.

As the portal winked out of existence in front of me, I knew that my chance — probably the only chance I'd ever get — was gone.

Holly continued to eye me, a poisonous look. A damning look. *You really* were *working with her*, Holly said. Not a question, but a statement of certainty. *My own brother.*

Suddenly, I had a very, very bad feeling. "No, Holly, you don't understand —"

I understand enough, she said. *I'm not stupid, you know.* She sounded arrogant and forceful, yet naive and immature. My sense of dread increased, hearing her talk that way. I could feel the power swelling inside her.

"Holly, please. What are you —" I never got the rest of my question out.

In an instant, Holly blazed with fire again, nearly blinding us all, and that fire flowed from her with a form and substance. It coalesced into a shape — first a ball, then flattening and extending in tendrils. Those extensions reached out toward me, toward Margrethe.

Holly looked at me coldly, and I readied for the worst, for whatever she would throw at me.

Then, she dismissed me. She simply turned away from me, like I was no one of consequence. The tendrils of her power shifted quickly, all focusing on Margrethe, a hundred writhing snakes who had decided I wasn't what they wanted for dinner.

The shape of Holly's power continued to gain form, each tendril become a finger or claw, the flattened ball becoming a hand. It reached for Margrethe and surrounded her, a grasping fist of force.

I had seen this before. This was Sol's way.

"Holly, no! This isn't you, this is *him*! Don't let him take you over like this!" But my words were ignored.

"Holly?" Mom said behind me, tinged with worry. "Honey, what are you doing?" She hadn't been on the roof to see Sol grab Naima's son with a fist of power, but she'd heard the tale. Knew this was too similar for comfort.

I turned to the others and pleaded with them. "Mom! Pip! We have to stop her!"

Trust is a bitch. Just when you lose it is usually just when you need it. And I needed them to trust me at that moment. They didn't. In their minds, I had teamed up with Margrethe behind their backs, and in a way, sure, I had, although I never technically gave her an okay. Didn't matter. I couldn't be trusted. Mom and Pip stood ready but motionless.

In the end, we did nothing, even me. Three superhumans watching, waiting, not acting. I immediately regretted my inaction. We all did.

When Holly attacked, it was fast and it was brutal. The hand of her power — its fingers ending in pointed talons that made it more like the claw of a monster than something from a young girl — closed down around Margrethe. The Norse God of Vengeance barely had time to grunt out her last breath of air.

I knew every cell in Margrethe's body was fighting, but Holly was simply stronger. In the blink of an eye, Margrethe was crushed, her once powerful body warped and collapsed. It was horrible to watch.

Then, not trusting that Margrethe's cells wouldn't simply put her back together once she was let go, Holly did something I would never have believed possible. Especially not from my own sister.

With the power of her mind, Holly pulled little sparkling flecks — the thorns, no doubt — from Margrethe body, and flowed them into herself, a glowing river of stars. First they came in a bright mass, thousands of dots floating toward my sister. Then the tide ebbed and the number of lights decreased, slowly at first, but soon noticeably, until at last only a few flickered their way from Margrethe to Holly. As the last dot seeped out, Holly's monstrous claw opened and the lifeless, broken form of Margrethe slipped to the floor with a sickening thud.

Holly had already shown that she could do things no other being of power could do. Now she went one better. She proved, beyond any shadow of doubt, that she could be the end of us all. Like a vampire, Holly consumed Margrethe's power, leaving nothing but an empty shell behind.

Would it even matter now if Sol consumed her, or she consumed him? She was all powerful, and nothing we could do would stand a chance.

What hope did any of us have after that?

7

For a long time, we all stood shell-shocked in the sitting room.

Not long after killing Margrethe, Holly let her power — and its bright light — slip away, and she floated herself down into her wheelchair. I don't know if she was exhausted or not, but seeing her slumped in that chair reminded me of the old Holly. The one I actually did know. The one I would do anything to protect.

I chased Sol across the country once to save my sister. Now, she was right in front of me and I felt there was nothing I could do. Sol and Holly both were before me, merging into one being more powerful and horrible than anyone could imagine.

And I was powerless to stop it.

I became furious. At Holly, at Sol, but mostly at myself.

Every step of the way, every day of my life, I bounced around from moment to moment without a clue. I wasn't a dumb guy, but I never, ever thought ahead. I never, ever had a plan.

I *had* to get Sol out of Holly. No more questions. Even if pulling him out brought Sol back into the world, that was better than a world where Sol and Holly were one and the same. With her power and his dark influence, she could kill us all. She could be 10 times the villain that he was, terrorize the entirety of the world. All would cower at her feet.

I had to get Sol out. Even if it meant killing my sister.

Let me be clear — I didn't want my sister to die, and I would do almost anything to make sure that didn't happen. My goal was to resolve everything and leave Holly alive and kicking. But if the only way to get Sol out meant killing Holly, I was suddenly ready to do it. All at once, I knew this to be true. Even if Holly had to die, it was the right thing to do, for the world.

Something important inside me died in that moment, I think. The part of me that, forever, held family above all else. I wanted to believe in that still, but to do so would be to ignore the truth staring me in the face, that my sister could destroy the world, and therefore might have to be destroyed. My mind bristled against the truth, but I became certain of the path I had to take.

And for perhaps the very first time in my entire life, I had a plan.

* * *

With a stern look on his face, Marcos set about finding a location to bury Margrethe.

It was his property, his place to decide, a fact we all seemed to sense without talking about it. After 10 minutes, he returned. "Bring her. Follow me."

Using power alone to carry Margrethe would have been simpler and cleaner, but it would also have been impersonal and undignified. Of course, Margrethe was far from petite, so I had to boost my muscles when I tried to carry her the old-fashioned way. It was so strange, being so close to a woman who had tried to destroy me, even kill me. She seemed lighter than I would have expected. In death, she was pale and limp. I realized, as I walked, why human beings had been performing burial services and other funeral rites for tens of thousands of years: because death is the ultimate humiliation, the final and biggest dismantling of spirit a person could endure. At least, by treating the deceased with care, by acting out some ceremony, we could try to send them off with something resembling dignity. So I carried Margrethe out among the tall pines, with the others trailing behind me. Except Holly. She stayed back. That was probably for the best.

Finally, Marcos stopped in a small clearing. "Here. Do I need to get my shovel, or… can you?"

Pip spoke first. "We can do it."

And then Pip and I used our powers to move the earth and bury our former enemy, Margrethe Vit, the Norse Goddess of Vengeance, sending her on her way to Valhalla, or the pearly gates, or maybe nowhere at all, depending on what you believe.

As Margrethe disappeared into the loamy earth, I couldn't help but think of Bobby, how he also ended up in a deep hole, never again to see the light of day again. I'm sure Pip was thinking the same.

* * *

Afterward, I was obsessed. My greatest desire was to figure out where Carrie was. I wanted to apologize, see what I could do to make things right. But I had to do what I had to do, and that meant let Carrie go and take care of Holly. As I had learned so keenly with my mother and Pip, forgiveness is not always ready to be given anyway. I would have to deal with Carrie later, if there was a later.

Pip didn't talk to me. Not in words. Neither did Mom. But for each of them, their eyes told me their feelings, as plain as words on paper. What Holly had done was wrong. It was terrible.

It was time for me to takes steps I thought were necessary. If nothing less, I figured they follow along out of shock.

I was sitting alone by the lake when Marcos cleared his throat behind me. "John?"

Rubbing my bleary eyes, I wondered how much sleep I'd actually had the night before. "Yeah? What's up?"

Marcos didn't sit down. He seemed tense. Which was completely understandable considering what he had witnessed in his living room, and the fact that he just had to pick out a burial plot on his own land. "I… I don't know exactly what to say. You all are my family, and I love you. I've tried to help, in every way possible. But…" He paused, struggling for the next words.

"But you've gone as far as you can," I said, my voice calm. I understood. Really I did.

Marcos nodded. "Yes. I never — this whole —"

"It's fine, Marcos, you don't have to explain. You've done so much for us. You never asked for all this trouble on your doorstep. You could never have expected what might happen." I could sense both sorrow and relief flowing from him in waves. "Besides, I don't think you have a *third* house where we can crash, do you?" I tried on a weary smile, but he didn't return it.

"John, things are very complicated," he said. *That* was an understatement. "I want to believe in the goodness of not only mankind in general, but in my family. In you, in your sister. And that's hard. I can't rectify what I want to believe with what I saw."

"I know," I said. What else could I say?

Marcos fixed me with a look that said more than words. When I was a kid, he was just another of the many faces at our family reunions. When he showed up on my doorstep and became my teacher, he turned into something new, a person of influence over me. All along, he was the elder, the one with knowledge and wisdom. And somewhere along the way, he became a friend. Now, though, he didn't know what to say. It was clear that time had changed our roles once more, and now I had to take the lead. I knew what I had to do. What we all try to do when we part with ones we love for the last time. Let him go with something resembling dignity.

"We'll leave," I said. "All of us. I promise. I have a plan. I know that's strange. Since when do I think ahead, right? But there's one final thing, if you could. One last thing to help us, and then we'll leave you in peace."

Marcos nodded and sat down beside me, hearing me out. To his credit, not once did he laugh or insist I had lost my mind.

8

They were coming, fast.

"We need to go!" I said, but nobody was moving, at least not quickly enough to satisfy me. I tried to herd the others out the door, but they bristled at my efforts.

Mom looked troubled. "We get it, John, but *where* do we go? We came here because it was remote, but they still found us. Now what?"

"I told you," I said. "I've got that covered. I know a place we can go where they won't find us. Then we can deal with Sol in peace." Technically, at least part of what I said to my mother wasn't a lie.

I probably should back up for a second and explain. I *did* have a plan. And part one of that plan was to call Deputy Director Barry Wilk and tell him where to find us.

Yep, I called the feds on us. So there was no doubt in my mind that Wilk and his agents were converging on the lake house at that very instant. We had to go.

Only Marcos knew what I'd done, and he was quiet. I don't know if that was because he trusted me or because he truly was tired of the insanity of living with superhumans, but I was glad for his silence nonetheless.

"What about Marcos?" Mom asked. For a moment, I thought she was reading my mind, but I was being careful to lock away my thoughts from everyone around me. Keeping secrets from superhumans is a bitch and requires constant vigilance.

Marcos shook his head once, looking at the floor. "I've made up my mind," he said. "I'm staying here. I'll do what I can to throw them off your trail." Still Mom scowled.

"Okay, so we're settled?" I said, standing impatiently by the door. "Marcos stays here, the rest of us..." I gestured into the air, a zipping motion. We needed to fly. Literally.

Mom leaned toward me and whispered. "About that, John. I don't think I can do it. I haven't really practiced *flying*. I can do it in controlled situations, but it still freaks me out. Doing it under pressure, well, there are no guarantees. It just never seemed like something I'd need to do."

"It's okay, Mom. I can help you. Carrie flew with me, and you can do the same." I nodded and smiled, trying to be reassuring. "So, can we go now?"

No, Holly said suddenly and forcefully. She was back in her wheelchair, slumped slightly forward in that strange way that made her look completely harmless, although nothing could be further from the truth.

"We need to, Hol," I said.

No.

Something about her face gave me pause. She seemed... what? Not just annoyed, though there was definitely that. It was something more. She seemed... scared? Maybe that was too strong. Anxious. Worried.

And you know what? Anything that scared or worried my massively powerful sister was a good enough reason for me to stop and figure things out, even with the government about to come crashing through the gates. I stood beside Holly and leaned toward her. I was just planning to ask her what was wrong in a low voice, to see if she would tell me privately, but that's not what I ended up doing.

I ended up falling into that old routine, our thing for so long. I pressed my forehead against hers, and to my shock, she let it happen. It felt strange, in more than one way, but I took it a step further. I reached out with my mind, to contact hers.

What's up, Hol? What is it?

Nothing, she said abruptly, and I thought for a moment she'd kick me out of her head. But she didn't.

Come on, sis. You can tell me.

Holly remained silent. I realized the others only saw us there together, heads touching, and had no idea what was happening. And after a moment, I figured she simply wasn't going to explain.

Then an image flashed into my mind, through our connection. An image of the edge of space, and a hole in the sky. Of three massive shapes coming through that hole.

Why was Holly showing me this — the moment when she almost killed me with her uncontrolled powers, and then created three monsters to terrorize the world instead?

In the vision, we started to fall.

And I felt the fear in my sister. Fear of falling? Maybe… but not quite.

What is it you're trying to tell me, Hol?

Still we fell, through the clouds and the emptiness of sky.

Emptiness of sky.

Holly tensed at the thought.

Is that it? The sky?

Sol's voice shattered the moment. "I love the power of the open air, don't you, old friend?"

I almost fell away from my sister, but she pushed the vision harder, filling my senses, and I saw Holly alone in the sky, falling…

…and losing control…

…to Sol.

Is that it, Holly? Something about being in the open sky helps him?

Yes, she said. *He gets stronger.*

Like when we fought, soaring through the sky, back there in the city.

Yes, that was him. It was hard for me to get control back.

It suddenly made sense to me. Each of us with our powers, we all had… specialties. Holly was incredibly powerful with her mind. I had my little rage boost. And Sol had always been good with air. He was the first to fly, as far as I knew. The one to make a fist of power from nothing more than the air around him. Hell, wind was even the thing that carried his essence into Jake Weissman. I fed these images into Holly's mind, and I felt her understand. *That's why we can't fly to escape? Because if you get into the open air, Sol gains power?*

Yes.

Well, shit, I thought to myself. And I made a mental note.

I agree, Holly said. I guess I hadn't thought that to myself after all. Or maybe, when someone's in your mind, you can't keep your thoughts to yourself. Which made me realize there were other thoughts in my head I definitely didn't want to broadcast.

Like the fact that I had called Barry Wilk myself. Mom and the others thought it was the other way around. That one of Wilk's agents had dialed Marcos's cell number and Marcos had been foolish enough to pick it up. But that was just the story we agreed upon. I didn't want Holly stumbling onto the truth. Then I'd never get any of them to follow me.

I snapped back, breaking both the physical and mental connection with my sister, and staggered a step.

"John!" Mom shouted. "Are you —?"

I waved a hand in reassurance. "I'm fine. But I understand now. We can't fly." *Can I tell them, Hol?* I asked her with my mind, and she nodded, just barely. "Holly says Sol gains power in the open air. So we need to stick to the ground. But that means we *really* need to go, like right now."

"You can take my car," said Marcos.

I put a hand on his shoulder, knowing this was likely to be a permanent goodbye. "Thank you. Really." Marcos stood straight and tall, hands clasped to his sides, and I knew immediately what he would do, and what I needed to do.

Facing each other, we bowed.

"We can't repay you for what you've done, Marcos, but at least we can leave you with your car. I think we need to stay out of sight, at least at first. Go through the woods."

I pushed through the door and into the front yard with both Mom and Pip following. A moment later, Holly was hovering beside me. Turning left, then right, I gave them each a sideways grin. "So, is everyone ready to run?"

9

Once we finally got going, getting everyone to move quickly was the easy part. The threat of Barry Wilk represented a clear and present danger to each of us. Because Barry meant Naima and Naima meant *poof*! No power. If those two got close, Mom, Pip, Holly, and I would be spending some quality time with Wilk's superhuman dissection team, and we wouldn't have any more Get Out of Jail Free cards up our sleeves.

We ran through the woods, a path that initially took us past Margrethe's burial site. That soured everyone's mood, and although we moved swiftly, it was in silence for the first hour, with me leading the way.

Pip jogged next to me as we ducked between pines. Occasionally we'd run directly through an unseen spider web that left us swatting at our faces. "Where are we going, John?" she finally asked.

I nodded over one shoulder, indicating whoever might be on our trail. "Away from them." I wasn't ready to be more specific, simply because there was too far to go and I didn't want to start an argument that could delay or even derail the plan. Soon, we might need a car, if we were lucky enough to stay unseen. Without flying, we had to find some other way to make better time.

There's another option, Holly said, letting that statement linger on its own.

I knew what she meant, or at least I thought I did. Kill Naima, end the threat. The way Holly killed so easily. Maybe it would even work. Maybe, if we could erase Sol and kill off Naima, the rest of us could live in peace.

No.

I mean, erase Sol, kill Sol, send Sol to the heart of the sun, blow Sol into a million tiny bits, sure. I was down with whatever was necessary to get him out of my life, remove his danger from the world. But Naima? Her only crime was that she worked against us. That was merely a difference of opinion on what was right for the world, and I couldn't possibly justify killing her for it. Barry Wilk either, for that matter. I didn't want the guy dead, I just wanted him to go away.

We should turn back. Let me handle this, Holly said as she slowed to a stop.

This is exactly what I don't *want. A debate.* I turned back. "No, Holly. We need to deal with Sol now, not get off track with Naima and the government." Were my motivations transparent? Was it all written on my face? I felt like it was. I was intentionally trying to provoke them into going where I wanted, and now no one was moving. As I carefully tried to avoid anyone's eyes, trying to make things look as natural as possible, my ears scanned the woods for sounds of approach. I wasn't ready to fight Wilk and Naima in the middle of some random forest. I needed us to keep going.

Mom and Pip had been on Holly's side for some time, making me the outsider. I knew my renewed position as leader was tenuous at best, and I'd have to tread lightly. What would stir them back to action, and keep them on my side? I needed something that they would agree with. "You can't go around killing everyone you don't like, Holly," I said. Well, crap. That was much harsher than my dimwitted brain thought it would be in the milliseconds before I said it. My shoulders fell, anticipating the backlash from my mother.

Instead, Holly answered. *Why not? Isn't Naima our enemy now, same as any other? I know you're all upset about Margrethe, but that woman attacked me. I only did what I had to. Now Naima is the threat, and here we are running through the woods. How long is this going to happen? How much of our lives will be spent running for our lives? I feel like I've been running for years, we all have. When do we stop and fight back? When does it change? When does it end? We'll never be at peace until we make our stand, and I say we do it now.*

Mom, Pip, and I stood in shock, mostly for the fact that Holly hadn't said so many words at one time in... well, maybe forever. There was a long silence, one that I figured I'd have to break, and frankly, I had no idea what to say next. My foot was still firmly in my mouth.

Thank God for mothers. "Killing a woman just because we don't agree with her isn't the way, Holly," Mom said, startling everyone. "Naima has a child. Would you approve if someone killed me, just because they didn't like what I was doing or what I had to say?"

"She's right," Pip said. "Holly, we just need time so you can deal with Sol. Then we can meet with Wilk and Naima and the rest of the government on our own terms, at some neutral location. They've got reservations, sure, but they've also seen us help a lot of people. It'll be like a Superhuman Summit. A safe way for both sides to figure out what's next. But not now, later. For now, we need to move."

I nodded, trying not to look too eager. People were seeing my side. Sure, Pip's Superhuman Summit might have been a delusion of grandeur, but if it would get them all moving again...

"Look, if there's one thing I see clearly, especially being the newest of our group here," Mom said, "it's that superhumans are no longer an anomaly. Something to be purged. We're here and we're staying. We're *people*, for heaven's sake. We're not aliens or a hostile power, not us. And the government needs to adapt to that reality. Because one day, who knows? There may be more of us."

And *that*, friends, made me think of my fears about Carrie all over again. Could there already be a new superhuman, um, on the way? I shivered at the thought.

"John?" Mom asked, shaking me back to the moment. "I hope you have some place in mind where we can be at peace long enough for Holly to do what she needs to do."

"That's the plan," I said, even though peace most definitely was not the plan.

10

"I need to talk to you," she said, interrupting the normal flow of operations. He didn't like it. He didn't like anything that disrupted his plans and schedules. John Black was potentially the worst at that, although he had some empathy for the kid. For me, I mean. He had some empathy for *me*. Weird to write about me in third person. Makes me feel arrogant and silly. How do people do this all the time?

Deputy Director Barry Wilk stopped in his tracks, knowing that Dr. Naima Ramadi was crucial to his plans and yet hating anything that acted as a speed bump on his road to success. Frankly, he was ready to remove the word *deputy* from his title. The director was old and tired and out of touch, and that was saying something for an agency that could tally its existence in terms of months. It was time for an upgrade, or so Wilk thought. "What is it?" he said, in a voice that was probably too curt.

"I want out," she said. "I can't do this anymore."

Wilk paused, considering options that were dwindling by the moment. The light in his field office was dim and giving him a headache. But what did he expect, attempting to lead this world-changing operation from a trailer parked by a forest in the foothills? "Naima, come on," he said. "We've talked about this. I realize you don't like the confrontational parts, but this will all be over soon. We need you for just a little bit longer and then you and Sharif can go. After that, you can do anything you want, lead a normal life, the thing you've been praying for."

Barry Wilk probably knew this wasn't true, but far be it for the truth to screw up his plans. The needs of the entire country outweighed the needs of one Dr. Naima Ramadi. "If you just finish this up," Wilk said, "not only will you have the money you've been promised, but I assure you that the government will make every effort to provide you and your son with a comfortable and uncomplicated life. That's what you want, isn't it?"

It was. It really was. And although Naima had been born, it wasn't yesterday. She could smell the stink on his words. They smelled like bullshit. "Things are never that simple," she said. "If only I'd never had this curse…" *If only I'd never heard of you people* is what she was probably thinking but had the courtesy and good sense not to say out loud. "I realize now that you all are two sides of a coin. You, Sol. He kept us where we didn't want to be and whispered lullabies in my son's ears. Now you do the same. To me."

Wilk scowled. "That's hardly fair," he said. "The federal government is nothing like that madman."

"And neither is John Black," Naima said.

Barry Wilk rolled his head around on his shoulders in frustration. "Listen, we've talked about this before. I'm not saying they're the same, not at all. But you have to agree that they're *both* a threat. A serious danger to the sovereignty of our nation." That was a mouthful, wasn't it? "Everyone knows that *Power corrupts and absolute power corrupts absolutely*. That's them. All of them. They have too much power, and we need to get a handle on all this before it's too late." You may have noticed that Barry Wilk loved to use that old *absolute power* phrase as justification for pretty much all of his actions. I wonder if he meant *my* absolute power or *his*.

Naima turned away. "If that's what you need to do, do it. But I don't need to be a part of it."

Wilk decided to play the warmth card. Be friendly. "What is it, Naima? Did something happen?"

She nodded. "He — John Black — he was *kind*. To my son. He didn't have to be. He could have used Sharif for leverage over me like so many others have recently."

"And that makes you think he's a good person and we should just leave him alone?"

"Basically," she said.

"What about his sister?"

Naima had no answer. She had seen Holly blow up a building and create a spinning vortex that sucked up Sol himself. Plus, while she doubted she got the same level of detail as the deputy director, as a government agent she'd seen some of the classified reports. About the giant monsters called Gorgols that the young girl had apparently *made*. Did she want someone with that sort of power roaming the streets?

"See?" Barry Wilk prodded. "We *are* in agreement, aren't we?"

"That's complicated," she said. "But I've made up my mind."

At that moment, Barry Wilk got an idea, and it was a terrible idea. Wilk, I think, honestly wasn't a mean or horrible person. He wanted success in his career, and he legitimately believed he was making the world a safer place. But even he knew this idea was extreme. He hesitated.

"What do I need to do to... I don't know what you call it. *Un*-enlist?" Naima said.

Barry Wilk chilled. He was all about loyalty, and what Naima was trying to do didn't suit him one bit. He looked her over, calmly and slowly. "Naima, please. What can I do to assure you that things are fine? We only need you for a little longer, then you and Sharif are free to do what you like. As long as you never exhibit signs of power — destructive power, I mean — the government will have no interest in bothering you again."

As long as you never exhibit signs of power. Sure, Wilk qualified it, but that was still a loaded phrase, wasn't it? What was power? People like me, or Sol, or Holly, we could wield massive strength and probably level cities. But Naima? What could she do? At the moment, not a lot, other than shut us down. But she had no clue how she came to have those abilities. Could she stop them from evolving, if they wanted to do such a thing? And if her power evolved, she would be right back in the crosshairs of the federal government. Without doing a thing.

"I knew this was a bad choice from the beginning," she muttered.

Wilk once again tried to appear warm and sympathetic, but it was harder because of his idea. His very bad idea. "No, Naima. Working with us was the best choice you could make. I'm only asking you to stick with that choice."

"I can't. I mean it. I want out." She looked away, which was perhaps the very worst thing she could have done at that moment. Because for Barry Wilk, it was so much easier to make up his mind when the subject of his very bad idea wasn't looking him in the eye.

11

Naima stormed into Barry Wilk's office. "Where is he? Where is my son?" A day or so had passed since their last conversation, and although she had been on the lookout for anything unusual in the wake of her announced retirement from government service, she hadn't expected Wilk to stoop so low as to abduct her son.

"How would I know?" Wilk replied.

Naima nearly screamed. "How would *you* know? Aren't *you* the deputy director?" She closed the distance between them, and even though she was shorter by several inches, she puffed herself up into her most intimidating pose and poked a finger directly at Barry Wilk's nose. "He isn't in our trailer, I can't find him anywhere inside the secure perimeter, and when I ask the other agents where Sharif is, they tell me they haven't seen him."

Wilk shrugged. "He's a kid. He's probably just playing hide and seek or something."

"No," she said. "Because that's not the only thing the other agents have said to me. Many of them suggested I come see you. Why would they do that, if Sharif was just out playing *hide and seek?*"

"He's fine. I swear. Calm down." Naima was stunned, realizing she wasn't simply being paranoid. Wilk *had* done something with Sharif.

Veins bulged at her temples as she squinted at the man she had called her boss. "If anything happens to my son, I will make sure you pay for it."

Wilk smiled smugly. "And exactly how would that happen?"

"If you don't return my son to me this instant, I will not only leave this agency, I will…" And then she said something pretty rash. "I'll join forces with John Black and his sister, and we'll actively work to bring you down."

Wilk recoiled dramatically. Then he paused, also dramatically. Then he started to laugh. "That," he said, "was exactly the wrong answer."

"I mean it," Naima said. "Give me back my son."

"Come with me," he said, turning and not bothering to see if she followed. Of course she would. He had all the leverage in the world. It had been crazy of her to want to have her son by her side when they were mobilized to find the superhumans, but she'd insisted. And since Wilk had to have Naima, and Naima had to have Sharif, well, there they all were. He led her to the door of his mobile field command office — a pretty fancy name for a 10-foot-by-50-foot trailer — and outside.

As they walked between the rows of other trailers and vehicles, each perfectly, governmentally nondescript, Wilk took on an almost casual air, strolling in a way that frustrated the hell out of Naima. "You're taking me to him." It wasn't a question.

"You'll see Sharif very soon," Wilk said, still sauntering along. He finally stopped in front of a trailer, identical in appearance to the others, but — as far as Naima could recall — not one that had been there the day before. In that sense, the trailer stood out to her. She had even tried the door when she was looking for her son, but she found it locked. Deputy Director Barry Wilk didn't try the knob at all. He simply went up the two steps to the door and knocked, twice. The door opened inward, and Wilk turned around with a smile, waving with some sort of twisted chivalry for Naima to enter first.

She fixed him with a stern look but stepped forward, determined not to be intimidated, and determined to find her son. As she entered the trailer, she saw a woman dressed in a light-blue coat, like a doctor or a lab technician, standing in front of an exam table. Naima took another step forward, scanning the rest of the mostly open space, but there was no sign of Sharif. She spun around to ask Wilk what exactly was going on, but the words never left her mouth. Barry Wilk had entered, closing and locking the door behind him. Inexplicably, as if they had come out of thin air, two dark-suited agents stood tall and imposing behind him. Naima recognized both as agents Wilk relied on to handle… *difficult* jobs. With eyes wide, she stared at her former boss. "I thought you were better than him — better than someone truly evil like Sol. Is this what you've come to, in the interest of getting your job done? Taking a child and bringing two of your heavies here to frighten a woman?"

Barry Wilk *tsked*. "Frighten a woman?" he repeated. "Are you insinuating that you're somehow frail and helpless? Isn't that a little sexist, doctor? Besides, between Red Hope, Luna, Shadow Ghost, and even yourself, women hardly seem to be the daintier sex these days."

Naima shivered. She knew that somehow her presence nullified the power of the superhumans, and that made her valuable to the government. But it didn't make her feel strong. If anything, since she first understood that she had this strange ability, she'd mostly felt weak and out of control of her life. Now, her foolish attempt to work with Wilk and his agents and somehow regain a normal life had backfired horribly. "Please…"

Wilk blinked and shook his head, ignoring her plea. "I don't believe you've met one of my colleagues. Please don't be offended, as she typically works in rather secretive settings. Actually, both of you worked in the bunker, very near to each other really, but separated by, shall we say, administrative protocol?" He smiled as the woman in the light-blue coat came to stand next to him. "In any event, today you will finally meet. Dr. Ramadi, this is Nurse Brooks."

The woman didn't extend a hand in greeting, and Naima wasn't much in the mood for pleasantries anyway. Instead, Nurse Brooks gestured to the two goons by the door and they stepped forward, each to one side of Naima. "What is this? What are you doing?"

Deputy Director Barry Wilk looked at her with cold eyes. "After John Black's mother broke her children out of the bunker, you yourself informed us that he had given her some of his own blood to save her life. Combine that with John's reactions when we took blood samples and the like, and we were on to something. In fact, once we dug out the bunker, we found that the Black family had conveniently destroyed all the samples we took. Which means *they* knew those samples were important, too."

"Okay so their blood is important to their power. And?"

"I believe the same is true of you," Wilk said.

"So you're going to take my blood?" Naima asked, confused. "Why didn't you just ask? You can have it. I just want my son back and then to get the hell out of here. Go ahead and take blood samples if you want." To emphasize her point, Naima slid one sleeve up to expose the smooth inside of her arm.

At the same time, Nurse Brooks pushed her cart forward, and for a moment Naima thought that would be the end of it. She'd give Wilk her blood, and then be done. But the nurse's cart carried two things, neither of which looked appropriate for drawing blood. The first was a tray filled with swabs and scalpels. The second was a strange electronic device about the size of a small suitcase, with thick glass sides and wires running to a power source and an electronic display.

Naima was a psychiatrist and dealt with mental and emotional disorders rather than the ailments of the flesh, but she thought the box looked similar to a devices used to transport organs. "What is this? You can't be —" The two dark-suited agents grabbed Naima by her arms and led her to the exam table as she struggled in vain. "Are you serious?" she shouted toward Deputy Director Barry Wilk. "You're a monster!"

"No," he said coolly. "I just need to be sure that when your abilities are needed, there will be no question of your willingness to cooperate."

"You'll be a murderer!"

Wilk scoffed. "Please, Naima. Give me some credit. I'm not going to *kill* you. We're only going to take what we need."

12

Why did you call them?

"Huh?" I replied, eloquently, as I ran through the woods. I almost missed a step at the sudden voice in my head. Well, that and the fact that the question was... troubling.

And what is Fin-Uh-More? Holly said. I assumed she was speaking only to me, because no one else was taking notice. I guess they assumed my previous intellectual question was actually a response to almost tripping rather than the reason for it.

I tried to play coy. *What are you talking about, Hol?*

Please, John. Floating along at my left side, I saw her expression darken. *I won't tolerate that anymore.*

Tolerate what?

Being treated like a fool. Or a child. She flashed me a look that was a clear reminder of what she had done to Margrethe.

I nodded toward her, half acknowledgment, half apology. *But you've been in my head, it seems, Hol.* I quickly double-checked my mental barriers. They seemed sound. If she could get through, she knew ways far beyond my comprehension. Frighteningly, I could easily imagine that. And if she knew my mind, she knew my plans. And then we were sunk. I purposely started thinking about TV cartoons, for two reasons. First, Holly used to love them, and we both knew it. Second, if she didn't want to be treated like a child, the image should piss her off. I knew it was risky pissing off my alarmingly powerful sister, but I had to know. When she didn't react, I thought I had the answer to my next question before I even spoke. *Are you in my head now?*

No, of course not. Because you're a— Holly stopped abruptly.

I'm a what?

Holly's face twisted in an angry mask. She didn't want to tell me, but she also didn't like being pushed into a corner and hiding. *It's usually easy to read your mind when you're asleep.*

Oh, wonderful, I thought to myself. *What teenage boy dreams was Holly plucking out of my head at night?* The possibilities made me shudder. I beamed my thoughts to her again. *That's not cool, Hol.*

Her body vibrated as she floated along beside me, slipping between trees much more easily than I ran around them. I had called her out, and that annoyed her. *I have to protect myself, John.*

Of course, you do, Holly.

Especially after that... woman.

I let that one go. There would be no seeing eye to eye about how Holly had killed Margrethe. No way. Maybe in the future we could talk it over, if we all lived that long, but this was not the moment. *Well, I'm your brother, and I'd appreciate you staying out of my head, okay?*

Then why did you call them?

Who?

Please, John, we already went over this. I know who you called and I don't like you treating me like I'm stupid.

I dodged past another tree. *Fine, Hol. I called them. I called Wilk and his government agents. You caught me.*

And you didn't tell anyone but Marcos?

Yes.

Not even Mom?

Nope.

Why?

Because I... I hesitated.

Holly completed my thought. *Because you have a plan.*

Yeah. Boy, did it sound stupid coming from someone else. John Black, lifelong scat-of-the-pants operator, finally has a plan. The likelihood of success now seemed essentially nil.

You want them to chase us, but I'm not sure why. And you want to go to Fin-Uh-More. What is that?

You don't know? She'd read my mind. How could she not know?

No, she said to my mind. *I wasn't expecting to uncover a deep secret plot, John, and I only got so far before you woke up.*

I chuckled, out loud, and Mom noticed. She shot me a quizzical glance as she stepped over a log, probably wondering how any of this was funny. I smiled sheepishly. "Sorry, but this reminded me of a video game. Some of the ones I play, they give you an objective, and sometimes they're really far away and you just have to run endlessly through the woods toward it. If only we could Fast Travel," I mused. I know I was over-explaining, but all of it was a lie, or at least subterfuge. I hadn't been thinking of a video game at all. But my excuse was enough to make my mom roll her eyes and go back to focusing on her own thoughts, watching out for spider webs and other minor pitfalls. Good thing there were no pools filled with alligators or quicksand to contend with. I didn't see any convenient hanging vines.

Back in reality, we did possess Fast Travel — flying — and still we couldn't use it. That *was* frustrating.

Why do you want the government to chase us, John? Holly asked.

To finish this, once and for all. Not just with Sol, but with everyone. If we're always looking over our shoulders, wondering where they are, hoping they don't find us, this will never be done. It was almost the straight truth, too. Knowing she couldn't — wouldn't? — read my mind while I was awake was at least somewhat reassuring.

Didn't you just tell me you didn't *want to kill Naima or Wilk?*

I don't. That's not how we finish things. We can work things out with those two.

John, you're older than me, but even I think that's naive. Everything *will be done, with* everyone? *Doesn't that seem like wishful thinking?*

Ouch. Holly just called me out. And maybe, probably she was right, but I had a plan and I was going to see it through. It had to work. *It's the best I've got, Hol.*

Hm. She left it at that, silently thinking as I plodded and she floated.

I had an idea. *Okay, Holly. If you've been in my head, you tell me — what is my goal? Am I trying to hurt you or help you?*

You're trying to help me, she said quickly, and for a moment, I felt victorious. Yes! She actually knew the truth. Maybe that would help when the time came. *Or at least you think what you're doing will help.* And that sufficiently burst my bubble.

I need you to trust me, Hol, just a little bit.

She jumped ahead. *So you can pull Sol out of me?*

I shrugged. *Well, yeah, pretty much that.*

Holly glided silently along, not giving away what she thought or whether she would help me or fight me. Finally, she returned to our conversation. *What if you fail?*

Then I fail. At least I'll have tried, I said.

No, she said. *I don't mean fail to beat Sol. If you face him, I think we all know it could go either way.*

Such confidence my sister had in me. About the same amount I had in myself, I suppose, or maybe even a little more. I figured I was doomed. *Then what?* I asked.

Holly glided to a stop, turning toward me, and for a moment, no one else noticed. Which is a good thing, given my reaction to what she said. *I mean this, John. What if you fail to pull him out of me, and instead, he pulls you in? Do I then have to purge you both?*

13

In the end, I had to explain my plan to everyone. We came out of the woods onto a wide and flat two-lane road. I'll give the gang credit. We didn't end up needing a car. Superpowered running is, I guess, a little better than normal running. Crickets chirped from all around us, creating a wall of sound that was somehow peaceful. Nearby, a long growth of green dotted with white flowers gave off the smell of honeysuckle, a scent that reminded me of simpler days, the time before power ruled our lives. There was no traffic, but that was understandable. It was midweek, getting on toward nightfall, and we were in the middle of nowhere.

Or thereabouts.

Because, really, we were right where I wanted us to be.

To our left stood a large brown wooden sign stood with raised letters painted in gold.

FINIMORE CAVERNS
Begin Your Journey to the Center of the Earth!

Well, that seemed overblown. Despite the supposedly incredible depth of the caverns, I assumed we'd remain firmly within the outermost layer of the earth, the crust. I was pretty sure they didn't have an elevator to the inner core. Although, come to think of it, if they did have one, I would definitely use it to my advantage.

Above the painted letters, a large, almost billboard sized photo showed happy people rappelling into a massive dark hole, their helmet lights picking out spectacular rock formations from the blackness. Spelunkers doing some spelunking, the way spelunkers do. Yes, I will take any opportunity to say that word, as many times as possible. Of course it's juvenile. Did you forget who you're talking to? The photo itself was illuminated by a floodlight, its brightness just becoming apparent as the sun's rays diminished in the west. A parking lot and squat, one-story building were set back a ways from the sign.

So this is Fin-Uh-More, Holly said, allowing everyone to hear.

Mom glanced at us in that almost casual way parents do, when you know they're about to assert their authority. "Okay, it's time for some information. John, what's going on? Holly, do you know?"

Holly shrugged. That left me. Might as well own up to it. We had arrived, after all. "This is where I wanted us to go. This is where I want to do what needs to be done."

Mom, God bless her, looked calmly at the sign, saw its happy tagline, glance at its smiling spelunkers (I told you I'd use it whenever I could), and then turned back. "Here? What are we going to do, live in a cave from now on?"

Pip laughed. "Let me guess. There's a magic ring down there somewhere. It'll make us all invisible so the government will leave us alone." I shot her a look, but that only resulted in her covering her face while she grinned.

He's been guiding us toward this place since we left Marcos, but I don't know why, Holly said.

I took a deep breath and looked over the wide, empty parking lot and the small building on the other side. This was it? This was my big idea? I was out of my mind. We were utterly and completely going to fail. I deflated, shoulders slouching forward.

Mom approached and put a hand on my arm. "John, what is it? Tell us why we're here. Don't lose faith in yourself now, after all that's happened. And don't lose faith in *us*. We're a family." She glanced at Pip. "All of us. If this place is important, just tell us how."

Okay. The time had come to make things clear to them all, to my family. Once more, I inhaled. "This is our last stand," I said, and that was sufficient to wipe away the edges of Pip's smile, turn Mom's furrowed brow into wide eyes, and get Holly's full attention. "Back at Marcos's lake house, it was me. I called Barry Wilk and told him where to find us."

Mom gasped. "John — why?"

Pip looked at me like I was a traitor. But I'd seen that look before from her, and maybe I'd see it again. For now, I had to move on. "Just listen, okay?" When Mom nodded, I continued. "This all may seem convoluted, but I needed everything to come together here. Somewhere very, very deep. Somewhere *dead*." I could feel their confusion, so I tried to explain things in a different way. "Mom, do you remember when I was little — really little — and there was that field trip to Xanadu Caverns?"

"Yes, but…"

"But that place *sucked*, right?" I asked, prodding her.

Mom was Mom. She deflected. "Well, I don't know if it *sucked*, but it was at least underwhelming."

"Right, sure. Let's call it that. The most I remember out of that trip was that me and Steve Martucci dug through a box of fool's gold in the gift shop. We really wanted those little yellow blobs, even though we knew they were worthless. Even though we knew it was *fool's* gold. And that's sort of what Xanadu Caverns were. They weren't all that deep, not all that memorable, but they were the semblance of the real thing. If that was the fool's gold, this place — Finimore Caverns — is gold. It's the real deal."

"I'm so confused," Pip interjected. "We're here to compare holes in the ground?"

"No, no," I said, waiving my hands. "This isn't about comparing caves. I just needed to get us to the deepest place."

Pip squinted at me. "Then tell us. Why?"

"Okay, if you believe me, or I should say, if you believe *like* me, then you believe our powers come from these little triangular shapes in our cells."

"The thorns, you call them," Mom said.

"Yes, the thorns. And I believe that those thorns came from ice melting off a comet and falling through the atmosphere." I could see the skepticism in their faces. "It doesn't really matter if you trust me about that or not, because the fact is, we have power, and we know for certain that our power is in our bodies, in our cells, in our blood. Pip — you remember. I cut off your arm."

"You don't want me to remember that," she said curtly.

"I am sorry about it. Really. But my point is that your body — your cells — came back together and made you whole again."

"Okay, and therefore… *cave*," Pip mocked. "Makes perfect sense to me. I'm on board. Anyone else?"

"Mom, Holly. What about Sol?" They both looked at me the way people side-eye the raving lunatic in the street, wondering when it might be time to call for help. "When I destroyed Sol in the desert, Holly's storm was raging. It took his cells and blew them around until they chanced upon Jake Weissman. And then those cells — with their little thorns inside that will do *anything* to stay alive — entered Jake's body and Sol corrupted him into Ranger. Then Ranger gave way to Sol himself, returned by piecing himself back together from the little thorns." I paused, looking to each of them in turn, trying to see if they were following my train of thought. I was not met with an overwhelmingly positive reaction.

"And...?" Pip said. "So far this is more of a history lesson, John. What's the point?"

"Just this — our powers want to live, beyond possibly even our own lives. They traveled in a comet to get here, meaning that even in the dead of space, they found a way. If the thorns are exposed to other living cells, they will figure out how to carry on, rebuild. Given that Holly refuses to fly because it *increases* Sol's power over her, and the fact that the thorns have survived in space already, I could only think of one other way to kill them."

"And that's here?" Mom asked.

I get it now, Holly said, although her face didn't seem to radiate confidence in my plan.

"You do?" I asked.

You want to take Sol so far into the earth that nothing else is alive down there, and then you want to bury him there for all eternity in a place where his powers can't just jump to some other form of life and carry on. Is that about it?

I smiled, a broad, satisfied smile. "That, Hol, is precisely it. And maybe — just maybe — if going up in the air makes him stronger, going down in the earth weakens him."

My sister frowned. *How are you going to keep Sol down there? A bunch of rocks, no matter how heavy, won't be enough. Even if it takes a while, he'll just dig his way out and be back. What's the point?*

"That's why I need Barry Wilk and the government," I said. "To bring Naima with them. So that when I bury Sol deep in the ground, he doesn't have any power at all."

I still don't understand, Holly said. *If you, me, and Naima go into the caverns, none of us will have power.*

"Well, I admit that my plan needs help. Specifically, it needs other people for it to work. Naima will have to listen to me, do as I say, so we can control the sphere of her influence — who it touches, who it doesn't."

Pip spoke up. "And the rest of us?"

"When Wilk gets here, he'll want to take us away, capture us. So I need you to be my Red Hope."

Pip stood taller. A part of her always enjoyed being the hero. Being the savior of the people. "Fight him, you mean? Give you time?"

"Yes."

She smiled. "I'd be happy to kick that guy's ass even if you didn't ask me, but since you did... sure. No problem." Reaching up to the hilt protruding over her shoulder, Pip loosened her sword, a smooth, practiced move. She'd be ready. I was sure of it.

"And me?" Mom asked.

I gave my mother an apologetic look. "I know you want to be with your daughter, and with me, but I don't think Pip can hold the entirety of the government's forces back by herself. I need you with her. I need you to be Luna. I need you to be a beacon in the dark of night, a ray of hope for us all, and the bane of Barry Wilk's existence. Can you?" Mom glanced back and forth between me and Holly, and maybe, probably, a tear was forming in one eye. But then she steeled herself and nodded, and that was that.

And you need me to fight Sol with you, Holly said. *Be the Shadow Ghost*. It wasn't a question, it was certainty.

"No," I said, and Holly's face wrinkled into confusion. "I need you to remember that I'm your brother and I love you. I just need you to be my sister."

I'd be happy to say Holly smiled and we had a heartfelt family moment at that time, but she didn't. So much had happened since we were innocent children in the back yard, having a family cookout. Instead, sister and brother stood staring at each other, unsure what to say for quite some time.

14

Past the parking lot, our options were to enter via the gift shop — most likely loaded with security cameras and alarms — or just go over the perimeter fence. It was solid brick, more than eight feet tall, topped with nasty-looking barbed wire, and it extended in a curve as far as I could see. "We just have to get over the fence — you can fly that far without trouble, right, Hol?" My sister didn't answer, instead floating over the wall and out of view. I guess a brief trip 10 feet or so in the air didn't trigger her Sol anxieties. "I'll take that as a yes." The rest of us followed, starting with my mother. I'll admit it was still weird to see Mom fly, even though I'd tried to train her and should have been used to it.

Inside the wall was a hill, sloping gradually upward, carpeted with ragged grasses of varying heights, some as tall as me. There was a growing wind sweeping across the hill, laden with pollen and the fresh smells of the world turning green, mocking my reasons for coming here. To find some place dead. A rock pathway was bordered by short poles connected with small black chains, guiding us toward the top of the hill. When we arrived, we found a wide concrete platform, semicircular in design, with four T-shaped metal posts along the far edge, leaning out over the abyss of Finimore Caverns' gaping maw. Each post was connected to a massive coil of sturdy cable that ran up and over a grooved wheel at its top. *For rappelling*, I thought. *Well, I guess that's one way to get down there.*

The giant hole beyond those posts revealed nothing but utter darkness, falling into the depths the earth. Significantly sturdier guard rails ran the length of the hole opening, curving around the area where the rappelling posts were mounted, with a large, sturdy gate latched and closed at the center. And, of course, there were many, many red signs warning of danger. Reading those signs, the warnings made sense. The first drop we were staring at was, incredibly, more than 200 meters deep. But I knew that it was really the baby of this cavern system. I'd seen enough ads on TV during my misspent youth — okay, fine, it was only a few years back — to know that Finimore Caverns' impressive first descent was just the warm up. True deep-earth aficionados preferred the second drop, not far from the base of the first. That one was more than a kilometer, straight down.

On the left side of the platform was an option more appropriate for the faint of heart: stairs. Leaning over the guard rail, I saw an endless zigzag of metal steps, and I wondered just how many it took to go down so far. *And that's another way to get down there. Not that I'll be taking the stairs, either.*

Seeing the dark pit before me, I didn't feel relief at reaching my goal. Instead, I was on pins and needles, ready to burst out of my skin at any sound or movement. I didn't feel ready at all, and my plan seemed like an utter joke with no hope of success. I paced the concrete platform.

Behind us, the low building that housed the requisite gift shop sat silent and dark. Through its windows and past the darkened displays selling trinkets, we saw no movement in the parking lot. In the sky, we saw no approaching helicopters. Nevertheless, everyone was tense.

Pip flicked open the simple latch of the gate and swung it wide. She walked to the edge, peering into the darkness. "What now?" she asked casually, as if the drop was nothing to her. Of course, given her powers, it was.

"We wait," I said, stating the obvious. Looking around, I figured we already must have tripped a hundred silent alarms. The gift shop was invariably locked down to prevent theft, but out here on the hill, next to a huge open hole, there had to be some measure of security to keep crazies from killing themselves in a huge cave at night. Someone would be checking in on us soon, and if that someone *wasn't* Barry Wilk, well, then they'd have to give him a call. I suspected Wilk was pretty tapped in to every level of law enforcement.

What if I don't want to do this? Holly said. She had lowered herself to sit on one of the benches that ringed the platform.

"You have to," I said. I had noticed something. Something that either no one else noticed, not even Holly, or no one wanted to talk about. I first picked up on it back at Marcos's house, by accident. But now, every time I looked at Holly, I saw it.

Why?

I walked to my sister and leaned toward her, my forehead nearing hers. It was our old ritual. Forehead to forehead, brother and sister, together. I almost thought she'd pull away, but perhaps tradition and history still meant something to her, to us all. I stopped before we came together and reached out to brush back her hair, sweep it away from her face.

Then they all saw it. There was a patch of flaking skin in the middle of Holly's forehead.

"What?" Mom asked, confused. "Dry skin? What does that mean?"

"Like Ranger," Pip said in a serious tone. She understood.

"Yes, like Ranger. Sol consumed Jake Weissman from the inside. It changed Jake's body." I scanned Holly and noticed another small blotch on one arm, touching it gently so the others saw it, too. "It looked like this."

"Oh my God," Mom said, covering her mouth with one hand, staring at the odd patches of skin on Holly like they were infested by a demon. Which they pretty much were.

Pip gave my sister a grave, concerned look. "Listen, Holly. I have been with you and I support you. I know you're so, very strong. What I'm about to say is not a slight, not an insult. You're in danger. Your life, your *soul* is in danger of extinction. If what happened to Ranger happens to you, you won't exist anymore. So we've got to do it John's

246

way now. We've got to work together, get Naima to work with us, to get Sol *out* of you. Not because you're weak, but because you aren't. Because he's a cancer, and the only way you can truly fight a cancer is to cut it out. The sad truth is that if you only suppress him, you'll never know when or if he'll come back."

Holly wouldn't make eye contact with any of us. I reached out with my mind to see if she wanted to talk to me privately, but I might as well have said hello to the brick wall or the hilltop. She was closed off.

Then we heard it. Helicopters, far in the distance, getting louder by the second. As the last purple tint of the sky gave way to black, we saw dots of light approaching in the air, mirrored by other lights coming in pairs down the road. Soon, the sound of engines was all we could hear, blotting out the quiet of the evening.

"Get ready, everyone," I said, taking up a position directly in the middle of the concrete platform, facing the building, with the depths of Finimore to my back. As if she didn't want me to be the center of attention, Holly floated just next to me. Pip and Mom arrayed themselves each to a side.

"We never did think of a good group name," Pip said, smirking at me.

I smiled. "Bobby always liked *Trio Supremo*." We both laughed.

Pip looked side to side. "Won't work. There are four of us now."

I thought Mom and Holly were ignoring us, but I was wrong. Mom chimed in. "We're a family, like I said. All of us. Just call us the Family."

Pip screwed up her face, considering the name. "It's not the most awe-inspiring superhero team name I've ever heard..."

Mom grinned back at her. "Tell me a name that's more important?"

Pip couldn't. Nor could I. I don't think any of us expected the name to stick, but at that moment it didn't matter. All that mattered was that it was us. We were the Family. And we were together.

The first wave of vehicles pulled into the parking lot and crunched to a stop on the gravel, their headlights tracing eerie beams through the billows of dust they kicked up. We heard doors open and close, the muffled sounds of people shouting orders. In no time, the front door of Finimore Caverns' gift shop was torn from its hinges and a swarm of agents passed through. They burst out the back door to the base of the hill where we waited, splaying out in a semicircle that mimicked ours. Finally, a lone figure walked through their midst and stood at the center of the group. Barry Wilk. "Well, well. You told the truth, John. The gang truly is all here. Nice to see you all together."

"Don't come any closer, Wilk," I said. "And don't bring Naima any closer either."

The deputy director chuckled, which completely confused me and the others. Let me just say that even a foursome of the most powerful people on Earth can look much less than intimidating when they have baffled looks on their faces. "I guess you didn't hear," Wilk said. "Dr. Ramadi has retired from government service."

"What? When?"

"Oh, very recently," he said.

"Then —" *Then what?* I thought. *How could Wilk possibly expect to capture the four of us without Naima?* But that wasn't my bigger concern. I had dragged the four of us all the way to Finimore Caverns. I had secretly called the government in to try to capture us. I had laid out a plan that needed my mother and Pip to fight while Holly and I worked to extract and destroy Sol. But most of all, I had based my plan on something that I thought was an immutable fact: Naima being there to take away Sol's power. And she hadn't shown up. Before it ever really began, my plan shattered into a million pieces and crashed at my feet. I was devastated. I was angry. I felt hopeless. I felt rage. I had to say something to Wilk, because now I was pissed. "Then how could you possibly hope to overcome us?" I asked, my voice booming and bold.

Wilk shrugged. "Well, let's just say I might have an ace up my sleeve, John." He nodded, and the agent to his left raised a squat weapon with a wide barrel, pointing it toward us at the top of the hill.

A gun? Wilk thinks he can stop us with a gun?

Just then, there was a pop and I saw the agent with the gun jerk from the recoil. As if my world went into slow motion, I could clearly trace the large projectile flying through the air, my powers immediately in full force. I watched it zip directly toward Pip and expected to see her body sluice into some impossible shape to allow whatever they had shot at her to pass by harmlessly. It didn't.

Instead, the projectile — something much bigger than a bullet — slammed into Pip and knocked her down, sending her sprawling back through the open gate and helplessly toward the brink of the deep hole. Looking like a discarded rag doll, Pip came to a stop just inches from the edge.

"Oh *shit*," Mom said, and, truth be told, I completely agreed with her sentiment.

15

All of a sudden, half a dozen other agents produced weapons just like the first. From above, a helicopter spotlight shined on us, and with my enhanced perception, I could see another of the wide-barreled guns pointing down at us. We were surrounded by the same kind of weapon that had just felled Pip, a superhuman. What magic did the government have up its sleeve?

Barry Wilk clapped once, hard, a sharp sound that snapped me out of the daze I fell into when Pip was shot down. "Hot damn, that worked better than even I expected," he said with a smile.

We all retreated through the gate, as if its bare metal bars gave us any protection from the new reality we faced. Mom rushed to Pip's side. "What have you *done* to her?" she shouted.

Wilk was positively gleeful. "Well, you know government bureaucracy. Everything has some long-winded acronym, and so does this." He pointed to the weapon in the hand of the agent next to him. "My dear superhumans, meet the TSND-1. That's *Tactical Superpower Nullification Device*. And the *1* just means it's the only one we have. At least for now. But those letters are a mouthful. I prefer to just call it my secret weapon."

I was incredulous. "How?"

"Right!" Wilk said. "Exactly! How? How did we make a weapon that could nullify superpowers?"

I didn't destroy everything. That must be it.

Wilk pretty much read my mind. "You might be thinking we got something from your samples, but no. Well, except for the fact that you thought those samples were important. That was good to know. Nope, this device, friends, is much, much simpler. And I know, it's bad form for someone like me to *explain* himself, because it gives people like you hope. But seriously, this is too good — too foolproof — not to tell you. No wait, I have a better idea. Guess."

"What?" I asked stupidly.

"Guess. Guess what my secret weapon is." Wilk waited.

To my side, I saw Pip stir. She was alive. Mom checked her over. "Are you okay?"

"I…" Pip started. "I can't feel my powers."

What had Wilk done to her? Some kind of projectile that took away superpowers? How? What had he figured out that the rest of us hadn't in all the time we had these abilities?

I saw my mother reaching down, and I turned. Her fingers were inches from the ball-like projectile they had fired at Pip. "Don't touch it!" I yelled, and Mom flinched away.

Still, she studied the strange round thing laying on the concrete deck next to Pip. "It's covered with something, like scales," she said. "And it's having an effect on me, too."

I shuddered. If Mom was losing her powers, that meant Wilk had fired a single shot and taken out half of us. Not good. "Get away from it, whatever it is."

Mom shook her head. "I'm not just going to walk away from Pip — she's hurt."

Frustrated, I wheeled back toward Barry Wilk and his agents. "No guessing games. Tell me. What is that?" I tensed, and several agents reflexively trained their new and devastating weapons on me. Reaching out with my mind, I crumpled the barrel of the nearest one, rendering it useless.

Deputy Director Wilk stepped in front of his agents and raised a hand. "Stop right there, John."

"Why should I? I'll destroy every one of those things, and then we'll see how confident you feel. You caught us off guard the first time. That won't happen again." That's when I started to wonder why Wilk hadn't shot us all down at once and just given us his joyful explanation afterward. Maybe he was bluffing. There were a lot of guns around us, but maybe they weren't all loaded with the government's unbelievable new ammunition.

Wilk turned and spoke to the agent nearest him. "Bring her up." The agent nodded and muttered something into his walkie-talkie. Moments later, another agent pushed through the door of the gift shop, dragging a very unhappy prisoner with him.

Even mad she was beautiful, curls of red hair hanging in front of her eyes. Eyes that were locked on me with anger and sorrow and disappointment. But mostly anger.

Carrie.

"No," I said. My eyes were daggers aimed at the hand of the agent as it squeezed her arm, guiding her forward. "Leave her out of this, Wilk. I mean it. If you harm her, I promise you you'll regret it."

Wilk smiled. "I don't plan on doing any such thing, *if* you behave yourself. But if you bust up any more of my fancy little weapons, I'm not going to be happy with you."

"Carrie, I'm sorry," I said, ignoring Wilk. "I'll get you out of this." But she turned away. So, yeah, that plus her expression were my clues that she was still really pissed with me. "And look, back there by the lake, I said some really stupid things to you, and hurt your feelings.

I'm *really* sorry about that. I wish I could take it all back and say what I really want to say."

"You're doing this here? Now?" Carrie said, with a sneer that looked so strange on her face and hit me like an ice pick to the heart.

"What I really want to say is that I love you and I want us to go back to the way things were before I started acting weird. I'm an idiot, and I hope you can forgive me."

Carrie's expression softened and she opened her mouth to say something, but Wilk interrupted. "Listen, love birds. This is all very heartwarming, but I have a duty to the people of this country to do my job, so that's exactly what I'm going to do. John, you and the others will each walk toward an agent holding one of these weapons. Once you get close, we will verify your powers have been nullified with a brief test. After that, you'll be taken into custody."

Wilk's certainty that we would just give up caused the fire in me to flare. "And what if we don't?"

He shrugged. "Then we shoot more of those cool new projectiles at you and take you into custody anyway. And if you get really fancy with me, don't forget I've got your girlfriend as insurance."

I didn't want to just give up. I couldn't. But, what choice did I have? He seemed to have outmaneuvered me pretty darned well. So much for my brilliant plan. The stupid plan that dragged us all to this place, only to fail. Still, I stalled, trying to think of some other option. "You didn't tell me what your secret weapon is." There had to be something.

"You didn't guess," Wilk replied.

"Fine," I said. "Here's my guess. They're filled with blood from Naima."

Wilk grimaced and nodded. "Close. Close. But a projectile filled with blood would probably shatter and be messy. I'm not actually trying to spill blood here, John. Plus, I wanted to make sure the effectiveness of the weapon was on the outside, the part that touches you. Maybe it would work to have blood in the center, but this way seems more certain. So I'll go ahead and tell you. Those *scales* your mother mentioned? Those are samples of Dr. Ramadi's skin, kept in stasis through a pretty amazing bit of biotech within the launching weapon itself." Wilk pointed to the extra-wide barrel. "Down here, there's a cooling system, all very advanced stuff. Suffice to say that's Naima's living flesh that rammed into your friend over there."

It didn't make sense. "So you're telling me Naima retired from service, and decided to give you a bunch of skin samples on her way out the door?"

Wilk smiled. "Well, *give* is probably not the word she'd use."

"You monster!" Mom gasped. "You sliced that woman up to make *bullets*?" She looked in horror at the skin-covered projectile beside her.

Wilk raised both hands, palm out. "Dr. Ramadi is perfectly fine. The samples we took aren't going to hurt her in the long run, and her wounds, though many in number, will heal." He looked at me with a smug grin. "In other words, she can go on providing us the means to make these projectiles for a *very* long time. And the good news about using my secret weapon is that, unlike Dr. Ramadi herself, these guns don't talk back."

That was exactly my problem with the weapon. My plan hinged upon Naima and my ability to talk to her, have her near when I needed her to render Sol powerless, then retreat to give my power back. A ball with skin samples wasn't going to give me such options, even if I dared to try to use it.

I'm not going to let them take me, Holly said, just to me. *I'd rather die.* I should have known she'd been too silent. Beside me, I felt a rising force growing in her, and I could see what was going to happen. Holly was going to kill, the agents were going to shoot, and then we were all going to be captured and packed away in an underground bunker for the rest of our natural lives.

There had to be another way. Just thinking that, but not knowing how to overcome the situation, made me want to scream.

So that's what I did.

I knew what it would do. I had been through it before, back at Naima's garden. The strange power yell I learned from Holly, but modified.

Holly's yell repelled me. My yell would knock everyone out.

I had to do it.

In one fluid motion, I reached over and grabbed Holly by the arm and tugged, leaning us precariously over the deep pit of Finimore Caverns. Then I screamed with all the fire and rage and power I had, 10 times what I had done in the garden.

If it was possible to be too successful, I was. I didn't just knock out Holly, or Wilk, or the agents. I knocked out everyone.

Including me.

And as everything went dark, Holly and I fell down, down into the unknown darkness.

IV

1

We tumbled, end over end, into the great abyss, toward a distant dark plane of earth that rushed up at us like an exclamation point.

Well, I assume we did.

Because I was completely unconscious, as was my sister. Thankfully, my little force yell didn't knock out our powers, it just turned off our minds for a little while. So we'd hit the bottom and live, though it might hurt.

* * *

There was no plan, not anymore. My belief that I would enter the caverns with a completely willing Dr. Naima Ramadi and Holly Black, and walk out with Sol dead and gone, well, those were the wishes of a fool.

I woke up first, sprawled on a stony table of rock, and that told me something important. It was cool and damp and dusty, and even the slightest sound sent wet echoes off into the distance. Maybe my attempt to protect my mind had done some good. Or maybe having stunned myself once before, I was getting used to it. Either way, if I had gained a little time by coming back to consciousness first, I planned to use it.

Shaking out the cobwebs in my head, I reached out with power to sense the space around me. Holly was a lump a dozen or so feet away, hidden somewhere within the tumbled folds of her white dress and her blanket of dark hair. I used my powers to lift her next to me. Except for the awkward angle of her hanging head and the tangled mess of her hair, you could almost trick yourself into believing she was the normal, floating-around Holly. Shadow Ghost, that is.

I eased her forward, using another tendril of my mind to get my bearings in the deep dark. To one side, I felt it. A vast emptiness. The second and much deeper drop of Finimore Caverns was close by.

As a gauge, I expanded the radius of my perception to get a sense of what was around us, and I felt pinpoints of energy — all the tiny living things down in the cavern, many too small for the naked eye to see. We had descended far into the earth, but there was still too much life nearby. We had to go deeper.

Using my powers to guide me through narrow, twisty tunnels, I carried my sister toward the next drop, and without hesitation took us over the edge. It's weird, being so far down and so high up at the same time. I had been in the air above skyscrapers, but somehow this was worse, at least the way it played with my mind. I couldn't see a thing in the dark, but with my powers, I could sense it. The nothingness below. But there was no time to waste. I had no idea when the people on the surface would be up and about, renewing their efforts to capture us. I needed to move fast.

We flew downward, Holly's hair and dress fluttering with the speed. It seemed like it took forever, but eventually I felt the bottom approaching. Darkness still ruled my normal vision, so it was almost a surprise when my feet hit something solid and I could stand again, knowing that Holly and I were now more than 1,200 meters below the surface of the planet.

I reached out in a sphere once more, and for a moment, I thought that was enough — I couldn't sense any life around us. Then, that momentary joy dissipated when I made out the tiny creatures, infinitesimally small dots, living somewhere within the rock, or in crevices between rocks. We needed to go deeper still.

My knowledge of what exactly to expect beyond Finimore's second drop was limited. Frankly, I had hoped we would be deep enough, but even knowing a few tiny living forms were with us was enough to push me onward. I had to find someplace completely dead.

I stretched my mind farther and farther, eventually locating a gap in the rock well below us — nearly another kilometer down, but this time accessible only through solid earth. Okay, there may have been some convoluted path though the caverns that would eventually get us there, but we didn't have time to put on our backpacks and be explorers. So I just blasted a hole and down we went. More like a corkscrew, actually, but all the same, we descended, and quickly.

When we arrived in the gap, now more than 2,000 meters below the surface of the earth, I saw a glow.

There were so many things I'd seen that amazed me — superpowers in action, the thorns in my cells, giant monsters from the sea, all that — yet so little now actually surprised me. For a moment, this did.

Light began to illuminate the ruddy rocks around us, like we had transported a little sun with us, deep into the ground. How was it possible? Bioluminescence? Some vein of glowing lichen I knew nothing about?

Nope.

It was my sister. She was coming back to consciousness, and she was most likely pissed. As her mind woke up, so did her eerie white light, emanating strangely from her body. Holly became our flashlight.

That was... different. She didn't sound thrilled, but not as mad as I expected. *Did you knock everyone out, or just me?*

"Everyone," I said, my words reverberating off the stone walls. In the glow made by my sister, I saw that the gap we'd entered was much larger than I anticipated, more like a vast underground hallway.

A power yell, like I've done before, but one that knocks your enemies out? You'll have to show me how some time.

"Sure. Trade you for the black-hole, portal thing you can do."

Holly was silent, but I sensed that she wasn't too keen on that trade.

"Hol, we need to act fast. I need you to let me in."

I don't really want to do that, John.

"Johnny," I said.

What?

"Call me, Johnny, Hol, just like you used to. Remember when I said I needed you to be my sister now?"

I do. But I don't remember you saying I had to be your little *sister.*

"*Touché.*" I gave a small bow and Holly nodded. I think she almost smiled. For a second, it was like we really were siblings, and ones that could maybe get along. "So, will you?"

I don't know.

"Okay, Hol. I get it. This is a big deal. Tell me what you're worried about."

I don't know that I want you to save me, she said.

"What does that mean? You don't want to be saved?"

Holly sagged in exasperation, letting out a gasping sigh. *No. Honestly, no. I don't want to be "saved." Why do you always have to make it like that? You save me. It's never Holly does something herself. It's never even as simple as working* with *me. It's always my big brother trying to save me. Right from the start.*

"Don't you think that's a little unfair, Hol?" I said. "It isn't like I traveled across the country and got you back from Sol because I wanted to *belittle* you. I didn't do it to make myself look good, or you look bad."

Yeah.

"Yeah, what? You don't believe me?"

No, she said. *I believe you. I've seen enough of your thoughts to know that much. But the end result is the same. Black Sword, international superhero. But Holly Black? Nobody.*

"The only thing fame has gotten us both is the government trying to take our powers away. Celebrity isn't exactly all it's cracked up to be." I studied my sister's face carefully. When you live with someone your whole life, you think you know them, down to the smallest detail of their appearance. But now, looking closely, I realized Holly was so much older than my mental image of her. I realized that, without even trying, I might always have been treating her like a little kid. And I realized that if someone had done that to me, I might hate it, too. But there in the middle of her forehead was that warning sign. The flaking skin that told me Sol wanted to come out again. "Hol, will you let me in? Will you let me help you defeat Sol, once and for all? This isn't about me being a hero, and it isn't about you being weak. If you say no, then I can't do a thing. You have all the power here. But soon enough, Barry Wilk and those government agents with their new guns will find us, so I need you to decide now."

Holly didn't answer, instead looking down toward her feet. For a moment, I thought we were done, that she wouldn't accept my help and then we'd just be waiting for something else to happen, like Sol taking her over, or Wilk firing his crazy Naima-bullets at us and hauling us away. Or maybe we'd just suffocate or starve to death. We were a couple thousand meters deep, after all. I opened my mouth to say something, just to break the silence, but then I saw it.

There, in the middle of the radiance of my sister's glow, a tiny swirl of black appeared, rapidly growing in diameter. A door. A door into her mind where I would find what? Sol, yes, but what else?

Holly barked a short laugh. *We're about to get to know each other a whole lot better, big brother.*

2

I was in a maze of twisty passages, all alike.

Sure, I had used my powers to enter people's minds many times before, read their thoughts, implant my own. But in comparison, that was like a slide show, brief flashes of another person's life. This? Well, this was different.

I *was* Holly. She was me. Was I in her mind, her spirit, her soul? Her essence? Or maybe the better question was whether *I* even existed anymore.

No, I must have, because I had distinct enough thoughts to recognize that I was there, experiencing Holly. Did that mean she was experiencing me in a similar way?

For that matter, how did time work, inside another soul? I had stepped into Holly's spinning portal vortex and instantly found myself someplace new, but it almost seemed like I had slowly woken up from a deep sleep. Had it been seconds, hours, days?

"Hol?" I asked to the void.

No answer.

"Holly, can you hear me?" I fumbled down dark passageways, not really having any sort of goal in mind, just moving. "Holly?" Still, no answer. Could she really not hear me, or was she just being... I don't know. Herself? Difficult? With Holly, it was hard to tell.

I then I realized how dumb I was. I reached out and immediately knew the answer.

I felt confusion, concern, and an awkwardness that at first I didn't understand.

All of Holly's emotions.

The confusion and concern told me she couldn't hear me. That we wouldn't be able to directly communicate to fight Sol. Not a good start.

But the awkwardness? She wasn't kidding when she said we'd get to know each other better.

And it wasn't some major discovery, or maybe it was. Because it was *everything*. I realized that, if I tried, I could see her ideas, thoughts, and memories, like rooms in a house.

There was a boy, Blake. I had never met him, but I could see him. On Holly's bus. She thought he was quiet and beautiful, although he'd never said a word to her. But she wasn't the Holly Black that Blake knew, the girl in the wheelchair who couldn't talk. That Holly Black, the one whose thoughts I was seeing, wondered what Blake might say to Shadow Ghost. Would he —?

That door closed, and stretched, turning into a long, dark hallway, bending around new corners as it grew.

Holly was hiding her thoughts from me. *That's* what the passageways were. That's why I was trying to get through them without even knowing my destination.

I glimpsed Holly with our dad, and my heart skipped a beat. Then that door closed, and the thought disappeared into a new set of passageways. "No! I want to see that," I said, knowing my words meant nothing, and were heard by no one.

Then my stomach lurched as I dropped. These hallways weren't just left and right, forward and back, they went up and down, too, and now I was plummeting. I hit the bottom and hoped my powers would save me as usual, but at that moment, there was nothing. Luckily, the pit she'd made wasn't all that deep. So I earned a bruise or two, nothing more. More importantly, I discovered that within Holly's mind, I guess, I was just me.

The passageways shifted and curled, with new openings and doors, all deliberately set to confuse me.

I ran.

I realized with terrible certainty that if I couldn't find my way out of the maze, I would be lost. Holly, simply by trying to hide her memories and thoughts, was burying me. I took lefts and rights with no rhyme or reason, no sense of direction. I ran up slopes, and when those got too steep, I took another random turn. *Up and out*, those were my thoughts. *I have to get up and get out.*

I ran. I climbed. Still the maze changed and remade itself and flipped and expanded. It seemed hopeless.

The tunnel-like hallway curved in front of me, into a surreal loop back on itself. I was getting nowhere. "Holly! Stop!" I yelled, and still no one heard me.

I ran and ran and ran, and one thing became clear. However time might work here, I knew at least that bodies worked differently. I wasn't getting tired. I could run and run and run. It might do me no good, and I might simply go on like that forever, but I didn't have to slow down. I didn't have to catch my breath.

Was that even air I was breathing?

The darkness of twisting tunnels collapsed again, and turned around me, and there, in the utter darkness, I got mad.

What took me so long?

I made light.

Yep, just like that, I knew exactly how Holly had done it, creating that radiating glow she did, and so I did it, too. But wait? Did that mean I had my powers here after all? Yes and no. Mental powers seemed to be possible. Physical powers, not sure. More than anything, I couldn't yet understand the rules that governed this place — if there even were any. And I needed to, more than anything.

I kept running. And there was a light. Not my light, something else. Something to run toward.

The dark passageways folded again, and I couldn't be sure if I was still headed toward the light or hurrying myself farther into the depths. Gravity worked strangely inside another person's mind.

"Holly, cut it out!" I screamed, still running. The glimpse of something beyond the dark tunnels started to affect me. Not to give me hope, but to tear it away. To make me realize something else was out there, but I was hopelessly lost. "Holly!"

All at once, the crazy stretching of the hallways stopped. A hatch appeared just above me, and without a sound, it fell open. Up inside it, there was only more darkness, but I had to try. I tested my ability to fly, and was surprised to find that I could. Still glowing, I floated into a dark chamber, narrow but very, very tall. Almost like the depths of Finimore Caverns, which, being stuck in Holly's mind, seemed like another lifetime. Except I was still there, in the caverns, inside Holly's mind. Yeah, I know. It still didn't really make sense to me either. But up and up I went, until finally I realized that *up* would be never-ending. The chamber was slowing stretching to match my pace. "Holly, please!"

Something changed, once more, and while it didn't seem like her efforts *stopped*, they at least *slowed*. I reached the top, and there I found the sort of round door you might see on a submarine in a movie. I spun the locking wheel and the seal loosened. More importantly, bright beams of light seeped through the cracks, eclipsing the dull radiance I emitted.

Finally, the hatch fell open, and I flew through it into a wide, open world. A sun was setting far in the distance. Was the direction west, considering it was inside Holly's mind? Was *west* even a concept, here? Nonetheless, I floated above the open hatch, at the top of a tall hill, overlooking a panoramic landscape that I could only describe as beautiful. Around me were mountains reflecting the hues of the setting sun, forests falling into the calm dark of night, rivers mirroring the last glints of light. It was too much, too amazing to see. In other words, it was the creation of someone's mind. It wasn't reality.

The clouds weren't moving. Instead, they looked like they were sculpted exactly into their place.

The trees were just a little too green, a little too perfectly formed. The distant mountains seemed impossibly tall, with picturesque formations of brilliant white snow capping their wildly purple forms.

But all of it was *my* reality now. I was there and needed to figure out what was next. I didn't know if a minute of my time was a minute in the real world or not, but I knew I didn't have forever to locate Sol and figure out a way to get him out of my sister.

Scanning the horizon, it suddenly became clear. Far off to one side, there was movement in the air. A small set of clouds roiled in a dark and ominous ball, pouring rain onto one section of the forest and blinking with flashes of lighting that bounced between their angry puffs.

There was a storm, and I knew its source. Something that threatened not just to rain or thunder or blow fierce winds.

It was something that sought to destroy the very essence of my sister, the impossible beauty all around me, and that was something — someone — I absolutely would not tolerate.

"I'm coming for you, Sol," I said into the growing wind as I drifted to the ground. Clenching my jaw, I took a step downhill toward the blackness as thunder rolled in the distance.

3

Walking across the pastel landscape of Holly's mind, I almost forgot to pay attention to where I was. It was such a spectacle that even flying over it seemed like a crime. I *had* to walk. Had to see this intense new world, a place that I knew was wholly my sister. *Everything* was so gorgeously over the top that noticing any one detail, even one patch of dirt I was walking over, was difficult.

But something struck me as familiar.

I had been here before.

I stopped, looking around. I was at the edge of a grove of trees, with thick bushes filling in the underbrush. Through those bushes, though? I was suddenly sure of what I'd see. It was a deviation from my path toward Sol, but I realized it was one I had to take. I turned aside and pushed into the dense cover of the bushes.

Like everything in Holly's mind, the bushes themselves were *more* than normal bushes. Their thickness obliterated anything beyond, meaning I had to push all the way through before I even got a glimpse of the other side. Reaching forward, I shoved both hands through the last, thick section of foliage.

And there in front of me was a road.

Inside the collapsing hallways I had first entered in Holly's mind, everything seemed like it was built by people. But her landscape? It was utterly devoid of any human trappings. Just nature. Until now.

I leaned forward, twisting my head side to side. I *knew* this road.

I spoke aloud to no one, just to hear a voice. "Route 22. The long straightaway just outside of town. Which is that way," I said, pointing to my right. "Once it gets into town, it's called Tucker Street. And that way..." — I turned left to see the road rise up a long, sloping hill — "...leads out of town." I was still mostly deep inside the thick bushes, so I pushed a little farther out. Across the street, slightly to my right, I saw the fence that ran around the lumber yard, and the small side road that led back to the warehouses.

Like the one where Bobby shot himself that one time.

The time when I left in a daze and bumped into three bullies, Roger, Lawrence, and Zach.

Where the side road dead-ended onto Route 22 there was a stop sign. That was where I'd used my mental powers to force Roger to drive out in front of a cop, my lame attempt to lash out at him for revenge.

And that placed Roger's car directly in the middle of the road when my father came over the hill.

I caused the accident that killed my dad.

I stepped fully out of the bushes and stood at the side of the road, finally noticing that a car was parked not too far away, idling.

I'd expected to find was my father's car crumpled in a tangle of metal, upside down in the ditch beside the road. What I found instead was my mother's car — the specialized van she drove Holly around in.

Of course. This wasn't *my* memory that I had stumbled into, the memory of the crash. This was something from Holly's head. Something later.

The entire scene around me — how it was staged, how it was presented — seemed reverential. I walked over to the van, almost afraid to make a sound.

Someone was inside.

I stopped beside the rear door and looked in the window, seeing the side of my sister's face, a face that had aged in reverse since I last saw her 10 seconds or 10 years ago, out in the real world of Finimore Caverns. "Holly?"

She didn't answer. She didn't move. She just sat there, staring forward. Following the angle of her eyes, I turned past the front of the van.

There were splotches of color, highlighted by something red, flapping in the breeze. A ribbon, tying up a bouquet of flowers. It was set carefully by the side of the road, upright and staked into the ground.

Beyond that, I saw what Holly's eyes were locked on: our mother, facing away, wearing all black. It might have been the same dress she wore to the funeral, and I could see her shoulders shiver as she silently cried at the exact spot where she lost her husband. Where I had killed him. Where I had killed my own father.

"Mom?" I started, my voice cracking. But something was changing. The dense bushes at the edge of the road began to grow and expand, intruding between my mother and the van, even the van and me. "No, Holly! Let me see this!"

But it wasn't mine to see and soon I was enveloped in a wall of thick green. Turning, pushing through, eventually I realized that I'd only be permitted to move one way — toward the distant storm. "Okay, Hol. I get it. No time for this other stuff. Gotta hurry up."

I let the bushes guide me, like the green walls of a hedge maze. Eventually I went back through the trees, back to the pathway. Speed was a necessity, so there would be no more walking. Lifting myself effortlessly into the air, I aimed for the darkest section of sky and zipped toward it at a low altitude. Within moments, I had come to its edge.

The storm was wide, dark, and curved, like the wall that surrounded Finimore Caverns, but, you know, a whole lot higher and without the gift shop. No, it was more like Holly's sandstorm, back in the desert when I first defeated Sol. Well, when I *thought* I had defeated Sol.

But this time, I wasn't in the center of that vortex, I was on the outside, looking in.

And, weirdly, the edge of the storm was incredibly well defined. There was a strange point in space where the storm just *began*. A harsh wall ahead of me.

Heedless, I dove forward.

And as my outstretched hand came into contact with the edge of the storm, it was sliced, forming many lines of red.

I pulled back.

Well, that hurt, I thought. Despite the fact that mental powers seemed to work here, I had to remind myself that I wasn't in the real world. The rules were definitely different, and the storm I was now confronting looked to be a major problem. I stared at my hand, expecting it to heal itself, but it didn't. It remained scraped and raw, with thin lines of blood welling up.

If Sol could keep an impenetrable wall of high winds and jagged dust swirling around him, what chance did I have of resolving things? Or at least, how could I get to him before, back in the real world, Barry Wilk did whatever he intended to do?

"Sol!" I shouted into the vortex. "What are you, chicken?"

I never said I was very good at taunting.

Something in the storm rumbled, a booming, earth-shaking sound that reminded me of laughter. Or, damn it all, a chuckle. *His* chuckle. The bastard.

Other than that, there was nothing. The storm just continued spinning, and I continued standing there like a dope. I had to do something.

Behind me, there were trees. Normally, I might have qualms about killing a bunch of trees and trashing Mother Nature, but I had to remind myself that these trees were in Holly's mind. No real trees were harmed in the making of this story.

I used my mind to tear a large oak from the ground, plucking it out as easily as you might pull a weed. It was dozens of feet tall, but moving it with my mental powers, I was able to ease it across the harsh border of the storm, so that half of it remained outside while the other half plunged deep within.

In no time, the leaves were stripped off the tree. Thin branches went next, then larger ones. Finally, the bark was flayed from the massive trunk and the bare wood underneath slowly pulped and ripped apart. Counting in my head, I estimated it was 30 seconds, all together.

That's what you get, John. Thirty seconds of cover, I told myself. It would have to do.

Thankfully the swirling storm went in only one direction, slicing left to right. If Sol got wise and changed directions on me, I'd be doomed.

Once more, I pulled a huge tree from the ground, then added another and another. Hovering in the sky, I slammed them together, so their trunks nearly touched. Branches broke and leaves fell away as I compressed the trees into each other. Three looked like too few, so I added a couple more, staggering them so the new ones lined up in the gaps between the first three.

It was the tallest, crudest, strangest-looking shield I'd ever seen, but it was the best I could do. With my mind, I floated it to the edge of the storm wall, standing the trees straight up, so that the roots dragged along the ground and the bulk of the leaves were high above me, while the thickest parts of the trunk were right at my level, offering the most protection.

That was my theory, anyway.

I took a deep breath. "Here goes."

Quickly, I flung the trees into the storm, running alongside them and into the dangerous swirl. And what do you know, it worked. I almost laughed out loud. As my feet ran forward, I kept the tree shield to my left, moving beside me, as fast as I could go. *One, two...* I counted seconds in my head.

The only problem was that dust was everywhere. While the trees blocked the wind, I could barely see. *Five, six...*

I heard a ripping sound above me as a huge branch was torn from one of the trees and flung into the swirl. Leaves and smaller branches rained down on me, but still I ran. *Nine, ten...*

I started to get pelted by something sharp — bits of bark peeling off the trees. *Twelve, thirteen...*

I tried to go faster, with no idea how long the storm might go on. *Fifteen, sixteen... More than halfway. I hope.*

Suddenly a pain stabbed into my left side. Glancing over, I saw that a breach had formed between the trees and high winds were blasting through. With my mind, I jammed the trees back together harshly. *Nineteen, twenty...*

Another breach, this time sending the deadly storm shearing across the back of my neck, slicing into my flesh. Warm blood spilled into my shirt and down my back. *Twenty-three, twenty-four... Come on, come on!*

I tried to compress the trees further, but that was a bad idea. The two in front lost some sort of structural integrity and were ripped apart, barely missing me as they broke into pieces and flew off in the wind. I had only three left, and they were thinning quickly, the branches and bark long gone, and only the dwindling cores left. I tried to keep them pressed tightly without doing any more damage. *Twenty-seven, twenty-eight...*

Another tree shattered, this time the one in back, clipping my leg as it tore by into the storm winds. My calf was ripped open and bleeding. *Thirty, thirty-one... On borrowed time now.*

Still I ran, but it was hopeless. The last of my tree shield would be gone any second. *Thirty-three, thirty—*

With an awful shattering sound, the trees gave way and the wind took them, almost taking me, too. I was thrown into the storm with no protection, still running as best I could, but staggering to my last steps.

And then, it all stopped.

I fell face first into the eye of the storm, a place so oddly calm I almost believed I'd died and gone to heaven. But, I could still feel the strong winds just behind me, cut off by the same sharp edge I'd seen on the outside. Starting to push myself up, I realized just how close I'd come. Everything ached, especially on my left side. My clothes looked like I was starting one of those new fashion trends, with tons of artfully placed rips and tears. My neck and leg were sliced raw, and I realized both arms were bleeding as well. I looked like someone had attacked me with a giant pad of steel wool, abrading the skin down to pink newness in the good spots and raw, bloody redness in the bad.

Slowly, I got to my feet, scanning my surroundings. And there he was.

Sol.

Just sitting there, in his typically pristine attire, a cornflower-blue shirt that looked like it had been pressed *after* he put it on, and dark pants. He had Italian leather loafers on his feet, because I guess that's what you do when you're a fashionable monster. But what I noticed most, there in the middle of his well-tanned face, below his perfectly coifed dark hair, were his teeth.

They gleamed at me in a broad smile.

I could almost believe he was happy to see me, his smile felt so warm and genuine. Too bad I already knew it was like the grin of a rabid hyena.

I tensed, readying for the fight, the final fight I planned to ever have with Sol.

But he just waved a hand, graciously. "Please, John Black, my old friend. Take a moment. You've had a rough time just now. Catch your breath. Then, we can just talk."

"I'm done talking to you," I said, hands raised in fists.

Suddenly, a swell rose from the ground below me. Assuming that it was his first assault, I stepped quickly to one side, but something about it was fascinating. Roots crawled out of the dirt, thickening and forming legs, then a seat, then a back. Glancing toward my enemy, I saw the same object under him. A chair, grown from the depths of the earth.

Sol had made me a chair? He wanted me to sit down and chat, like a couple of children having a tea party? I stared at the newly formed chair, then at Sol.

He gave me a broad smile, gesturing calmly toward the chair with one hand. "Welcome, John. Welcome to the surreal."

4

"Say what you want to say, but make it quick," I snarked, flopping down into the chair Sol had made. Not because I trusted him or acquiesced or any of that. Because I was tired and bleeding and needed a rest. At least for a moment.

The second I touched the chair, the swirling storm around us fell away, dissipating into nothing but dying wisps of dust in an instant.

"Always hasty, my friend," Sol said. He was acting so chummy and nice it boiled my blood.

"I've told you. I'm not your friend."

Sol smirked and nodded. "I understand your point of view, really I do. Perhaps more than you realize. But what other term would you have for us besides friends? We are obviously so much more than acquaintances."

"Let's go with mortal enemies," I said, crossing my arms and wincing from the sting as I scraped across my raw flesh accidentally.

"As you wish," Sol replied. "But that does bring up the question of why? Why are you my mortal enemy, John Black? And what if I don't wish to be yours? What if I truly wish for us to be friends? Eternally, since that is the time we will have."

"Maybe one of us isn't going to be so eternal after all."

"Yes, John, yes. I know about this plan of yours. But I know it's already crumbled to dust in your hands. You want to use Naima to take my powers away and kill me, but Naima isn't with you."

I nearly gasped. *How does he know? Is he—*

Yes, John, Sol said in my head. *Yes, of course I'm reading your mind.* He laughed out loud. "Did you forget where we are?" Well, I must have looked dumbstruck, because he decided to explain things to me. "John, we are *inside* your sister's mind. These physical manifestations you see, your body, my body, this landscape, these trees. All of these are just thoughts, synapses firing inside the head of Holly Black."

"Then, what? We don't physically exist any more?"

"That's difficult. I truly wrestled with that possibility when I first arrived here. Oh, and by the way, you are right that time moves differently here, because we are not bound by the rules of the natural world. I, for example, feel like I've already spent a lifetime here. You've been here only a short while, perhaps what seems like a few hours of time to you. I suspect in the so-called real world — though, of course, I'm not there to verify this — perhaps only seconds have passed. Maybe less."

Then I still have time, I thought.

You're so persistent, John, Sol said to me with his mind. *I've always liked that about you.*

"Get out of my head," I said angrily.

"Apologies." He gave a polite nod, like doffing a cap he wasn't wearing. "Anyway, I do think you and I still exist, because our minds are here and sentient. We are *distinct* from Holly, although all of us are currently intertwined. You have no doubt heard the popular myth that human beings use only 10 percent of their brain capacity. Of course, science has proven this to be incorrect, that almost all areas of our brains are active almost all of the time, but still... Have you ever been concerned that your mind would run out of space?"

"Of course not."

"Exactly. When you save something on a computer, space is limited depending on its finite available storage. But with the *mind*, an organic, living thing — particularly one like ours with, let's say, special capabilities — the available storage is essentially limitless. I believe when we each arrived here, Holly's brain simply *made space* for us."

"That doesn't make any sense to me, but since I'm sitting here and talking to you, with my own ideas, and my own confusion, I guess it has to be right."

Sol chuckled. "Well, look there, John. Progress. You and I just agreed upon something." I slow-clapped my hands briefly in mockery. "You jest, but perhaps you do not realize that we've always agreed. On everything."

"That," I said pushing back in my chair, "is the biggest joke in history."

"Yet it's true." He was serious. Sol was delusional. "John, did you ever find it strange that you and I just *found* each other? That we have these same powers? We are different parts of the same thing. Now and always."

"What the hell are you talking about?"

Sol leaned forward, and the intensity in his eyes struck me. "John, I am *you* and you are *me*."

My mind was tingling. My whole body quivered with confusion. "The hell I am."

"Everything *I* have done, it was because of *you*. You, John Black. You at the governor's mansion. You in the desert. You atop Babilu Tower."

"Don't forget me at the amusement park in Playa Beach, where you stalked me like a pedophile creep."

Again, a dismissive smile. "John, because of you, I came back from the ultimate nothing. Even death cannot separate us."

My internal fire kicked in hotter, and I nearly spat my reply to his accusations. "I'm not responsible for you, you monster. You've killed how many people in cold blood?"

Sol's eyes widened. "Oh, is that it? Are we here to discuss good versus evil?"

"Isn't that obvious?"

Sol nodded. "It is to me. It is indeed. But is it to you? Who's the *good* here, and who is the *evil*?"

"Please. This is boring and stupid."

"Really?" Sol finally snapped. "I know that in your head, you consider me to be evil. You've just now accused me of murder. I assume this is evidence of my evil, yes?" He didn't wait for an answer. "What about you, John Black? Have you killed?"

I blinked. That was a low blow. Yes, I had killed. Sometimes by accident. But sometimes willfully, in my rage.

"Ah, you see? If killing makes you evil, then what are *you*, John? Aren't you evil?"

"No."

"Then what are you?" Sol tilted his head expectantly.

"I'm the good guy," I said. It sounded just as stupid coming out of my mouth as you'd imagine, and as soon as I'd said it, I felt foolish. And wrong.

"The *good guy*," Sol repeated. "The guy who flung living humans off a

282

skyscraper, to their deaths."

"Those were *your* henchmen, doing your dirty work."

"Yet still living beings, incapable of harming you, wouldn't you agree? You showed no mercy. No humanity."

"Be quiet."

"Ignoring the truth doesn't make it untrue," Sol said. "What about your supposed *friend*, Pip?"

"What about her?"

"You were so enraged by her that you cut off her arm."

"It got better."

Sol smiled. "You make light of it, but I would assume Pip might not find the moment so trivial."

"Pip is up there somewhere above us, fighting with me. Fighting *for* me. I might have done something terrible to her, but she and I are good now."

"Fine, John. If you've made your peace with her, then I suppose I should let that one go. But there is one more thing. One more bit of evidence to reveal your true heart. You know this."

"Stop talking." I knew what he was going to say, and I desperately didn't want to hear it.

"John, you must face the truth. If you call me evil, you are, at the very least, just as evil as I am. In fact, I daresay that I'm not evil at all, and my actions have always been directed at creating a better society. I've been thinking of the greater good. The big picture. The long run. But you? Your actions have been petty and thoughtless. You've acted in haste and anger to satisfy your momentary wishes, and to lash out at those weaker than you."

"Enough," I said.

Although his feet remained locked against the base of his chair, Sol stood, suddenly brazen and strong. "It is *not* enough, John Black. There's one more thing you and I have in common, one more undeniable truth. You and I are both guilty of patricide. My father fell at my hand, and your father at yours."

I wanted to jump up and fight him, but his words crushed me with their truth. I was responsible for killing my father, and it was the most self-centered, petty act I ever committed. I could never forgive myself for it. And it was utterly and completely me. I killed my father and I was his murderer. The act *was* me.

"So now you see the truth. Now you know that you and I are not opposite sides of a spectrum. We are not yin and yang, good and evil. We are the same. If you truly believe that I must be destroyed, wiped from the face of the earth, because I am evil, then the same rule applies to you."

"I—" All I could do was sputter.

"Think about perspective, old friend. To the downtrodden, the poor, the hopeless, the pathetic souls who came to me to form the Way of the Sun, what are you? You are the evil that destroyed their lives."

"And what about the rest of the people in the city?" I said. "The ones who didn't want to live under your dictatorship? *You* are evil to them."

Sol sighed. "These labels are useless, because they are not mutually exclusive. The real truth is this. You and I are both the good in the world, the hope of the world's future. And you and I, John Black... we are both the world's evil."

5

The earth shuddered, and I didn't understand why. I was speechless. Sol was right.

If he had to be killed because he was evil and a real danger to the world, what about me?

Sol sat back down never having taken a single step toward me. He seemed content to stay in his chair, like he was rooted to it.

A few dozen feet behind him, the ground split open with a low, rumbling moan that made me think our strange world was giving up on life. The split turned into a rift which turned into a wide, gaping hole. Slowly, something rose out of the hole.

Something massive and dark.

Something covered with rough, stony scales.

When her eyes broke the surface, all I could do was stare. She went onward, up and up, rising out of the living earth, her giant amber eyes pinned to me, glowing with hate. Then the stench of her presence rolled over me like a putrid wave.

"Gorgol Alpha," I muttered, disbelieving. I staggered to my feet to stand beside the odd chair of twisted roots or vines Sol had made for me.

Still she rose, until finally her full height was revealed. Two hundred feet of deadly monster stood directly behind Sol, and he sat in his chair like he was reading the Sunday newspaper.

"There is one important distinction between us, John," he said, shouting over the crashing of rocks and booming thuds of Alpha's arrival. "I am not concerned with such trivial matters as good and evil. I know what I am doing is right, and just, and *necessary*. And I do not intend to die." With that, he flicked one well-manicured finger in my direction, and Gorgol Alpha attacked.

Alpha was the physical incarnation of my sister's rage, taking the form of a giant monster that had scales like massive boulders, fingers and toes that ended in claws longer than I was tall, and teeth that looked like razor-sharp mountains, ready to gnash me to a pulp.

I thought Sol's little sandstorm was a challenge. It was nothing compared to Gorgol Alpha.

She raised her clawed foot high above our heads, and stomped downward, directly toward me. I ducked, rolling to my left, just barely avoiding her. My chair was not so lucky. It was pounded into oblivion by the force of the blow.

What the hell am I going to do against that *without physical powers?* I asked myself, knowing there was only one possible answer. *Run!*

So I did.

With Sol's storm dead and gone, I could see the forest once more, far in the distance. I headed for it, hoping to at least find something to hide behind. Considering Alpha could casually stomp every tree into toothpicks while she was looking for me, it wasn't really a long-term solution to my situation, but it was better than standing in the open and hoping she'd have a change of heart.

Sol remained calmly in his chair but called out to my back. "Run if you like, John Black, but Alpha is considerably faster than you."

There had to be a way. Physical powers were apparently off limits here, but mental powers worked. I had already plucked five trees out of the ground with my mind. Might as well add to my lumberjacking street cred. I yanked another with my mind and shot it like a missile toward Gorgol Alpha.

In midair, she swiped it away, sending it crashing to the rough terrain, broken into pieces.

I sent another, and another. Alpha dispatched them all.

Tearing out a whole section of trees, I flung them at Gorgol Alpha as I ran. She smashed them all aside and I realized I was destroying the very thing I was running for — some kind of shelter. I also realized how dumb running was, and started using my brain, which seemed to have been frazzled by everything that Sol had said. I lifted myself and began to fly, at top speed. Soon Alpha was a speck behind me.

I laughed.

Alpha and Sol were quickly receding into the distance, until I noticed that the landscape below was moving in the opposite direction. I was flying backwards, not away from Alpha but directly back to her. More precisely, someone was pulling me backward. Sol.

I fought against his power and achieved a sort of balance. I pulled away, he pulled me back. In the end, I was at a virtual standstill hundreds of feet in the air. Gorgol Alpha, meanwhile, pounded forward, closing the distance quickly. I struggled to break free, my internal rage fire blazing. It gave me enough of an edge to keep moving, but my speed wouldn't keep me out of Alpha's reach for long.

I was straining so hard my breath grew ragged. In the surreal landscape of my sister's mind, I saw puffs of steam coming from my nose. My rage fire produced physical effects in Holly's world, it seemed.

Gorgol Alpha got closer.

I screamed, the same deafening, knockout-blow scream I'd done in

Naima's garden, then more recently at the top of the cavern entrance.

"That's an interesting new technique, John," Sol yelled from below, still casually sitting on his chair. *Thank you for teaching it to me*, he added in my head.

I screamed a second time, but it was useless. In Holly's mental world, my powers simply didn't work the same way.

Which is why it hurt like hell when Gorgol Alpha swiped at me, knocking me from the sky like you'd swat a slow-moving fly. I'm pretty sure she broke several of my ribs, possibly ruptured an internal organ or two, probably gave me a significant concussion. But my more immediate concern was the harsh ground, now rushing up to finish the task of killing me.

I had just enough mental awareness to break my fall. Instead of splattering the ground with my remains, I hit with a thump and rolled into a heap. Another rib cracked audibly and must have punctured my lung, because suddenly the act of breathing was the most painful thing I'd ever felt in my life.

I wanted to scream again, but there was no air, too much pain, and it was hopeless. I felt Gorgol Alpha's footfall just behind me and knew that in seconds, she would complete the job of crushing me to death.

How could this be? How could I be in so much physical pain, in a place that wasn't physical at all? If I died in Holly's mind, was I dead forever? It was uncharted territory, but I didn't want to risk finding out. I had to do something.

I was filled with rage. Rage at the futility of it all, my helplessness, my failure against Sol, my inability to help my sister. The complete senselessness of everything.

Why?

With what felt like one of my last breaths, steam once more puffed out of my nose like a cartoon bull seeing red.

And then I saw a bull.

Not a cartoon bull, and not even a real bull, but a massive bull monster rising before me. It was nearly as tall as Gorgol Alpha, and its body was solid as stone. It had the form of those broad-shouldered longhorn steers you see in old Westerns, and stood puffing steam out of its nose in time with my own. The bull glared and pawed the ground with one massive hoof, ready to fight. Its horns were huge and curved, starting out white near their middle, ending in long, black, deadly points far on each side. The distance between those points must have been a hundred feet or more. As I rumbled with anger, the bull's tail flicked and I saw it wasn't a bull's tail at all, but almost a chain of boulders whipping back and forth, ending in a scorpion-like curved tip.

With absolute clarity, I realized the bull was me. Or, more accurately, I had created the bull.

Holly could make giant monsters that were the living incarnations of her anger, and in Holly's world, I had done the same. I guess with all of our minds intertwined, we three — Holly, Sol, and I — were learning from each other.

The monstrous bull squared off at Gorgol Alpha, with me still curled in a painful lump between them. But seeing the bull gave me hope, and through the hurt I gathered enough strength to shout. I decided my rage monster needed a name.

"If you're going to fight me *by proxy*, Sol — if you're going to use Gorgol Alpha — then let me introduce you to my own version, Gorgol Tau!"

Sol, always smug, smiled at the name. "*Tau*, you say? Perfect, John. You have always been bull-headed. Time is running short for you, but this may be an interesting way to pass these final few moments." We glared at each other, him still in his chair, me broken and propped up on one elbow. Eyes locked, we nodded in unison.

And without another word, Gorgol Alpha and Gorgol Tau smashed together, claws and teeth facing off against horns and hooves, with enough force to shake the entirety of the world.

6

I sipped shallow breaths, wincing at the pain, as I dragged my broken body toward a nearby rock. It was just large enough that I could prop myself up, but its jagged edges poked at my abdomen and caused me to see stars.

I blinked and looked straight upward, noticing that the sky was still frozen in Holly's mind world, never changing in however long I'd been here. The clouds were perfect puffballs, reflecting the long rays of the sun with intense colors. But they weren't moving.

Time was nearly standing still.

Then an object tore through my line of sight, tumbling end over end. It was a slab of stone large enough to crush a car, raining smaller bits of rock and dirt down upon me, into my eyes. I blinked and looked away, to the fury and combat playing out in front of me.

Gorgol Alpha staggered backward from being rammed in the chest by Tau. Sliding to a stop, Alpha tensed. She bent forward and opened her giant, tooth-filled maw, emitting a sound like a thousand blaring horns mixed with the trumpet of an elephant. In response, Tau snorted and this time more than simple steam or smoke came out. Actual flames shot from Tau's nostrils.

In spite of the pain, I smiled. My rage fire had become a real fire. Fire from the snorting nose of a massive stone bull. For some reason, it made me think of Bobby. *I know why. Two giant monsters squaring off? He would've thought this was pretty bad-ass.*

Something tickled at my mind. Something about Sol. What was he doing? I was broken and bloodied and near death. If he simply got up from his chair, walked over and punched me in the gut, it would probably complete the job of killing me that my punctured lung was slowly achieving. If I died, would Gorgol Tau even continue to exist? Couldn't Sol achieve victory easily? What the hell was he waiting for?

That's it, I thought. *You're not waiting. You're* stalling.

Inside my head, Sol chuckled. Damn that chuckle. *You can be rather dense sometimes, old friend.*

Between us, Alpha leaped forward, slashing her massive claws across Tau's wide shoulders, ripping into his stony flesh. The bull bellowed in pain and rage, twisting his head to stab at Alpha with the tip of one horn, but Alpha pushed the blow aside, tearing at Tau once more. The giant bull lashed out with his tail, stabbing into Alpha's upper thigh. The monster responded with another shrieking trumpet blast, although this one was tinged with pain.

What are you stalling for?

Another chuckle. *Oh, John. Is this the part of the story where the bad guy explains his entire plan, to give the good guy hope and a chance? No, thank you, friend. You'll just have to see for yourself in time.*

Tau whirled, kicking out with his powerful back hooves, slamming Alpha in the midsection and pummeling her backward.

Or, Sol continued, *perhaps not. You don't seem to have a lot of time left, John. And in this world, if you succumb, you will be gone forever.*

"How—" I began to say, but the sharp pain in my chest stopped me, so I continued speaking to Sol with my mind. *How would you know? You don't make the rules here.*

You're right, John. This world is your sister's, not mine, at least for now. But I know that if you give up, you will be consumed by her mind.

That's what happened to Ranger — Jake Weissman — when I was inside his mind. Once I was able to take over, his spirit gave up, and now he's simply gone.

Alpha roared once more and dove for Tau's backside, biting into his less-protected lower flank. Gorgol Tau let loose a bleating cry of pain, flailing and kicking wildly to escape. His tail flashed in the air, threatening to stick the point into Alpha once more, but Gorgol Alpha swatted it aside.

I'm not giving up. You're not going to win, I said.

Sol seemed completely calm. I could feel his confidence, just as I could feel my own lack of it. I could barely breathe. What hope was left? *It's interesting, being in another person's mind*, Sol said. *I've done it twice now, and I have to say it's quite educational. Of course, Jake was a less — shall we say, complex? — subject than your sister. But Holly? Oh my, the things she can do. The things she has taught me.*

Stay out of my sister's head, I warned pointlessly. We *existed* in Holly's head.

I won't dignify that with a response, John. The portal your sister can create is magnificent. To produce living things out of her own mind, it's an achievement unrivaled in human history. And I know every secret of it now. Plus, as you saw recently, Holly has added the ability to take another superhuman's power. Oh now, that changes the game, doesn't it, old friend? Imagine if I had that ability a few years ago, back in the desert? You and I would not be here now, because you would not be here now.

Gorgol Tau spun and one of his horns gouged into Alpha's leg, gashing it open. Blood rained down to the ground in gruesome buckets of crimson. I smiled, suddenly full of hope. Tau had taken injuries, but he was hurting Alpha, too. Tau could win.

Alpha was enraged by the injury, grabbing the offending horn with both of her mighty clawed hands and tugging Tau forward. Then, as

Tau's own momentum was about to crash the two beasts together, Alpha released her grip with one hand and balled it into a fist, smashing it into the bull's forehead. Tau bellowed again in pain.

Sol continued. *Once I reach my goal, I will have all of Holly's abilities. And all of yours.* He didn't even chuckle this time. He outright laughed. *I know previously I said that you and I were destined to circle 'round each other for all eternity, John, but I no longer believe that. Holly has shown me the truth.*

Tau dug his massive hooves into the dirt, trying to pull back from Alpha but failing. Alpha kept her grip on the bull's horn, then reached out and grabbed the other horn with her free hand. They stood in a deadly face-off, but Tau was at a distinct disadvantage. His horns were his main weapon, but locked in Alpha's grasp, they were neutralized. In that position, his dagger tail could only flail helplessly behind him, unable to connect with the other monster.

John, once things are complete, there will only be me remaining. Jake Weissman, Margrethe, and Petrus are already dead and gone, as is your friend Bobby. Soon, you and Holly will be gone. That leaves only two others for me to address in the aftermath. With the strength of both you and your sister inside me, it will be trivial for me to destroy Pip.

And your mother.

I gritted my teeth, unable to take in much air at all. The stabbing pain in my chest threatened to overwhelm me, and I thought I was close to losing consciousness. If that happened... I didn't want to think about it, but there was no cavalry coming to save me. All would be lost.

I had to keep myself together.

I tried to ignore Sol, focusing on Tau. *Fight! Come on!* I shouted with my mind but in this place, who did it reach. No one? *He's going to kill my mother!*

But, no. It was too late. With her claws dug into each horn, Gorgol Alpha roared directly into the face of the bull, a defiant and horrifying sound. Then her muscles tensed and she snapped both horns in half, tearing them violently from Gorgol Tau's head.

The bull staggered. The bull fell. For one fleeting moment, Tau tried to regain his feet, but Alpha turned the two horns around and stabbed them into the fallen bull's back, a twisted matador delivering a pair of killing strokes.

I felt a mirror of stabbing pain in my chest, and an echo of wailing despair. Gorgol Tau, my incarnate rage monster, puffed out a last plume of steam and died.

Above his body, Gorgol Alpha stood tall, lifting her head and roaring at the sky.

And as if the beast was made of nothing but motes of dust, Tau's body disintegrated and blew away in the breeze. In moments, nothing remained except his blood that stained the land.

Hope was lost. I had lost. I closed my eyes.

7

Nothing else stood between me and death at the hands of Gorgol Alpha, and the giant monster wasted no time in seeking to complete the task. She pounded over to my pathetic form, where I was lying broken, bleeding, and helpless, propped up on a rock. Alpha raised one foot to stomp me into eternal oblivion, then froze and put her foot down again.

Sol spoke in my mind again. *I have asked Gorgol Alpha to wait a moment, John. Because I simply have to let you see something before you die.*

I was furious. *Just shut up, would you?* I blasted at Sol. *If I have to die, at least let me do without listening to one more damn word from you.* Despite the pain, my rage fire blazed brightly within.

I'm afraid that I cannot comply with your last wishes, old friend. The time has come, and it is glorious.

I sighed, once more watching puffs of steam come out of my own nose. *What, then? Say it and let this all end.*

Very well. Here it is. Your sister is giving up, too.

What? Raising my head, I tried to look past Gorgol Alpha's towering bulk. *What are you talking about?*

Sol grinned, still sitting stupidly in that chair. *You must feel it. Holly has been holding open the portal she made, waiting for you. It has been tapping all of her strength, and soon her strength will fail. But here's the crux of her problem, John. She loves you. She refuses to close the portal until you come back out of it, and so she is willing to sacrifice the last of her strength. For you.*

I shuddered with fear and disbelief. My sister...

And you, John? You lie there about to die. Meaning that your sister is doing all this for nothing. He chuckled again and looked down toward his feet. *Meanwhile, I am so close to being able to take over her body. Do you remember when you blasted your force at Jake Weissman, the Ranger, and it ended up dislodging the last fragments of him, and resurrected me? Well, with Holly, there will be no explosion, because there will be an implosion instead. I have tapped into every aspect of your sister, and when her strength fails waiting for you, I will pull back, imploding her inward, and she will cease to be.*

Sol stood, but once more he wouldn't walk away from the chair he had made, and suddenly I realized why. He was rooted into the ground, physically. Tendrils of his body extending downward into the soil. Into the world that Holly's mind created. Sol was attached to my sister like a parasite.

He waved a hand and Gorgol Alpha once more raised her deadly foot to crush me, letting loose an earth-shaking roar of victory.

8

I closed my eyes again.

Maybe you're thinking I gave up. Maybe Sol thought that, too.

But, nah.

The truth is, I was way too pissed off to give up.

For a second time, Gorgol Alpha froze above me, but this time not from a command by Sol. She looked past me, and even though the beast had nothing resembling human emotive expressions, she appeared to be in shock.

Without turning, I knew what she saw. Gorgol Tau had reappeared.

"What strange magic is this?" Sol said, standing in front of his chair, still literally tethered into my sister's mind.

I realized a few things at that moment, critically important things. First, my rage hadn't died with the original Gorgol Tau, meaning that there was still more of it within me. More rage to expel. And second, if nothing else was true of existing inside Holly's head, everything physical had to be mental. Because physical things, here, were just manifestations of Holly's mind. And mine.

I'd like to say that with this revelation, I stood up, taking a long, deep, pain-free breath, sucking in to fill my restored lungs before laughing loudly in Sol's face, but I couldn't. My physical body was still trapped and near death, a manifestation of the odd rules of living within Holly's mind. At least that much she dictated.

But behind and far above me, the new Gorgol Tau struck the pose I wish I had, puffs of fire and smoke coming from his nostrils.

How did I do it? Make another rage monster? Simply put, I wasn't willing to stop. I wasn't willing to fail. I changed the rules of the game. I guess I don't believe in the no-win scenario.

I coughed, spitting up blood, still reclined against a rock, still broken and straining just to draw a breath. But a thought struck me, some arcane fact from long ago. I think my dad told me about it, since nerdy language stuff was one of the many intellectual topics he thought was interesting. Sucking in a harsh breath that felt like a spike to my chest, I asked Sol a question. I deliberately spoke aloud. He needed to *hear* this shit. "Did you know that, in ancient times, *Tau* was the symbol of resurrection?" He goggled at me and my bizarre pet, the giant monster behind me. "Well, I guess you know now."

Sol seethed, gritting his teeth. "This matters little, John Black. Tau and Alpha will simply fight again, and once more Alpha will win. You can resurrect this... *thing*... as many times as you want, and all it will do is expend time. Time your sister doesn't have."

I smiled. "So, we agree on something again. This has been a day full of surprises, hasn't it?"

"What do you mean?" Sol stammered.

"I mean that you're correct — if I just make a new Tau every time Alpha wins, we'll be here for a very long time. So I want to change things up a little." I nodded upward, gesturing for Sol to look over his shoulder.

He did. And I want to hope that a tiny bit of him died as he saw what stood there.

Another Gorgol Tau.

Sol staggered, almost pulling away from the roots that tied his body into Holly's mind before composing himself. His game was the long game. Stall as long as possible until Holly weakened. He composed himself. "Let them all fight!" Sol shouted, tossing one arm in the air, his normally well-coifed hair flying in a wild tangle atop his head.

If Sol was playing the long game, that meant that I had to play a short one.

Once more Sol gestured for Alpha to attack, and my two Taus closed ranks, coming together with her as their focal point. But I raised my right hand in a calmer reflection of Sol's gesture. "Hold on," I said. Then I pointed off to Sol's left, and he turned to see what stood there waiting for him.

A third Gorgol Tau.

I flicked my wrist and a fourth appeared on the other side. Then a fifth and sixth.

In no more than a dozen heartbeats, I'd made a herd of deadly bull monsters, an Army of Tau. Yeah, Sol was right. Especially when it came to giving up and dying, I *could* be bullheaded.

Desperate, Sol flailed at his champion. "Fight!" he screamed at Gorgol Alpha, imploring her to action.

And, to her credit, the giant monster did the only thing that was going to help her cause against such overwhelming odds. Against all of these beasts fueled by the rage of one broken person, lying helplessly against a rock.

She stomped me into the unforgiving, stony ground.

9

As I lay dying, my army came to rally around me.

How I even had any blood flowing, or breath moving, or any strip of consciousness, I couldn't tell you, but then again, Holly's mind was not the normal world. I somehow lived on, ever so slightly, smashed to a pulp and gurgling my last breaths. But it was long enough to see all my Gorgol Taus as they surrounded Gorgol Alpha.

I had to feel bad for Alpha. She was simply Holly's rage, being manipulated by Sol. She wasn't my real foe. That honor belonged to the suntanned jerk himself, standing rooted into the ground beside a chair made from odd twists of earth and vines.

But my time was at an end. I don't even think I was breathing. How could a broken, crushed body? I think I was holding on simply from the remaining oxygen in my cells. Those cells with their alien thorns. I almost wanted to will the thorns to say goodbye to the last few molecules of oxygen, their last connection to life. But of course, here there was no oxygen, no cells, nothing real. I was just an idea, and this world was about to forget me forever.

This is it. Goodbye, I said, hoping some hint of it would reach Holly's mind. Sure, that sounds rather dramatic, but in my state, I hardly cared for such labels. I just wanted my sister to know she'd have to proceed on her own against Sol, if she could. If she had any strength left. *Holly, you have to do it yourself now. I failed.*

As if they were all waiting for me to die, Alpha, the Taus, and Sol all stood silently by, watching.

And then a feeling came over me, whooshing through my body like I was being filled up, chilling me to the bone. Something massive and unprecedented and universal was *wrong*.

Something had come, and come for me alone. I felt a power directed toward me, like magnifying sunlight to kill a bug. It was large and very powerful, and whatever was behind it, I had become its main focus. The whole situation might have been scary had I not already been squished to death.

A sound like wind came into my head. I thought I was hallucinating. There were no words, but I could feel a presence.

Was it God?

The windy sound came again, but this time I heard three beats to it, a cadence. *Whoosh-whoosh...Whoosh.* Then it repeated, gaining even more clarity. *Gaaaaah-ahhhh-Jaaahhh.*

It *was* God. Not an actual god from any actual religion mind you, but the God of Here.

Holly?

Geeetttt-uuupppp-Johhhnnnn.

"Holly? You can hear me?" I said aloud.

Hold on. How exactly had I said that aloud? My lungs couldn't even have been described as "collapsed," they were more like "road-kill-splattered." But air came out and I spoke. I sucked in a breath.

And realized there was no pain.

I looked down, and there my body was, fresh as new. I wiggled my fingers with glee.

Get up, John, Holly said once more.

So I did. "Thank you, Hol. Don't know how I can repay you for that one." I waited for a response, but that feeling of focus left and she didn't speak to me again. Who knows how much extra energy I made her use, energy she really couldn't spare.

That meant the rules were still the same. Time was of the essence. Sol was making inroads with every passing second, while Holly was running out of steam. And somewhere, Barry Wilk and his government agents still wanted to lock us all up. I had to act.

Snapping my head to the left, I made a circling gesture with the index finger of my right hand. "Army of Tau — time to end Alpha's reign." In near unison, they snorted their agreement, puffs of smoke and fire blasting from their nostrils. They pawed at the earth with their massive bull hooves, tearing out truck-sized clots of dirt and debris.

Slowly, deliberately, they surrounded Alpha. She roared her defiance, turning to meet them, but never able to face them all. It seemed like she was waiting, perhaps waiting for Sol to come to her rescue. When he didn't, I assumed his connection to my sister took up too much of his focus and he could only stand there watching. Finally, realizing she was all alone, Alpha decided a good offense was her best defense. She dove for the Tau closest to her outstretched front arms and twisted past his horns. With lightning quickness, she went for his throat, tearing into his flesh with deadly force.

That Tau fell, bleeding out rapidly. Alpha turned to the next, and I was afraid. She was so very powerful.

Then she roared once more, but it was different. Not defiance, not rage, not anger. Something new.

Agony.

From her belly, I saw the bloodied tip of a horn protrude. She'd been speared by one of the Taus behind her. Soon another joined, and another. Alpha raged and flailed, desperate, but they were all around her. She couldn't get away, she couldn't defend herself against so many.

In a slowly compressing swirl of giant bodies, the Army of Tau pressed in on Gorgol Alpha, and more than a dozen horns pierced her flesh.

Alpha inhaled, probably feeling a pain similar to mine just a short time before. Then she released a shriek of such pure rage that I felt I'd never hear anything like it again. And somewhere, buried in the many tones of that final cry, was the voice of a young girl screaming out all of her anger forever and ever.

* * *

Gorgol Alpha fell. She had her claws deep enough into two Taus to take them out with her, and her fall alone dispatched a couple more. In the end, there were half a dozen dead Gorgols lying on the ground.

It amazed me, once more, how sad and pathetic, how lonesome and lost, a giant monster could appear when it was motionless, helpless, and dead.

I thought about Gorgols Sigma and Omicron, the ones I had killed. The feeling of guilt I had, despite the destruction they caused, was palpable. I realized it was because they came from Holly.

But time was running short, I still had a small army of bull-shaped Gorgols, and Sol remained tapped into my sister's mind. I had to change that.

"Sol!" I shouted, standing tall. "Break it off, now, or die!"

He smiled. "Break it off? You mean disconnect myself from the mind of your sister and give her back her life? No, my friend, it is far too late for such a thing. In moments, all of this will be decided, and you will be eradicated. She is nearly spent. You can *feel* it. I know it. Look around you, John Black." Sol waved his hands in a circle, boldly, triumphantly, even though he was the one rooted to the ground and faced with my horde of murderous, giant monsters.

But there was something...

The world seemed, I don't know, *thinner*. Perhaps darker as well. The strange sky with clouds that never moved nonetheless seemed to be fading into night.

"Enjoy your supposed victory while it lasts," he scoffed at me. Sol was a serious scoffer. Is scoffer a word? Whatever. One who scoffs. Only douchebags scoffed regularly, and Sol was definitely one of those.

"Your choice," I said. "You've seen what my Army of Tau can do." Funny how names stick quickly sometimes. Army of Tau. At least it was a better name than Trio Supremo. Sorry, Bobby.

Slowly, the giant, stony bulls turned their blood-soaked horns to face Sol. Slowly they moved to surround him, so many thunderous beasts kicking up dust. Holly made the rules in Holly's mind, and Holly had decided to save me. Not only was it an unexpected reprieve, it was something Sol couldn't begin to hope for if the roles were reversed. If any one of my Taus crushed or gored Sol, he would not be brought back to life. And good riddance.

I realized with a certainty that *this* was the way to do it. This was the solution to killing Sol forever. Kill him in Holly's mental world, where nothing at all could bring him back. Where the thorns in his cells were helpless.

I strolled between the legs of my massive bull Gorgols like you would take a walk among the trees on a pleasant day in the park, coming to a stop just a few dozen feet from Sol, face to face. But inside, I was all anger, and pent-up energy, ready to finish things once and for all.

Thunder rolled in the distance. Or at least I thought it was thunder.

"Did you hear that, old friend?" Sol said. "It has already begun."

"What? Another one of your little storms?" I seethed.

"Hardly," he said, scoffing again. See what I mean? "No, John. That is the sound of Holly tearing apart. Of her mind succumbing to mine. And *you* brought this on. Because she is your sister, because she wasted her energy to save you, I have won." And Sol chuckled, a final, triumphant little laugh, so smug and joyous and horrible.

"Listen to me carefully, Sol," I said. "I'm going to make sure you never, ever laugh at me like that again." Rage fire boiling over inside me, I pointed directly at his chest. "Army of Tau! Kill him!"

Stirring into action, one of the giant beasts just next to me snorted loudly, sending a plume of fiery smoke over my head. Then the bull stomped forward on giant hooves, twisting to whip its deadly scorpion tail into Sol's heart and destroy him forever.

Sol puffed himself up, broadening himself like he was daring the attack to come. Then he closed his eyes and held his arms out like someone having a religious experience. "Now," he muttered softly.

And the entire landscape shook in a massive earthquake that I knew had nothing to do with tectonic plates and everything to do with Sol's mind tearing Holly's mind apart.

Around me, the Taus struggled to keep their feet, not expecting the very ground they walked on to be their new enemy. The one who had been about to strike down Sol staggered and his attack went wide, stabbing into the dirt.

I struggled to stay upright as the earth heaved, an act complicated by the fact that I had to dance and dodge to evade the randomly stamping feet of the two Gorgol Taus nearest to me.

Sol slowly clenched his hands into fists, and the shaking of the ground worsened. All I could do, all the Army of Tau could do, was hold on. But not Sol, with his tethers into Holly's mind. He was rooted firmly, lashed to the mast as a maelstrom of dirt erupted all around.

"Tau! You must stop him!" I shouted, trying to be heard amid the chaos.

One of them responded, the one just to my left. Trying desperately to keep his feet, he somehow plodded forward. Finally, teetering on three legs, Gorgol Tau raised one massive stone hoof to crush the life out of Sol.

There goes your eternity, Sol, I thought.

And at that moment, it seemed time slowed to a crawl. I could watch the descending foot of the monster as it came down to destroy Sol, but it was in slow motion. There, in the center of the maelstrom going on, Sol snapped his eyes open and locked them on mine.

He strained to complete the task of taking over Holly. And still the hoof fell toward him.

At the very last moment, I saw the tendrils binding Sol to Holly turn to dust and fall away, and I thought he had won. But his eyes... no. His eyes burned with a hateful obsession, staring at me. *Damn you to the pits of hell, John Black.*

In the strange slog of time, I realized what had happened. With death coming for him, he disconnected from Holly. Sol gave up.

No, Sol said, reading my mind. *There you are wrong. I will* never *give up.* He waved one hand and just to the right of where he stood, a shimmering form appeared. At first I thought he was creating something, but with our minds still connected, I realized that was incorrect. Sol was merely showing what he had visually concealed until this very moment.

A portal.

Sol seemed to have perfected some sort of unique trick that could hide something in plain sight, maybe fooling my mind, or perhaps just bending light in a strange way, like a movie special effect in real life.

Pulling his feet up from the ground to snap the last vestiges of connection to my sister, Sol stepped toward the swirling black hole beside him. *One thing you will need to learn, John, is this: Always have a Plan B.*

And then Sol raised his foot to step through the portal and leave me and my Army of Tau to suffer through the last collapse of Holly's mind.

10

Not so fast, asshole, I thought. *If I'm going down, I'm going down swinging.*

With haste, I flung a tendril of my mind out to lock onto Sol just as he stepped into the swirl of the portal and was sucked away.

And everything went black.

No, that's not right. The stony ground and motionless clouds and Army of Tau disappeared, but there was a light. Just a faint glow.

Somehow I'd been thrown to the floor and was lying on my stomach. I pushed up to see the source of the glow and there above me it hovered, like an angel. Like a ghost in the shadows. Shadow Ghost.

Holly floated as if in water, arms slightly parted to each side. I was back in the dim underground depths of the earth — the real earth — and thankfully not surrounded by a mob of government agents with their crazy new anti-superhuman weapons. The only thing I could see was Holly emanating a dim luminescence, with just the nearest bits of rock reflecting some of her light. It wasn't the beaming orb of light Holly could so easily create in her strongest moments. No, she was tired and very weak.

Abruptly, Holly fell out of the air into a heap on the rough stone below. I pushed myself up and scrambled to her side, realizing as I did that I could still see her. There was still some shred of light coming from my sister, which meant she was still fighting, even though now she appeared to be unconscious.

I reached out with my powers and could tell she was breathing and alive, but my attempts to speak to her mind were met with silence. Holly was out cold.

Trying to force my eyes to adjust to the shadowy darkness, I looked around. There was no sign of the portal that returned me from inside Holly's mental world. And no sign of Sol.

It was quiet, deep in the earth, like being buried alive. I reached out with my senses, trying to find any of the others — some beacon from my mother, Pip, or even Sol. I sensed nothing, other than my sister. Not a shred of life, not even a microbe or an amoeba or whatever the heck would live so far down in the dark. Caves often seem damp, but we were so deep there wasn't even any water nearby. Only dry, dead rock. I stretched my mind upward, straining the limits of my perceptions. High above us, little pinpricks of life appeared, but they were far away. I pushed farther, looking for something bigger, something human. When I felt I had reached my limit, I stoked the fire within me to push just a little farther. Finally, I realized that I simply couldn't do it. We were so far down that I couldn't sense anyone except me and Holly.

Where are you, Sol?

How could he possibly have escaped? Where could he go, two thousand meters down? It wasn't like there was a trap door or a secret hideaway.

I concentrated on Holly, digging deeper with my mind to see if there was some way I could help her. It was like flicking a more powerful microscope lens over a slide, seeing tiny new details suddenly come into focus. The glow, Holly's luminescence, was really a million or even a trillion tiny lights.

I tried to push some of my energy into her, to bring her back. At first, nothing seemed to happen, but slowly I realized she was taking it. My powers were filling up a void inside her, like recharging a battery. I smiled, there in the mostly dark, thinking that soon Holly would be up and around, and we could figure out what to do next together.

But the power trickling from me to her slowly increased. A trickle turned into a thin stream, then into something stronger.

I pulled back and realized that my unconscious sister had somehow dug in. I couldn't cut off the flow.

And there was something else about Holly that was strange. Something odd and familiar. I mean, she's my sister, and so of course she was familiar, but this was different. It didn't seem like Holly at all. It seemed like, well, me.

I realized I was letting myself get distracted, and the flow of power into my sister notched up just a little bit more. I knew what was happening, all too well. The way Holly had drained Margrethe, like a vampire. She was now doing it to me.

I had to break the connection. My fire pulsed into life, bright and angry inside me.

Something like a mirror of that action happened in Holly, another fire echoing my own. Once more, it threatened to take away my focus, so willfully I ignored it.

I pulled, harsh and fast. Holly resisted. My knocked-out kid sister was beating me. Although I was in mortal danger, I took a moment to acknowledge how foolish I felt. *Holly's new slogan: I beat other superhumans in my sleep!*

I raged and pulled again, as hard as I could, and with relief I felt the connection finally break, a rubber band stretched too far. Holly, still out, moaned pathetically, as if the other end of that rubber band has just snapped back into her face.

Skittering backward, I put some physical distance between us as well, suddenly afraid that touching my sister might renew the power drain. I sat leaning backward, both arms propped behind me, panting.

And I heard him chuckle in the dark.

I saw nothing, but he had to be near, somewhere. *What is the one thing you want that you no longer can have, old friend?* Sol asked in my head.

"What is this?" I said. "Riddles in the dark?"

No, John. Not a riddle. Simply the truth.

Suddenly the darkness swirled just above my sleeping sister, and a tanned, grinning face appeared, white teeth reflecting Holly's faint glow. Sol had done it again — made some kind of visual trickery that hid him in plain sight, just as he had done to the portal hovering beside him in Holly's mind. As he appeared before me, with Holly's light shining below, his face reminded me of my dad putting a flashlight under his chin to tell spooky stories as we sat around a campfire back on some happier day. Sol grinned a ghoul's grin. "The one thing you no longer have, John, is this. *Time*." Then he crawled over Holly like an animal, coming for me with a feral speed.

Quickly, I blazed with rage, trying to stand, but Sol had the element of surprise. He was rushing for me not only in body, but also in mind. A powerful cylinder of force compressed around me, in a way that precluded any evasion my thorn-filled cells could provide. There was no escape, not left, right, up, or down. Every side pressed in. Meanwhile, with a sharp mental tendril, he stabbed at me, a dagger to the brain, delving deep into the pain, fear, and regret he knew was there. *You are the evil in the world*, Sol repeated to me, over and over, pressing to plant that seed so deep I could never dig it up. *You are the evil in the world, John Black.*

I wriggled, but my body only became more stuck, in ever more unpleasant poses. For a second, I remembered some undersea documentary where a vessel had gone too far below the surface of the ocean and had been crushed into a tight ball by the pressure. My arms twisted awkwardly, pressing against my midsection. My legs squeezed together until I thought they'd snap.

Sol's mind poured into mine like a sea of stars, filling me with a light so bright it was blinding. I pushed and pushed and pushed, but still he kept coming, and I knew that his flood would end my life.

Do not struggle, old friend. This will all be over momentarily. Then, I can finally rectify things with your sister, too. Sol's face filled my vision, a heinous Halloween mask of contrasts.

This was the last thing I would see. Sol's face, with my own sister lying vulnerable behind him.

I sucked in every ounce of strength I had, knowing it was less that what it might be because of what Holly had taken from me. It had to be enough, though. It had to.

Dumping every bit of fuel I could into my internal rage fire, I blazed with light, pushing backward on Sol.

At that moment, I realized I could see.

All around us, the odd reds and blacks of the rock walls suddenly burst into view, as if a shard of the sun had fallen into this deep hole. Accidentally, I had learned Holly's trick. I was somehow making light with my power, and now my body was a glowing beacon of luminescence. The knowledge of what was happening strengthened me, and somehow I blazed even brighter, willing every cell in my body to live and rage with fire. I was the sun. If I wished, I could black out the sun.

But it wasn't enough.

Sol reached out with one hand and, although it seemed impossible, easily penetrated the invisible cocoon that held me fast. He put his hand around my throat, holding it firmly in a gesture of dominance, and used it as a focal point to continue his attack.

His light poured faster into me, and I was baffled by how this could be happening. How could my most powerful counterattack do *nothing* to him? I felt hope slipping away. If my best wasn't enough, what more was there?

His light. My light. Was his stronger? It didn't feel that way... it felt more like... what?

Light.

Light doesn't remove light. Take two lights and shine them in the same space, and one doesn't cancel the other. They both illuminate at the same time.

So what good was my light against his?

Hope finally left me, because I had nothing else. I realized I had no way to stop what Sol was doing.

I gave up.

Really, I did. I pushed and pushed and pushed with everything I had and nothing worked, until finally I just let go, and watched as Sol's light flowed into me, surging into every crevice, filling my head.

I let it happen. I was tired and I'd had enough. The only thing left inside me was a burning, horrible anger. At losing. I was mad, not at Sol for winning, because that's what Sol had always wanted to do.

No, I was mad at *me* for losing.

Get it over with, John, you fool, I said to myself. *You've failed like you always knew you would, so just end it. Quickly.*

I began to tug.

If Sol's power was going to overwhelm and consume me, let it happen faster. If I couldn't push him out, I could pull him in. Finish the job sooner.

I pulled and pulled and pulled, and I could feel Sol's glee knowing that

I had given up and was no longer trying to stop him, no longer acting in my own best interest.

Our faces nearly nose to nose, Sol smiled, triumphant.

Still I pulled, again and again. Harder now, really wanting everything to be done. I was zealous in my madness. If I had to die, then bring it on. Let it be done with.

And something snapped.

One of Sol's innumerable lights was plucked out and went dark.

In front of me, Sol's smile twinged at one corner, just a bit.

I yanked again, and three more lights were plucked out.

Suddenly Sol looked like someone who'd been rapturously devouring ice cream only to realize they were getting a brain freeze. Joy turned to pain. I dug deep with rage and pulled, mentally grabbing handfuls at a time.

Huge swathes of light went dark as the tendrils were broken. I continued.

"What are you doing, John Black? Stop this!" Sol shouted from inches away. He tried to reverse his flow and pull the light from my mind, but he was so extended that it couldn't happen fast enough.

And unlike when my sister had almost taken my power away, I was awake and angry. I wasn't going to let him go so easily.

I pulled more and more, and soon most of Sol went dark.

But my actions weren't like Holly's — I wasn't a vampire sucking up Sol's power.

I was turning off the lights.

This, I said. *This is the light we create. All of us. And the dark that our opposites bring about. This is what Naima does to us.* She had touched me and knocked out much of my power, but I understood that it had instructed me, too.

We all had the same power — Sol, me, Naima. It just mattered if your switches were on or off.

And I was turning Sol's off.

I pulled and yanked and tugged and snatched at his power tendrils like a madman, flailing, until at last I held the final few strands.

I panted, breathing harsh breaths into his face.

Goodbye.

Old.

Friend.

And then it was my turn to grin at him as I pulled at the last vestiges of Sol's power, plucking them out like dandelions. Killing the weed that was infecting the world.

I realized the pressure around me was gone, probably for some time, at least since I'd been ripping out Sol's power. I remained connected to Sol's mind, but he no longer knew how to connect to me. His mind felt like that of any other normal human I might push, someone to let me on the city bus unnoticed or lend me their phone or whatever. Sol's hand fell from my throat and he crumpled backward into a pathetic ball on the rocky floor of the cave.

Coughing and sputtering, he looked sad and defeated, curled on the ground before me. But his coughing soon turned to ragged laughter. "You think you've won, John? You think this is the end? Impossible! How many times must I come back from the dead before you realize we are in this together *forever*! I am eternal. I will *always* come back."

"No," I said. "Not this time. Because Sol is already dead. Now you're *you* again, just plain old Jose do Branco. Sol isn't coming back again, ever."

At that moment, something within him broke and he jumped up, reaching for me with hands like claws. Where once he had been manicured and polished, now he seemed like a wild animal. His shirt, which would normally be immaculately pressed, its tails neatly tucked, instead was wrinkled, torn, and flapping sloppily to one side.

I stopped his attack with little effort, making a fist of air to hold him where he stood.

Sol barked almost like a dog. "John Black. Know this. I will kill you, and I will kill Holly. And do you know what I will do after that?"

"Kill Pip, kill my mom, kill everyone else," I said with a sigh. "So creative."

Sol shook his head and spittle flew. "No, not everyone. Your mother I will keep alive. It will entertain me greatly to see how long it is before she breaks."

That was enough. Yes, there was good and evil in everyone, me and Sol both. Yes, I had done terrible things. So had he. But the difference was this: I didn't like it, and he did.

I didn't even like what I needed to do at that moment, but I knew it had to be done. Holding Sol away from me with the will of my mental powers, I began to bore deeper into the ground. "No. Not only will you never lay eyes on my mother again, you are done, forever. Get used to the darkness down here, because you'll never see the light of the sun again."

And down we went.

11

I wasn't taking any chances, so I blasted us hundreds of meters farther underground. Where nothing had ever lived. Where nothing could live.

There was no way Jose do Branco was truly eternal. He had become Sol and I'd previously defeated him by blasting him into a million pieces. But my error was that each of those pieces contained a thorn and each of those thorns both wanted to stay alive *and* had its own sort of Sol data bank stored within. By fate or bad luck, those cells ended up swarming a hapless park ranger named Jake Weissman and, slowly at first, they turned on him. Eventually Sol won the fight for Jake's body, and he was returned.

And when he was accidentally sucked into Holly's mental portal, he was full of power. Although power worked differently in Holly's mind, Sol had options. Either he could take over my sister and join his power with hers, or simply get out again. Either way, he returned to life as an even more powerful superhuman.

But now? Now I had taken away all of his power.

No, that's wrong. I didn't take his power away, I turned it off, just like Naima had been able to turn all of us off at some point. I figured out the trick.

Offhandedly, I wondered what Dr. Naima Ramadi would do if I ever had the chance to tell her. That her full and true powers could be switched *on*, that she might soar and blast and fight just like the rest of us. I bet she might like to meet her old friend, Deputy Director Barry

Wilk of the Task Force on Superhuman Affairs, and have a little chat. I smirked, wishing I could be a fly on the wall for that conversation.

Finally, Sol and I came to a stop inside a thin open vein of rock, a place where perhaps millions of years ago some global event had disrupted the normal accrual of sediment, switching from one form of rock to some other. The light from my body illuminated diagonal swathes in pale hues cutting across the otherwise dark stone.

I decided this would be the place to end it all.

Still carrying Sol in a fist of air, I deposited him on the far side of the opening. He landed unceremoniously on the cold ground and stayed there. I kept expecting him to launch yet another foolish attack, but he didn't.

"This is it, Sol," I said. "The end."

He didn't move. He didn't even look at me.

"Did you hear me? I'm going to be leaving. If you have any last words or anything…"

"How?" Sol said in a low, gritty voice.

I didn't answer.

"How did you do it?" he continued. "You were finished, and then…? How?" Sol slowly turned to look at me, his eyes glinting in the blaze of my powers.

I had to think about it. Like most things I had learned since discovering my powers, I didn't feel like I could truly take credit for it.

The hammer trick? Learning how to evade physical harm? That started with Bobby.

Making light? My sister.

And taking away our powers? That had been a combination. Naima was a pro at it, of course, doing it without even thinking, but we'd wrongly assumed she was somehow different from us. Once Holly learned to vampire another superhuman's powers, things became a little more clear to me. Our powers were somehow binary — on or off. Not gone. Not even Sol's were gone, even here deep in the ground. They were just *off*.

"I think it was when she touched me," I said. Perhaps it was foolish to say anything, but in a few moments I planned to leave Sol to a miserable, lingering death. I felt I could at least talk to him first.

"Who do you mean?"

"Naima," I said.

"Interesting. And what did this touch *do* to you?"

I barked a short laugh that echoed strangely within the small rift in the rocks. "It messed me up, that's what. I couldn't control my powers the right way, couldn't fly. I was a mess."

"And what fixed it, for you?" he asked, with a sweet sort of innocence.

I wagged a finger. "Ah, ah, ah. You didn't say the magic word."

"It was worth the asking," Sol said.

I nodded. It truly *was* worth the asking. Who knew how stupid I would be in answering, right? But the truth was that when Naima affected me, I was *never* turned all the way off. It was only partial. Perhaps because Naima's actions were passive. Mine, however, were quite forceful and active. So now, with Sol fully disconnected from his powers, nothing he could do would bring them back.

Nothing.

Sol looked around at the small rocky cave where we stood. "So, now what? You will leave me here?"

"Yes."

"And what will become of me, then?" he asked, and for once I think I heard the real Jose. The man who was just a man, full of normal insecurities and uncertainties.

"You'll die."

"Even though I have died, by all measures, at least once before?"

I nodded again, this time gravely. "There's nothing living down here. Nowhere for the thorns in your cells to escape."

Sol twisted his face into grimace. "You truly believe this? That there is something alien in our cells to give us power?"

"Yes."

"And that we ourselves are nothing special? We're merely accidents of time and space?"

"Yes. I think so."

"I can accept many things, John Black, but not that." Sol looked down at his hands as he wrung them together.

"Why?"

"Because I simply don't believe it to be true," Sol said. "We are not *accidents*. We are superhuman, you and I. We are eternal. We are forever intertwined. Wherever you are, forever, there I shall be as well."

"No," I said. "You won't. You'll be here."

Something about my words hit him hard, and his body seemed to collapse. I don't know why, but I felt sympathy. Sol was evil, but did he deserve this? I thought again about how we had *both* done evil things. Was this another entry my list of horrible deeds? And, if so, from whose perspective? Was it all a matter of being good in the eyes of the most people? God, I hoped there was something more than that.

Sol lifted himself back to a seated position. "Grant me one dignity, before you leave."

Why hadn't I left already? Because this was, in a way, a funeral, and I felt like there was something ceremonial to be done, yet I didn't know what it was. "What do you want?" I asked.

Sol extended his right hand.

On that hand, I saw ragged nails. I saw cuts and scrapes. This was not the immaculate Sol I knew, but instead some pathetic creature.

And all he wanted was a handshake before he died.

I raised my hand to meet his.

Something felt very strange about it. Perhaps my cells were warning me. Something told me not to do it.

So I paused, just feet away, our hands both hanging in the air.

What harm could come from a handshake? I thought. *The brief humanity of a touch?*

That was the problem. Touch.

Naima had touched me and set off a firestorm of binary switches I struggled to understand. Touch might be enough to give him hope. If he could connect to my light cells, his dark ones might be brought to life again. Light and dark, dark and light. No, touch was the very last thing I could ever do with him. I recoiled, pulling my hand away.

"Shake my hand, you uncivilized bastard!" Sol shouted, suddenly leaping off the ground toward me.

"Stay back!" I said, reacting with power, blasting upward through solid rock, beginning the long ascent back to the surface. But Sol kept coming, dodging rocks, each of which could now crush him to death. He scrambled, climbing toward me.

Sol, the man who was once just Jose do Branco, stood defiantly on a broken slab of rock as I hovered above him, his hair wildly tousled, his clothing torn and unkempt. "If you leave me in this hell, John Black, I will find a way. One day, you'll see. I will return to you and bring all of the misery you now give me back to you as a gift. I will bring it back to you tenfold! I will have my revenge!" Then Sol leaped into the air and swung his hand. It nearly touched me as it swept by. In Sol's eyes, I saw only one thing. Hate. A hate that was exactly what he always said he wanted to be.

Eternal.

With my powers, I pushed upward, sending a rain of massive boulders to crash down below. To each side, I pulled down the surrounding layers of rock and created the world's largest, deepest cairn, burying my nemesis in a lifeless hell for the remainder of eternity, or at least until the end of his life.

Without power, Sol could not survive the collapse. Without power, he could never again return.

The thorns were still within his cells, even though they were turned off. The same thorns in me.

And so it was that a silent explosion occurred, with a million screaming voices threatening to shatter my mind as Sol was crushed to death, finally and for good, under a mountain of stone, in the black veins of the earth.

12

Where are you, Hol? I had left her behind to do what needed to be done, and now, with her powers still weak, I could barely locate her again.

But there were only so many gaps to be found deep in the earth, and only one living thing left to aim for. My sister.

Leaving a pile of broken stone behind me, I rose into the large opening where Holly was still unconscious on the floor.

Who knew where Barry Wilk was then, or how Mom and Pip were faring in the fight above. If there was even a fight happening still. Maybe they had lost long ago and were now in government custody. Or maybe a mere heartbeat had passed since I'd faced Sol in Holly's mind. It was time to get out of this damned hole in the ground and find out.

As I scooped up my sister to carry her back to the surface, she made a short grunting sound, like someone unwilling to wake from a dream.

We floated up and out of the gap, then through the tunnel I'd created and back to the bottom of Finimore Caverns' second drop, the deeper one.

Holly and I both radiated light, mine much stronger than hers. But there was also some kind of glow beyond that, a faint shimmer that seemed a mile overhead. I floated upward with my sister.

It was surreal to think that things were truly over, at least with Sol. He was gone, finally. But where did that leave the rest of us?

What would Barry Wilk do now? Things had changed, and I firmly believed that while he could fire his Naima bullets at me if he wanted, it would take more than that — it would take a real superhuman and their real strength — to take away my powers ever again. I would show Mom, Pip, and Holly what I'd learned, and we could stop being afraid. Stop running.

Sure, we could tell Wilk that we weren't a threat, but I knew he wouldn't believe that. In time, though, he'd have to agree. Without Sol or Margrethe to stir up trouble, our lives would likely be lived out fairly normally, other than the fact that Pip might save a few people from a burning building now and then. Actually, that might be fun. Maybe I'd join her.

There was a strange warmth in my mind, something that made no sense to me at the time. I think now I know what it was, though. I think it was my sister, invading my thoughts, learning.

You! Holly's voice said, booming in the huge expanse of the cavern.

I froze, stopping our ascent midway, with nothing but air above and below us. "Holly! You're awake! That's gre—"

What have you done? Holly cried.

Blasting out of my arms, my sister hit me with a wall of force so strong and unexpected that I lost control of myself, tumbling back down toward the rock below. "What's wrong, Holly?" I said calmly. Ha. Did you believe that? No, I didn't say that at all. I just yelled like a maniac, *Aaaaahhhhhhh!* Finally, I caught myself and dropped down to stand on the stone surface.

Holly floated toward me, godlike, to alight nearby with grace.

She twitched as her feet hit the ground.

That was weird.

"What's wrong, Holly?" I did say it this time.

My sister's head shifted quickly, tilting to an odd angle, making her long, dark hair flop into her face. With strands hanging down over her eyes, she looked strange and frightening. This was not Holly Black. This was only Shadow Ghost. *What have you done to me?* She asked it with venom.

"Nothing, Holly, what? I... remember what we talked about? I went into your portal, to get Sol out of you. And he's gone now."

She twitched again, bent over slightly and clenching her fists. My sister was fighting something inside herself. Were Holly and Shadow Ghost somehow at war? How? Why?

You hurt me, she finally said.

"How? I don't understand."

You... killed me.

"No, Holly, you're right here. You're not *dead*!" What was she talking about? I waved my hands, trying to claim innocence for something that clearly hadn't happened.

Once more, my sister shook her head. *No, not me. You killed her. And you left... them... behind.*

Her. Them. "Oh no," I muttered. Suddenly, it made sense. Gorgol Alpha in the real world was a manifestation of Holly's rage. But *inside* Holly's head, even under Sol's direction, what was Alpha there?

I realized that the Alpha in Holly's mind simply *was* her anger, an unpleasant yet integral part of my sister's makeup.

And I had killed it.

Well, technically, *I* hadn't. Gorgol Tau had. Many of them. And I had left them behind in my haste to chase down Sol.

The rage that I had so long battled to control, the rage that had made me do things that might be considered evil, that I regretted. That rage was now inside of Holly, and her own normal anger was gone.

If Shadow Ghost had come to life, she did so with the rage of Black Sword.

My God. What had I done?

"Holly, listen. I—"

My sister dove for me like a lioness bringing down a weak gazelle. So I did the only thing I could think to do at that moment.

I rocketed upward, trying to get out of Finimore Caverns as quickly as my powers would allow.

13

I flew, not sure what gaining the surface might get me, yet knowing it was better than the fight waiting for me below.

But Holly was no shrinking violet. She followed, at an even greater speed. Within seconds, I had to dodge sharply to the left to avoid her slamming into me.

After that, it was a good, old-fashioned dogfight. The Red Baron looped in his triplane as I tried to evade in my Sopwith Camel. I really, truly wish anything about this fight was that funny, that lighthearted.

Instead, my sister speared at me again and again, and all I could do was spin, twist, and sluice aside. Several times she came so close, my body morphed into wild forms, narrowly avoiding the brute force of my sister's attacks.

"Holly! Stop! Let's talk about this! I didn't mean to hurt you!"

She flew toward me again, a human bullet, and I chose to continue upward to avoid her. As I rapidly ascended toward the ledge between the two big drops, I realized it really was getting lighter. Something had changed. Was it daylight already?

No, what I saw was artificial. Its tone seemed like it came straight out of an electric floodlight, not the broad spectrum that comes from the sun. Not that it mattered. Someone had turned on the lights, and I flew toward them desperately.

I gained the next level well ahead of my sister and then found myself back in a maze of passages. I could fly, but only if I liked bouncing off stone walls. I decided running would be fine.

Using the lights as a guide, I ran, turning left and right following the now floodlit path. Finally, I found myself at the bottom of the first drop.

The entirety of the deep well was brightly lit with massive lamps. But in the opening, far above me, the sky was still pitch black.

Standing at the bottom of Finimore Caverns' first huge hole, I shouted up. "Hello? Who's there?"

I expected Wilk or some government loudspeaker. Instead, I heard my mom. "John?"

"Mom? What's going on up there?"

I could see tiny heads peering over the ledge so far above me. "John, where's your sister?" Mom said with fear in her voice.

I waved a calming gesture, trying to reassure her. "Don't worry, Mom, she's —"

Holly burst into the open area, her internal light dwarfing the floodlights around us. *You nearly killed me!* she shouted in her mental way that everyone could her.

"No, Holly, no!"

Once more, my sister dove toward me.

"Oh my God, what's going on down there?" Mom shouted, high above. "Holly, stop!"

And, unbelievably, the Power of Mom worked. Holly stopped. And hovering there, just feet from me, she seethed.

"John, Holly," Mom called. "Tell me what's happening. Please!"

Don't listen to him, Mom! He can't be trusted. He hurts people, Holly said. *He is the evil in this world.*

Those words...

"Stop it, Holly!" I said. "I was trying to help you."

And did you?

"Yes, of course. Sol is gone."

Pip gasped. "Really? You did it? That *sound*. We heard it — well, *felt* it. That was him dying?"

"Yeah, he's gone," I said. "But what about you all? Where's Wilk? Where are all the government agents?"

"Routed 'em," Pip said flippantly. "Once their little beanbag guns were empty, they took off in a hurry. And those things weren't too hard to avoid once we knew what we were up against. They didn't even have all that many. Most of the guns weren't loaded. Wilk was bluffing. Oh, and by the way, your mom was awesome."

"Looks like we all won, then," I said. I wish I felt any joy in that, but instead I felt the hot stare of my sister beside me.

At what cost? Holly continued, raging.

"Tell me what happened between you two," Mom said. In the end, she couldn't care less about Wilk or Sol. She cared about us.

I spoke in a low voice. I realized speaking in a low voice when we were hundreds of meters apart wasn't too helpful, but both Mom and Pip had powers to augment what they could hear. "Sol attacked me with Gorgol Alpha, inside Holly. And I killed her — the monster, not Holly, of course!"

Alpha was me, Holly said. *You killed a part of me.*

"I had to, Holly."

My sister ignored me. *That's not the worst part, Mom*, she said. *He cut out a part of me and replaced it with something else. Something horrible. I will never be the same.* Holly shuddered in fear and revulsion.

Unseen by Mom or Pip, and possibly masked so that even their augmented senses wouldn't detect it, Holly stabbed at me with her mind. A spike of molten lava pierced my head, right between the eyes. I almost staggered to my knees, but to do that would've been the end. I couldn't, after all I'd been through. I had to stay alive, and eventually, I hoped I could reason with my sister.

I stood my ground, fighting back without moving.

From above, it probably looked like nothing at all was happening.

"Come up here, you two, and let's talk it over," Mom said. Always the rational one. She waved a hand, gesturing us up almost casually, not understanding the deadly struggle happening between her children.

Again Holly stabbed into me. Again I pushed back. It was nothing like Sol's flow of light. I would have happily taken that instead, knowing that I could turn it off. Holly's attack was fierce and unyielding, while the true core of her own strength was walled off from me. She had learned to combine offense with defense. Clever girl.

Then I felt the first of it. My power being sucked up, like a vacuum running in my mind.

Holly was going to do to me what she had done to Margrethe.

I pushed back against her attack, but, as I had known for so long, Holly's mental powers vastly eclipsed mine. I had to do something if I didn't want to be lobotomized and have my powers stripped away in front of my mother.

I became frantic, needing to do *something*. We were a few feet apart, and with some effort, I could have reached out to strike at my sister, but why bother? Her body would sluice, and her mental attack would continue.

Soon, I wouldn't have any powers anymore anyway.

I tensed, my arms pulling in reflexively at each side. Visions of the training Marcos had given me flickered like a dream over my vision. *Always defend the body*, he would say. But why? What good would that do when the attack was in my head?

My hand brushed across my belt.

Wait.

My *belt*.

That belt. That *double* belt that Pip had given me.

The one I could turn into double swords.

Holly's mental vampire fangs dug deeper into my brain, threatening to destroy my very core, so I acted. Maybe it wasn't even me. Maybe the thorns did it. All they wanted to do was live.

With a lightning flash of speed, I crossed my arms in front and grabbed at the two sides of my belt, whipping them from around my waist and immediately hardening them into something like steel. Then, with a crisscrossing action, I slashed, nearly blind from the pain in my head, just wanting *something* to make Holly stop.

To my horror, I succeeded.

My right sword sliced through Holly's neck, nearly taking her head off, cutting a deep gash suddenly full of red blood.

The spike inside my head disappeared in an instant. The tendrils draining my power fizzled and were no more.

Holly fell.

High above, my mother screamed, a sound I will never forget, will never be able to forget. The sound of a mother losing a daughter and a son at the same time.

Immediately I tossed aside the swords. They reverted to nothing more than belts, harmless curls on the rocky ground. "No," I said. "What have I done?" I ran to my sister.

I didn't dare to touch her, she seemed so fragile on the ground, her hair and dress tangled and tossed. I didn't know if she was even alive.

It's true. It really is true. I am the evil in the world.

Finally, she stirred, turning over so that I could see the wide opening on her neck slowly knitting itself closed. *John?* she said, confused.

"I'm sorry, Holly. I just needed to stop you."

I know. I know. My sister reached out toward me to hold my hand. To forgive me. To ask for forgiveness.

I felt such relief that she was alive. She had done things with her powers, and so had I, but alive, we could work it out. Maybe we needed each other to keep the evil at bay.

I took her hand in mine. "Yes, Holly, that's it. Let's go home now," I said.

Of course, John, she said, looking up at me with a faint smile that seemed oddly cold and distant. *But there's just one more thing.*

"What is it, Hol? Anything…"

I can't always live in your shadow, big brother.

As our hands touched, Holly turned my own revelations around and flipped off every tiny light in my body. She took my superpowers away, leaving nothing behind but plain old John Black, normal human being.

Epilogue

Every clock you've ever seen is a lie.

Why?

Because they circle around and around endlessly, time never ceasing. Nothing ever ending, just looping back to the beginning a hundred trillion times.

Unless the battery dies, of course.

But in reality, things end.

For me, they did. For Sol, they did. And really, for all of us, for the world, things ended.

Clocks might have ticked off another second, kept spinning endlessly around their dials, but events — *things* — end.

Our time came upon us without warning, all of us, even Sol. Although many of us might have wanted a change in our everyday existence, not one of us asked for what happened. How could we possibly have imagined it, anyway? The power, the fame, the struggles, pitting us one against the other. Men and women, or just kids like Bobby and me, people who originally had no reason to be friends. Some of whom had no reason to even know one another. Some of whom should have had no reason to ever be enemies.

But it came, and with all the torrent of a building tempest it stoked our winds and drove our waves, crashing them into each other violently. Like a storm, we raged and we were heard and we changed the world with our fury.

And like a storm, we passed.

The world is different now. We're considered normal, understood, manageable. Well, maybe not normal. But close.

And we're different, too.

I'm different.

How long will I be here, walking this planet? It's hard to say, after all I've been through.

After death.

But I know one thing, and strangely it's the only thing that gives me solace. Sol is gone. And, if it has to come to it, at some dark day in the future, when my body strives independently to carry on but my mind wishes otherwise, I know I can be overcome, too.

It's weird to find peace in the possibility of one's own demise. I'd ask you to try to understand.

But then again, you don't have to live forever, do you?

* * *

All right, maybe I'm being a little dramatic. Sorry. That's what happens when you've got nothing but time on your hands. Time to think. Well, time to overthink.

I've been held against my will a long time now. It's hard to remember how long given that I can't exactly see or even sense the passing of days. Or seasons. I tried to estimate the time, for a while. But when your whole world is a cube made up of nondescript beige walls with no windows, marking time is difficult. The fluorescent lights don't rise and set. Has it been six months? No, that's gotta be low. A year? Maybe more.

It's funny, ending up in the same stupid government bunker all over again. Maybe even the same room. They all look the identical, so who knows? I know Wilk said they dug out the facility Holly and I trashed, but I don't have a clue how the elevator shaft got remade, or the power got restored. Still, it did.

The whole arrangement, in my opinion, is tenuous. Holly got fame and respect, though she's become a sort of recluse, living somewhere in the bunker above me. For his part, Barry Wilk saved face by reaching a truce with the superhumans. I hear it earned him that director job finally. I wasn't there to witness the treaty signing, although I'm gonna guess it went something like this: *We, the superhuman Black family, give you back the world, except for this one former government bunker. Attempt no landings there.* But how long is an ambitious guy like Wilk going to honor that agreement?

The only one of us who returned to anything like a normal life is Pip, probably plucking hapless folks out of burning buildings on a nightly basis. Somehow, Holly and Wilk's détente either overlooked Pip or gave her a pass.

As for my forced retirement, Mom was in on the whole thing, but she always tells me it's just so she can keep an eye on Holly and try to help me out when possible. She promises to keep talking to Holly, to try to convince her to change. I guess I should be mad at my mom for conspiring against me and all, but I can see her side. Although imperfect, this way at least keeps both her kids alive.

Of us all, only I got the shaft. Get it? Shaft? And I'm a prisoner at the bottom of a giant elevator shaft? Okay, fine, that joke sucked. I'm a little off my game. I think it's a product of my environment.

I would have expected more from — crap, the door latch just clicked. Dinner time must have snuck up on me. Back in a sec.

* * *

I'll say this about my life, stuck here. It's given me plenty of time to write this all down. I mean, sure, every once in a while I have company, but that's mostly just for meals. Three hots and a cot. Like jail. You'd think I could at least count the meals to figure out how long I've been here, but I'll tell you this... It's harder than it sounds. When you get to meal 346, your mind starts to play tricks on you. Maybe it's 347. Or maybe you really messed up and it's 436. 437? Possibly 734. Numbers all sound so much *the same* after a while. Which means that, despite trying, that particular calendar method failed me, too.

The door slid open. At first, I didn't even look, choosing to remain seated.

"Hi, Mom," I said.

For a moment there wasn't a reply, which was strange. When my visitor finally spoke, her voice wasn't my mother's.

No, it's me, John.

I turned. "Holly? You — you don't usually —"

What? I don't usually come down here to see you? I know, I'm a bad sister.

"You know, Hol, if I was going to think of you as a bad sister, not coming to visit is probably the least of my reasons. Imprisoning me? *That's a lot* higher up the list."

Holly floated through the doorway, a tray of food preceding her. Even though I knew Holly had to float to get around, it was still strange to see her "carry" things by making them float in front of her. It was sort of like those cartoons where the character had hands but no arms, or feet but no legs. You've seen those, right? Tell me I'm not just imagining those things, manufacturing memories.

Hell, if I'm manufacturing memories now, all this writing I've been doing is going to be some pretty bizarro fiction. For what it's worth,

I'm pretty sure Ramona wasn't a hamster.

"So, you've come to set me free?" I asked. A boy can dream, right?

No, John. I still don't think I can trust you.

"You?" This conversation had baffled me many times before. "*You* can't trust *me*?"

We've been through all this, John. You're... erratic. I know that so well now. Now that you've... tainted me.

I nodded. "You've got me there. I definitely don't have it all figured out, and sometimes my actions have been inconsistent. But that doesn't mean I'm bad. It doesn't mean you can just keep me here." I had said all these things to her before. I didn't expect her to suddenly change her mind.

John, you attacked me with... those swords you use. I had to do something. Besides, I didn't hurt you. I just... stopped... you. You're perfectly comfortable here.

Standing, I grimaced. Holly stopped floating forward, not willing to come closer. If only I could touch her... "I attacked you, you attacked me. I did bad things, you did bad things. How is one better than the other, Hol? But you're right. It's comfortable here. Kind of the way I imagine it's comfortable for a bird to live in a steel cage. As long as you don't think about it, it works. Just let the days roll by."

I'll admit that you must be bored. Holly glanced past me, toward my desk and the computer where I spent my time. No, not a networked computer. No chance for me to reach the outside world. Just a box and a keyboard, a place where I could type out my story. She even did something to the computer so that it always says the date is the first of January. Like every day is New Year's Day here in prison, I suppose. So that kept me guessing, too. My sister is a thorough jail warden. *I let them bring you that when you requested it. Just trying to be kind. Are you still writing?* she asked.

"It gives me something to do," I replied, waiting for the next moment.

With the powers of her mind, Holly slid the tray of food toward my desk, setting it down next to the old monitor, a massive CRT unit borrowed from some evacuated government worker. Holly's attention was only off me for a few seconds, just enough to properly send the food on its way.

I jumped.

And with all the effectiveness of an ant attacking a Gorgol, I was thwarted. She didn't even look at me when she did it.

I hung in midair, like a decorative mobile over some insane infant's crib, one hand outstretched toward my sister, but never reaching her. It was worth a shot, you know? Just a touch and maybe my powers would return, and then we could deal with things more maturely. Or at least I could try to get the hell out of this prison.

Holly floated closer, until her face was only inches from mine. It reminded me of the times we touched our foreheads together, our sibling gesture of love. For a second, I thought she might do just that, she was so close to me. So close that I strained to have us connect, so I could regain what belonged to me. And yet I couldn't budge. Without power, my sister held me motionless and she didn't even break a sweat doing so. *This is exactly what I mean, John. Every time I deal with you, you do* something. *Something that makes me not trust you.*

I strained to speak, my jaw as frozen as the rest of my body. "Come on, sis! I didn't mean anything by it! I just want to get out of here. I'll leave you alone if you give me back my powers. Honest."

Surprisingly, Holly didn't believe me. This may have been due in large part to the fact that she was reading my mind. It may also have been due to the fact that I was lying. Would I do anything to Holly if I had my abilities back? Um, yeah. She had gone full-tilt power mad, and needed to be stopped. I could clearly see that.

Holly drifted away, toward the open door, then turned back to face me.

I'm sorry I came, John. I hope that, in time, you'll become someone more trustworthy. I remember our times together growing up, even back when it seemed like I couldn't say or do much of anything. You were always there for me. My brother. I remember it all. Dad, Mom, you. You and me, John. I hope one day we can be like that again. Do you remember?

Of course I did. I wrote it all down, didn't I?

As she floated before me, little black spiders popped into existence and began to crawl across her pristine white dress. First one, then a dozen. In just a few moments, it seemed like there were hundreds of them, and I don't even think Holly noticed. The ability to create life, and she used it without thought. Her powers seemed infinite and awesome and terrifying.

I don't know when I'll be back to see you, but one day I'll come again. I hope by then you're different. Like the brother I remember...

And then my sister said the one word that told me maybe, just maybe, there was still a chance for us to work things out.

...Johnny.

As Holly left, the door slid closed and the latch clicked.

For a moment, I remained frozen. Then, just when I thought she might leave me hanging in the air permanently, my body was released and I fell to the floor.

* * *

I slept. Other than writing and eating, it was the only other thing to do, really. I don't count bathroom visits as a legitimate pastime, sorry.

So I was asleep when the door latch clicked once again.

Something about it was strange — too soon. I wasn't at all hungry, so the space between visits felt odd to me.

341

I rolled over to face the door and saw my mother. Like I said, the fluorescents in my holding room didn't rise or set. They were always on. I'd become used to sleeping with the lights on. "John." That's all she said. Not a question, just a statement.

"Mom," I replied, mirroring her aloof tone. And, confirming what my stomach already suspected, my mother's hands were empty. There was no food tray. "Why are you here?" I asked, sitting up.

She took a moment to glance quickly down the hallway then entered my room, pushing the door most of the way closed. Given that she was my most regular visitor, her behavior was distinctly odd. Mom walked toward me with a furtive gait, like she was afraid of something both behind her and in front of her. Then she reached into one pocket and pulled out a folded piece of paper. "Take this."

She had brought me notes before. I had developed a strange pen-pal relationship with Dr. Naima Ramadi. It was interesting, getting to know more about things from her point of view. But when Mom brought those notes, she always left them for me on the desk.

Now she was handing me something, willing me to reach out and take it.

I did.

But as I grabbed the note, my index finger brushed against Mom's, so quickly, so slightly, that it could have just been my imagination.

It was my first physical human contact in months, years, however long I had been captive.

Without another word, Mom turned and rushed out the door. The latch clicked loudly, telling me I was once more alone and trapped.

But…

There had been that fleeting touch.

As a low tingle crept up my index finger, like the sensation of jumpstarting a leg that's fallen asleep, I unfolded the paper. The whole situation reminded me of passing notes in class. Don't let the teacher see.

Who would pass me a note, way down here? Who could? I thought. *Carrie. Gotta be Carrie. That explains why Mom's doing it. Why she's breaking the rules. Mom always liked Carrie.*

Well, friends. I was wrong. It was handwritten in a sort of clunky script, and even before I read the first word, I knew who wrote it.

I'm sure I was sitting there with my mouth gaping wide, but no one could see me, so I didn't care. As my shock slowly turned to wonder, then joy, I could only think one thing…

Son of a bitch!

* * *

Johnny, my man!

Well, well… Betcha never thought you'd hear from me, right? At least not like this — with you all locked up and me running free. I guess I know how you feel now. How it feels to come back. Thankfully, I didn't end up spliced into someone I couldn't stand. Can you even imagine how much that would suck? Nah, Charlie Nero's a decent guy. I like him.

Anyhoo, first things first. Gotta break you outta there, buddy. I'd tell you to stand by, to wait for a sign, but you'll know it when it happens. Subtlety's never been my strong suit.

See you soon, Johnny.

B.

THE END OF

IN THE BLACK VEINS OF THE EARTH

but

WILL JOHN BLACK RETURN?

Keith Soares

By day, Keith Soares runs an interactive game, web, and app development agency. But by night, his imagination runs wild. A fan of authors such as Stephen King, Robert Heinlein, Arthur C. Clarke, Brandon Sanderson, Justin Cronin, and Andy Weir, Keith writes stories of science fiction, the apocalypse, fantasy, revenge, and horror. He lives in Alexandria, Virginia, with his wife and two daughters, who are all avid readers.

Sign Up for the Keith Soares New Releases Newsletter

Get release news and free books,
including private giveaways and preview chapters.

Visit KeithSoares.com

Like Facebook.com/KeithSoaresAuthor
Follow Twitter.com/ksoares

PLEASE CONSIDER leaving a review where you purchased this book. Reviews are the best thing you can do to help an independent author like me, and even one sentence about your thoughts is enough.

Thanks in advance!

— **K.**

Made in the USA
Columbia, SC
20 May 2021